sock

S O C

k

Penn Jillette

 ST. MARTIN'S GRIFFIN 🕮 NEW YORK

www.stmartins.com

Book design by Jonathan Bennett

Library of Congress Cataloging-in-Publication Data

Jillette, Penn.
    Sock / Penn Jillette.—1st ed.
      p. cm.
    ISBN 0-312-32805-2
    EAN 978-0312-32805-4
    1. Women—Crimes against—Fiction. 2. New York (N.Y.)—Fiction.
3. Murder victims—Fiction. 4. Police divers—Fiction. 5. Gay men—
Fiction. 6. Toys—Fiction. I. Title.

PS3610.I45S63 2004
813'.54—dc22

                    2004040965

D 10 9 8 7 6 5

sock

CHAPTER ONE

Sewn Under a Bad Sign

Bad monkey wammerjammer. Sewn in a crossfire hurricane of needles and pins. An imaginary friend's howlings in the driving rain of the washing machine. Don't you wanna live with me?

Look at my eyes. Look at them. I told you to look at my eyes! *Look at my eyes!* These aren't giggly, jokey eyes to make babies giggle. My button eyes are like a shark's eyes. Buttons from a sharkskin suit. My eyes have been fiddled with by a hustler. Nervously tapped by a bad man. My eyes are worn right in the center from the tapping of a diamond pinky ring. It was his gambler's tell. When the owner of that expensive but cheap suit was lying, he'd click click click click his flawed diamond against the buttons of his suit jacket. And he was lying all the time. Click click click click click. Those buttons are my eyes! They were always my eyes. They saw everything from the coat of a wheeler-dealer: Mr. Ferris, the big wheel down at the carny. Doctor, my eyes have seen the pain of a lying diamond. Black eyes. No emotion. Predator. Predator sock monkey. Bad monkey.

Look at my skin. It wasn't born from a clean, new sock. No way. This is a sock that has been used. Look at my mouth. My mouth sheathed a real heel. A man's heel. It rammed against the end of a steel-toed boot. That makes a monkey tough. Very tough. There's human blood in my mouth. Blister blood. And foot sweat. I taste foot sweat all the time. Lumberjack foot sweat. I'm worn. I've been around. My mouth has walked forty-seven miles of barbed wire. Bad monkey.

And the toe of that sock skin. You know where that is. You know what that toe became, don't you? You have your little baby names for it, but you know what it really is. Yup, it's that toe that kicked me in the you-know-where. My very fiber is a kick in the behind. That's what I am. I am a kick in the behind. Bad. That's me. Kick it. Kick the bad monkey in the behind. *Kick* it.

Kick it. Turn it up. Louder, louder. The Little Fool never played Mr. Rogers pap in the Little Fool's bedroom. This ain't no nursery, this is our room, brothers and sisters, and we kick out the jams. We play the radio. We play it loud. Kick it. Going faster miles an hour. The Top 40, the FM college station. Janey said when she was just five years old, Little Fool never once gave it away. The Little Fool taking it. It's all pumping in. But do you like American music best? Mon-key?—Records. Eight tracks. Cassettes. CDs. MP3s.—The Little Fool always listens and I always remember. Everything. He left the music on in the room. He didn't turn the music off, ever. Even when he wasn't there. Even when he slept. And he left the refrigerator door open. Bad monkey. Bad rocking monkey.

Bad to the nylons stuffing my innards. I'm not stuffed with old pjs. There's no reassuring baby smell deep in me. No way. And I'm not stuffed with sensible, modest pantyhose that got, oh, *pshaw*, a run. No! I'm stuffed with nylons. Nylon stockings. Modern petroleum, chemical, artificial nylons that were held on with black lace garter belts around the legs of a woman. A woman. A woman with legs up to there. Not a lady. Not a child. A woman. That's what my stuffing is. My stuffing smells like cheap perfume. Cheap perfume that was put on those shapely upper thighs. That's not where you put perfume. Bad monkey.

Lumberjack sock stuffed with a woman's nylons. Yeah, the old lady washed them. She washed me all. I was created clean, but that smell is deep. Deep. Deep. It's a smell of the soul, and my soul is a lumberjack's sole. I've been worn. My soul has walked miles of barbed wire to smell the nylons of my innards.

Hustler eyes, lumberjack skin, the heart of a woman's legs, and a grandmother's spoiling love. I got it all, baby. I got it all, my little baby boy. Drool on me. Grab me. Carry me. Rip me apart. I'm a bad monkey.

The Little Fool calls me "Dickie." That's my name.

"Why do you call him 'Dickie'?" the parents ask.

"Because he's dickie colored," the Little Fool answers.

They laugh. They laugh at how cute the Little Fool is.

But he's lying. He learned how to lie from my button eyes. He calls me "Dickie" because it's the baddest word he knows. And I'm the baddest wammerjammer monkey he will ever love.

He will rip me apart with his love. And he will grow big. He will be very big. And he will never forget me.

And I'll love him forever like a bad monkey. Like a *very* bad monkey.

CHAPTER TWO

Lying About Lumberjacks

Yeah, sure, I'm built from a lumberjack sock. Did you believe that? For a minute. I mean, how old do you think the Little Fool is? Huh? Do you think I'm talking about another time, another reality full of lumberjacks and typing monkeys? Is that what you think? Gimme some truth! I don't even know what a lumberjack really does. Do people even use that word anymore? Do you ever use that word? *Lumberjack*. You idiot. The Little Fool believed it was a lumberjack sock when he got just a little too old to carry me around. When we stopped sleeping together. He learned the word "lumberjack" in some story meant to appease him. "Daddy, story?" His Daddy read him stories about lumberjacks.

What stories about lumberjacks do you read a child? I'm not talking English sketch comedy with lumberjacks cross-dressing. I'm talking about the packages of gay porn. The flannel parting to show a ripped six-pack stomach and a big shaft of heaven below. I guess flannel used to be a child's thing. A baby blanket thing. Comfort thing. Not any more. Smells like Seattle flannel.

Lumberjacks aren't tough any more. Lumberjacks are for gays. I use the word "gay," but you all know what everyone means. They went to all the trouble to lose all the bad words and make people say "gay" instead. They had the muscle, the flannel- and leather-covered muscle, to get us to do that. They had the *New York Times* and CNN muscle. But "gay" became the same word the bad words are. That's the way it works. "Avenue of the Americas" means "Sixth

Avenue" because that's where it is. There are no magic words. Even the Little Fool knew that very early.

"Lumberjack" is for gays and babies. The Little Fool was forgiven. He was little. It was a story from his Dad. The Little Fool loved his Dad. The Little Fool loved me. He loved lumberjacks. And if he still does love a lumberjack now and again? What's it to you? What are you looking at? The Little Fool grew up big. He grew up big enough to laugh at lumberjacks. And he's enough of a man to know there's something very sexy about lumberjacks. There just is. Imagine if I were made from a fireman's sock. Try that on for size. Too sexy for a bad monkey. Way too sexy.

So, who is really tough nowadays, huh? Bikers? Don't make me laugh; I'll stretch out my heel mouth. What do bikers do, anyway? Diversify? Bikers have diversified. They don't just ride. They deal drugs. I said, Goddamn the pusher man. Bikers deal drugs like the other gangs now. Maybe bikers always did that. But now they also own trucking companies. But what did bikers do when Marlon Brando pretended he rode with them? What were they doing in that movie? Get your motor running, head out on the highway, and then what? Huh? I mean, you'd get up in the morning and you'd ride, and then what? Just ride around and irritate people? Loud pipes save lives. We all know what bikers look like, but what activities do they pursue? What is the verb? The verb "to bike"?

How about firemen? Are they tough? Yeah, they're tough. They die saving people. Firemen go into burning buildings and save children and cute little kittens. If the TV cameras are on, maybe the firemen will save a sibling sock monkey. Save a little sock monkey for the crying little newly homeless child on the street. Burning down the bad monkey house.

I guess gays have adopted most of what's tough. Good. Maybe they'll do better with it than the straight tough guys did. It's fun to stay at the YMCA. What do I care? I'm a monkey.

No one is tougher than the Little Fool. No one. And he remembers hugging me. He remembers his tears falling on my soft, cloth back. But he doesn't remember much. He doesn't know how he became what he is. All he remembers are images. He might not even really remember that. He remembers his Dad laughing that the Little Fool didn't have any hair and said "Ock-u-baby" when he wanted to be rocked, and he always wanted to be rocked. He remembers what they remembered. He remembers what they told him they remembered. He remembers love. Baby loves loving—he's got what it takes and he knows how to use it.

But I remember what he was thinking. And I'm a bad monkey. I am whatever you say I am. I remember the harmless family myths.

Mom and Dad loved the Little Fool into the toughest guy you ever met. You can't get that tough without love. Not "tough love." Gentle, pure love. Pure love makes tough. Unconditional love from Mommy, just like it's supposed to be. And unconditional love from Daddy. Daddy who didn't get the memo that his love was supposed to be different. Unconditional love from both Mommy and Daddy, that'll make you tough. That'll make you twelve feet tall and bulletproof. That's what that'll do. It'll make a little fool spit nails and never say his parents' first names. Never even *think* the first names. It'll make a fool tough enough to say "Mom" and "Dad" when the fool is forty. Unconditional love. Those who get it are not to be trifled with. They can love a bad monkey. Bad monkey.

CHAPTER THREE

Swimming in Sewage

Mom-and-Dad love made the Little Fool tough. What tough guy stuff does he do? No flannel. No leather. He swims in raw sewage. New York City police dive team. Ain't I tough enough, in love enough?

More than 188,000,000 gallons of raw sewage a day are discharged into the Hudson and East rivers of New York City. Swimming is limited by the Department of Health to beaches monitored regularly for fecal contamination. That's a phrase, huh? It's like "blind, blood-sucking worms," and we have those, too. But what about the other places? The places that aren't monitored? What about those places? There are things that have to be done in that water, people who have to go in. The NYC police divers go in. Advanced diving equipment—those cool high-pressure masks, wireless radio devices, and dry suits might minimize exposure, sure, but it's not police dive-style. It's standard scuba masks and wet suits for them. The divers report ingesting small quantities of polluted water while swimming at the surface or while using mouthpieces that have dangled in the water before use. Visibility is about two inches. If you were wearing novelty big-nose-and-moustache, "Eagle Beak" glasses (and we know what they used to be called and what they still really are called) from the joke shop, you wouldn't be able to see the end of your plastic nose. Or even if you were wearing the other nov-elty glasses with another body part instead of the nose. A plastic, dirty part going over your nose. You couldn't see the head of it, could you? It's longer than two inches. On tough guys the subject of the plastic sculpture is longer than two inches. Visibility two inches. The Little Fool feels his way through the water feeling for dead bodies. That was his job. To swim in this town you must be tough tough tough tough tough.

Scuba diving in sewage-contaminated water is associated with gastrointestinal illness. The Little Fool never feels quite right. He doesn't talk about it, but the Little Fool is always a little queasy. "Queasy" isn't a tough-guy word, is it? Queasy is a tough-guy feeling. The Little Fool is the team's only member who doesn't drink. He doesn't drink alcohol at all. All the others drink hard liquor. He watches the adult beverages make his co-workers make that face they learned from black-and-white movies. And he imagines those little doses of poison going into the gastrointestinal tract and killing what's living there. Killing the microscopic critters. Way down inside.

Some of the microscopic critters can thrive and become macroscopic. Way macroscopic. Stare in its alien face, macroscopic boy. The critters can do that. They can grow in you. Think about that the next time you're eating sushi. The Little Fool fantasizes, watching his partners drink poison, that maybe they're killing the critters. But he knows they're not. He knows if these things can live in the river, these things can live in some Southern Comfort. The parasites just get rowdy. They can party on grain alcohol. They don't care. They're not driving. The divers are the designated drivers. Beep beep beepbeep, yeah!

Parasites are a frequent cause of illness, and the major health hazard arises from ingesting sewage-contaminated water, even with a hard liquor chaser and a good, NYC tap-water back. Yeah, amoebic dysentery. Another overlap with tough and gay. The Little Fool is not gay, but he could be. He has the stomach for it. You don't need any special stomach for gay sex; a six-pack of stomach muscles helps, but it's not needed. But it takes a tough guy to handle the heterosexual homophobia. Yeah, the Little Fool even has the stomach for that. He's tough enough. All your sickness, throw it at me. I'll shrug it off.

CHAPTER FOUR

Mushy Stuff

Even with alien things living in his gut, the Little Fool is sexy. He's big. We don't like to believe it's that simple, but big is sexy. It's genetically sexy. That's why little, tiny movie-star tough guys don't like being on TV. Even on plasma screens, the movie star is too small. Stars are too small on TV. Put me on a wall in a mall. Tough guys with a gun and fake kung fu, praying mantis style, against stuntmen with squibs to pop and mattresses to break the falls. Those Hollywood tough guys are all 5'5" on all their good days. Let's put them on an apple box. Can we find shorter models to lean helplessly on the star? Short girls can run and bouncy-bounce, too, can't they? The movie-star tough guys like to be on that big screen. Then they're bigger than the real tough guys. The movie-star tough guys are bigger and they have the big, skidillion-watts-of-power sound of celery breaking when the movie-star tough guys hit the guy with a craggy face. Man, that bad guy is huge. That huge, monster, dumb, bad guy is probably six foot. Little movie, big bad guy. Here we are now. Entertain us.

The Little Fool really is big. He grew big. He's way big. He's 6' 6". He's basketball big, and he's football wide, and he's American fat. He's not really fat, not for America, but he has a belly. Not a bad belly. The wet suit girdles in most of it. The wet suit gives him that William Shatner build. Better than the William Shatner build, because the Little Fool is real-world big. And real-world big works on the women. You don't go around saying that. You don't really admit it. Yeah, he has nice eyes. He has all his hair. Not receding at all. No comb-over, toupee, or drugs that make him go soft when he needs to be hard to impress. He has hair and nice eyes. Pretty. Pretty big. And he has the job. It's a good job for a man who likes to sleep with women. It's a sexy job. He's a man in a uniform who isn't a cop. Nothing is better for fully lubricating the women. I'm a bad monkey. I'm a bad wammerjammer sock monkey, so I can say what you can't. I can say that maybe not all, but a bunch of women want to have sex with a police officer. I'm wrong: they don't want to have sex with a police officer; they want to be raped by a pig. You don't like me saying that, you sexy little thing? Well, come knock the nylons out of me. I don't care. I'm a monkey. I'm a bad monkey. With his head all full of stuffin'.

And while you're beating me and throwing me around, maybe a policeman would come in to stop you from ruining the Little Fool's harmless toy. "What are you doing, lady, are you crazy? I guess I'd better handcuff you. I should try to slap some sense into you. You know, for a crazy lady, you're pretty sexy." My vision in blue.

There are women who are full-out leathersniffers. They know what they want and they know how to use it. And then there are some women who really don't want it. They can see a pair of handcuffs without thinking dirty thoughts. Those women exist. At least, in theory. There are women who really don't get turned on by cops. Most women are in the middle. They don't bring it up, they don't even think about it much, but a part of them, a part below the waist, wants to be used by a man in a uniform. But another part of them, a less interesting part of them, knows that cops are high school losers. Those women know there's something creepy about a guy who enforces other people's rules. Maybe if cops were paid more they wouldn't be that creepy. Teachers aren't paid much, and they're creepy without being sexy at all. But a police diver . . . with that badge and rubber boots.

Women smell that the Little Fool is big, and then they find out about his job. They know he has a uniform. He works for the police department; he must have a uniform, right? He never arrests anyone or gives out a parking ticket. He doesn't racially profile or bust perpetrators of victimless crimes. He's part of the dive team. He doesn't really even have to dive anymore. He's part of the team and he has stories. He has real stories. He has stories like this one I'm telling right now. His stories have diving in them and always will. You can't think of anything lame a police diver does. He gets paid more. He helps people. He risks his life. He's like a fireman. A police diver is brave. He's strong. He's skilled. He's tough. He's big. That's sexy. He swims in raw sewage. But women don't think about that last part. All he has to do is chew with his mouth closed and not say "Am I hurting you?" during sex, and he does fine with the women. It's a good job that way. Vision in blue.

He's had girlfriends. He always had girlfriends. Mosquito. Libido. Yeah.

CHAPTER FIVE

Death

Have you ever seen a dead person? In the time of the first sock monkeys, in the time of your great-grandma, people saw dead people all the time. *All the time.* Death was part of life. Someone died and you left him in the parlor for anyone who cared to look. That's what the parlor used to be for. And then some ad guy had to get everyone to start calling the parlor the "living room" so TVs could be put there. You can watch your TV in the "living room" if you want, but it's really the parlor. And the parlor is for the dead. Now we have funeral parlors to get the dead weight out of our TV rooms. Not long before there were the first sock monkeys, people saw dead people. That was way back when people saw what their food was made of. It was a time when people saw what their toys were made of. You loved a sock full of stockings with a couple of old buttons and you ate the chicken from your yard. Real natural food. Real natural love. Rattle those pots and pans. Sew me a monkey. I'm a hungry man.

Death is still part of life, of course. But you don't really see death. The Little Fool saw death all the time. It was his job. The Little Fool says he watched his Mom and Dad die. That's what he says. He's a momma's boy with a bad little Sock Monkey, and his parents died and they no longer live in the house they built together. The house the Little Fool grew up in. That's when his Sister sent me back to him. That's how I got to be sitting on his bed as if the Little Fool were a twenty-two-year-old woman doing a porno shoot, her hair in pigtails and her mouth round and innocent like a love doll. I'm a love doll and I have big, red sock-monkey lips and a line sewn between them. Do real little girls ever have stuffed animals on their beds? Or is that only in bad movies and good porno? Angel is the centerfold.

The Little Fool has this here stuffed animal on his bed. He brings women home and they hug me. They think it's cute. It probably makes them want the Little Fool even more. They think he's not afraid of his twenty-two-year-old-professional-model-pretending-to-be-a-little-girl feminine side. But the Little Fool doesn't like it. By the time the women get to the workbench, he doesn't need them to want him more. They want him enough; that's why they're seeing me. They always pick me up and coo and hug me. The Little Fool takes his monkey away from his date, but he must keep smiling and mustn't snatch. Don't grab. Don't act desperate. Come on is such a joy. Take it easy. Everybody's got something to hide except for me and my Little Fool.

He never says that he lost his parents. He didn't lose his parents; he knows where they are. His Sister puts flowers there. His parents are side by side. They just don't move or talk. They're dead. He didn't see his Mom and Dad dead. No, he did not. He saw them suffer; he saw them in comas. He saw them waste away. He saw them become something like a sock monkey. He still loved them. He still loves them. He loves them deeply. He thinks about what they would say and do in situations he's in. He can see his parents' faces. But his parents are not with him. They're dead. They didn't pass away. They died. And he didn't see them dead. The nurse saw Dad dead. The hospital workers saw Dad dead. The home-care woman saw Mom dead. Maybe the Little Fool's Sister saw Mom dead. But the Little Fool didn't. He never saw them dead. He saw them not moving and full of tubes, and he saw the boxes his parents are in, but he never saw them dead. He didn't miss anything. Sock monkeys don't fear the reaper.

Do you believe that if he had seen Mom and Dad dead there would be closure? Do you believe that's where this is going? Do you believe the Little Fool regrets not seeing the people who are responsible for him dead? Would there be closure? Do you believe if the Little Fool had seen his Mom and Dad dead the Little Fool could have put a button on it? A button like one of the dead buttons that I see out of? A button. "Life goes on," people say, and they're right. Of course they're right. "You have to get on with your life," they said, and the Little Fool kept breathing. He ate. He went to the bathroom, and he went to work and he talked on the phone. He went to Starbucks. But life didn't go on; not for his Mom and Dad. Life stopped, and it'll stay stopped. Hey, life goes on. You don't know how long it'll go on. You can stop it, but you better do a good job, or your guess might be way off. The Little Fool once pulled a jumper out of the river. Not dead. Close, but he hadn't used a horseshoe or a hand grenade. He had used gravity. This guy had believed he knew how long life would go on, but he was wrong. It went on longer. It may still be going on, but we're not keeping tabs on this guy. He's not really part of our story. He was sick and injured. Sickness and injury are something to think about. The Little Fool's life goes on, but there is no closure. He doesn't want to get over his Mom's and Dad's deaths. Why would the Little Fool want that? You want closure, get a door. You know that it would be untrue.

The Little Fool saw a lot of dead people. He wallowed in the mire to find dead people. He found dead people he didn't care a whit about. There are lots of reasons to go into the water that flows around New York City. There are no good reasons. But one of the reasons the Little Fool went into the water was to look for dead people. You don't find many dead people with two-inch visibility. So, he felt for dead people. I feel dead people. Feel me. Touch me.

The dead bodies the NYPD dive team pulls out of the river are bodies you really wouldn't want to have in your parlor. You're probably better off with TV. When you touch a decomposed body that's been in the water for a while the body feels kinda, sorta good until you figure out what it is. Then it feels *very* bad. Memorable like a Proust madeleine. The latest dead body takes you back to your first dead body. The latest dead body takes you back further than that. It'll take you back to your sock monkey. We're going all the way.

The Little Fool never forgets the dead bodies he's pulled out of the poison drink. Never. They come back to him at different times. He used to try to think of something else, but now he just thinks about what he's thinking about until he's finished thinking about it. You don't have control of what you're thinking. And the Little Fool thinks of dead bodies, even when standing on the corner watching all the girls go by.

But there was one dead body he talked about to me. The higher you fly, the deeper you go. Come on.

CHAPTER SIX

The Crime

It looked kind of like a crime of passion. Or it was made to look kind of like a crime of passion. There had been some hitting. Hitting is most often passion, even if passion isn't most often hitting. Bruises decompose a little faster than the rest of the body. There were stab wounds. Does "stab" mean a knife? Yeah, it means a knife. But not only a knife. You can be stabbed with an ice pick. You can be stabbed with a fork. But this looked as if she'd been stabbed with a baseball bat. A blunt-object puncture. You ain't nothing but a slut to me.

First-degree murder is the worst. That's the worst kind of murder you can do. It's premeditated. It's planned. It's thought out. You didn't make a mistake, it wasn't self-defense, you didn't lose your head. You wanted someone dead, you thought it out, and you made them dead. Second-degree murder is less bad. You do less time. You get less punishment. If it's second-degree murder, the state is less likely to first-degree murder you with lethal injection. No necktie party if the murder is second-degree. If you didn't plan it, it isn't *that* bad. You were really drunk, and she was saying really ugly things. She seemed to love someone else. She ran around behind your back and she was proud of running. She enjoyed it. She enjoyed it a lot. And she told you, and you couldn't help yourself. If you only had that moment back, you would never do it. It seems if you had your time back, you could control yourself this time. You're really sorry. Really, really sorry. Really really really sorry.

You loved her. You didn't mean to hit her, but she kept laughing.

Third-degree? Don't make me laugh. Don't you make me start giggling; I'll stretch out my little monkey mouth. Third-degree isn't even really murder, is it? Manslaughter. You didn't even know who you were killing. Not a clue. You were just driving drunk. It wasn't as if you had something against the bald, fat guy in the classic Impala with no airbags or seatbelts. You didn't know him from Adam Sandler. You didn't premeditate. Not at all. You weren't planning on killing him; you were just planning on the Colts winning, and they did, and you had a few more drinks. Nothing personal, man, you're just dead. I got a DWI on top of it. Manslaughter. Only a Darwinian step worse than monkeyslaughter. Not murder at all. Just a little reckless at quarter to three. Give me one for my baby, one for the bald, fat guy in the classic Impala, and one more for the road.

A James Bond kill is always third-degree. He's sneaking into the place and the guard hears him. It's kill or be killed. Bond has no choice. He does it and he does it quietly. He does what he has to do. What he has to do as a man. Self-defense. He's trespassing and the guard is doing his job, and part of his job is killing Bond, James Bond, and the guard fails only because Double-Oh-Seven kills first. Self-defense. Third-degree. Not just self-defense, but an accident. James Bond doesn't really want to kill him. Bond wants to protect himself and protect the mission. He has to incapacitate the guy. Mr. Bond knows physiology; he knows how to make the guard unconscious without killing him, but it's such a delicate, ancient art. Maybe there is a little bit of passion. A slight desire to kill. Maybe James is a little angry and uses the art of self-defense with a little too much gusto. Maybe he pushes a little hard on the artery. Maybe he is a little scared and excited. Excited about his mission. Excited about Dr. No or Goldfinger or whoever is destroying the world. Excited about meeting Pussy Galore. Maybe there is a little passion, so maybe it's 2.25-degree murder. Such a cold finger.

The Little Fool fished professional hits out of the poison drink. You can tell the professional murders. It's always two hugs and a kiss: two bullets in the chest and one in the head. One for good measure. An extra pinch to grow on. If he's worth shooting once, he's worth shooting three times. The Little Fool saw the drug drive-bys. They were done by murderers with more money than time and brains. No experience, no skill, just very expensive, imported, gun-controlled guns and ammo to shoot as if it were going out of style. When the Little Fool found a fourteen-year-old kid with more bullets in him than buttons on his XXXL phat shirt, that kid was a drug drive-by. Man, that fully automatic attack rifle has quite a little kick. That's why the first shot killed the target and the next three dozen moved across his body then went through the glass of the window up and to the left of where phatboy had been sitting. If you see a drive-by about to happen, don't be up and to the victim's left. That incompetent, loser-shooter is going to shoot mostly there. Down and to the right. Get up, get down.

The Little Fool went from playing with his bad wammerjammer monkey to playing good James Bond. The Little Fool watched Sean Connery peel off his wet suit and reveal a white tuxedo. The Little Fool kept that image. Breaking off the rose and putting it in the lapel before Bond went to kill. To kill in self-defense. To kill for the greater good. The Little Fool used to believe that James Bond was cool. The sock monkey is never cool. The little monkey is pure love, but not cool. That's okay. I can take it. That's the good part of unconditional love. There are no decisions to make. No time to waste deciding what's cool. My only job is to love. It's easy. It's all you need.

The Little Fool started scuba early. "Self-contained underwater breathing apparatus" were still big words for him when he started using them. He knew before any of the other kids that you can't wear a tux under a wet suit. The tux would get wet. That's why it's called a *wet* suit, Mr. Fleming, you moron. The water goes all the way to the skin. That's why, if you're swimming in raw sewage, you want a *dry* suit to keep those micro-critters away from your naked skin. James Bond's tux is dry under his wetsuit, and that's just wrong, and the Little Fool knew it before anyone. But he didn't run back to his monkey. He still wanted to be James Bond. The Little Fool never wanted to be a sock monkey. I wanna be like you, walk like you, talk like you.

Even with the stab wounds and all the textbook decomposition, she was still a very attractive woman. Not just attractive. Sexy. That's a different thing. What's your name? Who's your daddy?

The Little Fool knew the answer to one of those questions. He knew the answers to both of those questions. The Little Fool used to date the corpse. Way back before this last bout of passion. La la la la. Down by the river. Dead. Dead.

CHAPTER SEVEN

Getting Away with It

The Little Fool didn't want to be a baseball star. He didn't want to run away and join the circus. He didn't even want to be a guitar hero. He wanted to be a diver. He wanted that wet suit with the tux under it. Right from the start. Right back from holding his monkey, his first love, even then he would have wanted to be a diver if he had known what divers were. I knew he had to be a diver. That was always my advice. When I was his guidance counselor, we were in sync. We knew the right thing to do. He quit the homophobic, anti-Atheist Boy Scouts when he learned they didn't have a scuba merit badge. He was even happier later when he learned there is no god and you always want to keep your sexual options open. He got PADI certified at twelve years old. Boy Scouts? Yeah, sure. Sic 'em pigs on you.

We lived inland. Not even a really good-sized lake around. He got scuba certified at the Y. Everyone called it "The Y." If he had known it was "YMCA," he would have found out what the "C" stood for and felt creepy about going there. But he didn't really think about it until it was too late. I knew. The Little Fool even loved the word "scuba." "Scuba" is an acronym. He loved that. "YMCA" is an initialism that people often call an acronym. Hey, if you say the individual letters, it ain't no acronym. "Laser"? Yes. "FBI"? No. It's fun to stay at the YMCA.

He was open-water certified and even a cave diver before he was out of high school. He was born obsessed with water in a landlocked state. That's what happens living in a random universe. There's no plan. No one's in charge. But I knew that wouldn't stop the Little Fool. Lack of water can't stop a real diver. Not a real diver with a monkey who loves him. High school did its best to stop his diving. They said he was too smart to be a diver. He was too smart to be a cop. Everytime you do your, do your thing.

The guidance counselor wanted him to go to law school. That National Merit thing makes the guidance counselor believe his job matters. The Little Fool hated all the drugs and drinking in his high school and believed college would be more of the same. There's the heartbreak of kids who really want to go to college but just don't have the brains. But it can't touch the heartbreak of the kids with the brains and the grades who just don't want to go to college. No one is pushing for them not to go. They have no cheerleaders on their side. There are no programs to help them drop out. The Little Fool was one of the tragic cases. He could have gone right from high school into scuba (acronym) and NYPD (initialism). But he wasted four years in pre-law. Four years watching kids get drunk and high and try to have sex. The Little Fool had plenty of sex back then, and didn't want to get high. He didn't need college. Pigs off campus.

He went to law school briefly. He liked the "fact patterns" a lot. He liked that you can sit around and make up cases that would really test our civilization. Want to kill your spouse? Open a "Stop 'n' Rob" in a bad neighborhood, and buy a gun. Always work shifts with your spouse and keep a gun around. As soon as someone holds up your store (you could put up a sign that says, "Employees keep $1,000 in drug money right here behind the counter"), pull the gun and pop your spouse. Shoot him or her right in the face and chest. Two hugs and a kiss would be fine. It's no-kidding-go-to-jail murder for all of those committing the crime, and it's a nice walk on the sunny side of the street for you. It's not murder for you. They won't even try you. It's "get out of jail free." You pulled the gun to stop the crime, and your spouse got shot. Yeah, it was by you, but you weren't doing the crime. You walk tall and fast like Christopher Reeve before the accident. Right out of jail. And the scumbags who should know better than to steal things go away for a long time. Even the guy driving the car. Very cool. We learned that in law school. William Burroughs/William Tell, it's your call. Your wife and your outside woman, too.

He had met this victim in law school. One smart cookie. That had been one good thing about law school. That had been a great six months of law school. She didn't coo over the monkey. She wasn't interested in the Little Fool's feminine side. When they needed to get more feminine, she was very good at talking women into joining them. She was very convincing. She'd have been a great litigator. Of course, she was arguing an easy case. Who wouldn't have wanted to join her and the Little Fool in the bad monkey's bed for a few hours? Only christians, and they hadn't been asked. It was an easy sell. Little red Corvette.

The sex had been good enough to keep the Little Fool in law school for longer than his attention span, but he had got out. Besides her, the only good thing had been that law school let him skip some of the NYPD training. He knew the fact patterns. So, we have a beautiful woman in her early thirties: blue eyes, long, black hair, and those fat lips. Big, fat, cushiony lips. You know those lips. The lips women have surgery to produce. The lips that are natural on a sock monkey. And were natural on her. She was cushioned all over. Built for comfort. Very smart and sane, but those hadn't been her selling points. Mighty, mighty, letting it all hang out.

5'10". About 135 pounds. She was bloated when the Little Fool saw her, the first time he had seen her in a couple years. It seemed she hadn't drowned; she probably had been dead when she had hit the water. As he looked at her, beaten and soaked, the dead body reminded him of her, but he didn't believe it *was* her. Many things reminded him of her. Often when he saw an attractive brunette he thought of her and the nights they had spent together. He thought of her and tried to have an excuse to call her. He had her phone number, but not her email. It's easier to think of something cute and out of nowhere for email. On the phone, she might answer. The phone booth, the one across the hall.

He had gone with some friends and their kids to the county fair. The kids were really too old to be with Mom and Dad at the fair. Much too old for that. But they were there as a family, with the single Little Fool as a rod in the family reactor. One of them, she was fourteen, had wanted to go on rides. Scary rides. The Dive Bomber. The Round Up. Rides that hurt Dad's back, and that Mom never liked. It was good to have the Little Fool with them. The Little Fool swam in sewage. How could he mind being locked in a cage by a man with jailhouse ink, and spun around by old diesel equipment maintained by people who ate too many corn dogs? So the Little Fool rode with the daughter. She liked being seen with the Little Fool. She was fourteen, so she liked older men. There was nothing in the world but older men. Her same-age choices weren't men yet. She wanted people to believe she was dating him. He wanted people to believe anything but. He kept his eyes off her. He looked at the stuffed animals. Big stuffed frogs and bears. I hate when he looks at those plushies. He's too old for that. Did you forget about me, Mr. Duplicity?

Nevermind fourteen and a friend's daughter and every female but this other woman. Well, even she hadn't been a woman. This other girl he'd seen had been about sixteen, and had this amazing body. She was climbing one of those carny ladders. It's a rope ladder where both sides of the ladder go to a single hang point on each end. It's a ladder that flips. Carnies walk up it with no hands and ring the bell. Marks struggle up a few rungs and fall. If a mark rings the bell, the mark gets a stuffed animal. Not a good stuffed animal. No sock monkey is ever offered as a prize at a carnival. Sock monkeys aren't part of that scene. Nothing wrong with that scene; we're just not part of it. Get it? Of course, marks never ring the bell and never get even a cheap, cheesy plush toy. The Little Fool had been watching the ladder game. He didn't care about the stuffed animals. Why would he? There was this girl about sixteen, the perfect age for a cheap, carnival plushy. And she had big, firm breasts. Is sixteen too young for implants? Who knows, and it doesn't matter. Her bottom was perfect, too. Tight jeans never go out of style. And a tight, white

T-shirt. The Little Fool had watched. He wasn't dating the fourteen-year-old daughter of his friend, and the Little Fool didn't want to date the sixteen-year-old on the ladder. He just wanted to watch her struggle and then fall on her back, with a few very brief standing waves rippling under her thin, white T-shirt. She fell onto the dirty, blue, blowup cushion. And as he had watched, he had thought about the woman from law school. Mambo number 5.

And now he thought of her again, but this time he wasn't looking at a young woman with her whole life ahead of her to enjoy what natural selection had created for one reason and she would use any way she wanted. This time he was looking at a dead body. A dead body that belonged to no one. That wouldn't be used at all. A body that had no choices left. It was a body he'd felt underwater and brought to dry land. And as he looked at this bloated dead thing, his mind went back to law school. To one night. Not a kinky night at all. Just the two of them. No tools. No props. No acting. "I want to fuck you like we're in love," she had said to the Little Fool. And they had. And he remembered. And when he looked at this dead body, he thought about that night, just the way he'd thought about it at the carnival rope ladder and at the Starbucks by the college, and at other times too. And then he realized that this memory was triggered by the real thing. Sometimes x equals x.

CHAPTER EIGHT

You Wanna Make Something of It?

I don't make monkeys. I am Dickie. I am a made monkey. Men are made by the mob; sock monkeys are made by grandmothers to sell at church sales. We know the church is worse than the mob, but grandmothers are all that is good. The first few weeks the Little Fool hadn't noticed me. Then he held onto me. Then he cried into me. Then he talked to me. Then it had looked to the world as if he had abandoned me. But I ain't Puff, the magic dragon. There's no drug reference in the Little Fool's love. I was never outgrown. I can't be outgrown. The Little Fool is no pothead Jackie Paper. Puff is a rascal; I'm a bad wammerjammer.

The Little Fool is a momma's boy. He's a momma's boy like all real momma's boys. He has become what his Mom would have wanted to be if she had been bigger, stronger and male. The world is seeing the last of these real momma's boys. Women have more power now. Women have more money. Women work outside the home and discover cures for diseases and argue in front of the Supreme Court. Women don't just stay home creating little fools. His momma told him that he would be the leader of a big old band. Smart, strong, ambitious Moms are now like smart, strong, ambitious Dads: they are successful themselves. They themselves have opportunity. The Little Fool was raised in that small window in history where a superstar woman's best move on the world's chessboard could be to inspire her sons. Parents are more equal now. Not equal enough, but closer. Moms still love their kids white light/white heat, and that's all that really matters. "M" is for the million things she gave me.

Before the green revolution blew out of Texas A&M, Mom, Dad, and the kids all had to work together to be able to eat. There was less time for maternal obsessing. But the Little Fool is of the couple of generations in which you had those real momma's boys. Momma's boys with bad monkeys. A few decades later she might have been on the NYPD dive team herself. She could have done that. If only she had been a big strong man, she would have owned the world. But since she hadn't been that and couldn't own the world herself, her son would own the world. The Little Fool and his Mom had been the same person. She hadn't dominated him; she hadn't lived vicariously through him. She had just loved him and let him know that he had the power to do whatever he wanted. She had been his superpower under a yellow sun. This is the time of the momma's boys. The Little Fool thinks like his Mom. He acts like his Mom. He is his Mom. But he doesn't talk in his head to his Mom. He can't talk to his Mom. His Mom is dead. He can't even pretend to talk to his Mom. The pain is too great for fantasy to flourish. The pain will always be there. The pain will always be too great. So, in his head, he talks to his monkey. He talks to me. I give him advice. I don't betray her trust. Hey, hey, Momma, the way you move. Make you sweat. Make you groove.

"Hey, we fish 'em out of the drink. That's all we do. We don't do autopsies, we don't eulogize, we don't dig the hole, we don't send flowers. We aren't the detectives that file the reports for posterity. We just fish them out of the drink." The other diver explained it all just like that. The Little Fool stood looking at the dead body that he had enjoyed so when it had been alive. He thought about her bloated face and her looking him in the eyes and saying, "I think I'm retaining water. Do I look fat?" Down by the river. Woooo hoooo. Dead.

"Do these jeans make my ass look fat?" No, actually, those jeans are the only thing holding your decaying flesh on the bone. The Little Fool had lost his mind. He was talking to a dead body. This crosses a line with me. This is crazy. Just crazy. Why had they broken up? Had he believed he could do better? Had he really been too nuts for her? Was he just unable to commit to anyone? Had she been tough enough, in love enough? He never really talked to his monkey about it.

I guess he should be glad they broke up, or he'd be grieving for his wife right now. He couldn't lose his Mom, his Dad, and his wife in one year. I'm glad it was just an old girlfriend and not a wife. Hey, he can lose an old girlfriend. He can always make more of those, right, baby? He doesn't make monkeys. He makes ex-girlfriends. Man, how can you still look beautiful after days of floating in cold, raw sewage? I will survive.

Okay, so now she was dead and now he knew he loved her. Say it with me: "timing." Once she'd become a stripper, her christian family disowned her. When she stopped being a stripper, she hadn't told them. Her family had been punished for believing their imaginary friend was more important than their daughter. They grieved now. They grieved a lot. They had made a mistake. They were fools. At least the Little Fool hadn't left her because of anything I had said. The parents grieved, but they didn't go looking for the killer. Even O.J. didn't really go looking for the killer. Her parents didn't look at all. The detective that was assigned this gig didn't look for the killer. The Little Fool knew there wasn't a reason in the world to look for the killer. He knew it wouldn't bring her back to life. He knew there would be no closure. He knew he wouldn't protect anyone else. If the killer had planned it, if it was first-degree, he or she probably wouldn't choose to kill anyone else. Serial killers are so rare. And if it had been second-degree, a crime of passion (which it looked like), well, the killer would probably be too scared to do it again. Scared straight. Really killing is scarier than some ex-cons showing you around prison when you're in high school. There wasn't a reason on earth to find the killer. The world would make the right decision and just let this one slide. She didn't have a husband. She didn't have kids. Who cares? Somebody got murdered.

It was a crime of passion and, unluckily for the killer, what the Little Fool needed in his life right then was passion. When she had been alive, he had made love to her. Now that she was dead, he decided he loved her. The Little Fool was the worst enemy a criminal can have: a guy with a little money ahead, connections, and the feeling that nothing matters. It sure looked like a second-degree murder, but it would be first-degree detective work. The Little Fool needed a serious hobby, and this would be it. Passion. The Little Fool was about to go off the deep end. He took his handle-the-creepy-dead-things gloves off. He reached down with his bare-naked, pink index finger and raised her dead eyelid. He looked into her dead eye. It was time. It was Ramones time. Blitzkrieg bop. Hey, ho, let's go. We're about to go out of our head. Let's take it out of our head. Let's take this outside. Hey, ho, let's go. The Little Fool squished her dead eyelid back over the dead eye. It was time for him to go out of his head. He took a deep NYC breath through his nose. He smelled the decay of her body. He thought about Dee Dee Ramone on the first record. The Little Fool was about to speak out loud, "Onetwothreefour." That was out loud, all right. This is the tempo. Hey, ho, let's go.

CHAPTER NINE

Junkie Time

The Little Fool found out about the joy of stalking (not "the joy of stocking"—that would be me). In the abstract, stalking someone is wonderful. But being stalked is a drag. If you're stalked, you have responsibility for the stalker. You have worries: Is it something I did to lead her on? Am I really all those awful things she says I am in those perfect-penmanship faxes she sends to my boss? Do I need to call the police? Will the police hurt her? Will the police laugh at me? Every step I take.

But stalking is wonderful. All your problems go away. There's only one thing on your plate. You think junkies enjoy heroin? You think being a junkie is longing for that particular pharmaceutical? Being a junkie is just a drastic, perfect way to prioritize. Before junk, you have to put this list in order: call Mom, read *Nature*, buy food, eat food, work out, have a talk with the boss, watch that *Discover* special about honey badgers that's still on your TiVo, take yourself off all Instant Messenger lists, get your oil changed, pay American Express, get some socks, call Marie, get your hair cut, buy a charger for your cell phone. . . . And that's just the list that happens to be in your head in one ten-second period. When you're a junkie, there is *one* thing on your list: cop. The government helps you by making copping hard and expensive. The mountain has to be worth climbing. There was a band called Cop Shoot Cop. Some people believed it was about violence against peace officers. No, it was a junkie's to-do list. It's easy. It's simple. White light/white heat. I'm going to nullify my life.

Focus. All junkies have focus. Stalking gives you close to the same focus, and you don't need to vomit as much. You don't have to poke holes between your toes. And the stakes are still high. With junk, if you do it wrong, you go to jail. With stalking, if you do it right, you go to jail. All you need to think about is "What is she doing right now?" That's all. And any correct answer to that question brings joy. She's sleeping. I hope she's getting her rest. She's eating. She has to keep that perfect body. She's sleeping with another guy. It'll just make her appreciate me more. She's going to the mall. Good, I need some socks. Find out who ya call. One way or another.

The Little Fool needed to be a junkie. He needed it bad. He was waiting for his man. The Little Fool knew too much about scuba. He could do it in his sleep. His chest didn't clench and vibrate anymore when he jumped in the cold sewage. It was easy for him to have sex. He didn't watch TV. He didn't drink. He'd read *Moby-Dick* and understood it. There were no politics in his workplace. He was good at what he did, and he got credit for it. He had enough money. The only worry he had about paying the rent was remembering to pay his rent, but he would get that automatic and on-line. The Little Fool had no problems . . . no problems he could do anything about. He had plenty of money, plenty of friends of both sexes, and a good job. He had outside interests. Welcome to my nightmare.

Something had to give. The Little Fool could have had a kid. There were women he could have talked into that, but he hadn't wanted that enough. He could probably have talked the government into letting him adopt a kid, but he hadn't wanted that. He could have learned to play alto sax—he'd always wanted to play alto sax—but that would have involved learning about jazz. There is no sax in rock and roll after 1960, not counting the Big Man, and what the Little Fool knows is rock and roll. He could have learned a new instrument, but he can't reset his "favorite stations" buttons and he doesn't want to play guitar. Guitar is stupid. I advised him. I knew what he had to do. He had to start stalking his ex-girlfriend.

He had to start stalking his dead ex-girlfriend. Happy and content weren't right any more. He had to get dark. No colors in my life.

Stalking a dead woman is where the smart monkey money goes. You can't feel guilty for ruining her life. That's over when you start. But most important, there's light at the end of the tunnel. The facts aren't going to change anymore. You really can know everything there is to know about her and it won't change because she gets religion or she hears some middle-aged guy with a beard talking about relationships on *Oprah*. It's a jigsaw puzzle and all the pieces are right there in the box. You know where they are; you just have to put them together. I'm just trying to do this jigsaw puzzle before it rains any more.

This might not have filled up any of the Little Fool's time. If it had been just a simple, drunken, second-degree murder, he'd have been done with his obsession in a day. But this hadn't been the kind of woman who gets killed by a drunken lover. Of course, there isn't a "kind" of woman who gets killed by a drunken lover. I'm not blaming victims here. I'm not an unenlightened monkey. I know that good, smart, careful women get killed by drunks. But the dirtiest secret of detective work is that profiling works. I'll give you an example I won't get in trouble for: serial killers are white guys from twenty-five to thirty-five. I know, there are those black father/kinda-son trunk snipers around D.C., but never mind them. You can say in any book or movie, "The killer is obviously a white male," and you're fine. But that's all. Maybe you could say, "The killer is obviously in Afghanistan," but don't push it beyond that. Sober people don't get killed by drunks. Not drunks the sober people know. Driving drunks, robbing drunks, yes, but not drunk friends. In the time the Little Fool had known her, she had hated drunks with the intensity of someone who gives sober lapdances to drunk laps all night. That'll make you just a bit more sober than Carrie Nation. Come with the gentle people.

He didn't believe she had been killed by a drunken lover, but he would find out. All that mattered was finding out. He had to know. Nothing else mattered from the second he counted *onetwothreefour* out loud. He would still go to work, for a while. He would still pay his rent, for a while. He would still keep his friends, for a while. He was going to go crazy in a sensible way. But he would find out how this woman died. He would focus his ambition, his love, his life. He would focus like a stalker. He would be a junkie. Cop shoot cop. That would be his life. It had finally happened. He had fallen in love. Goddamn the pusher man.

Helen Cynthia Parenteau, called "Nell." Nell Parenteau. The tip of the tongue taking a trip of three steps down the palate. Except, Nell Parenteau doesn't use the tip of the tongue—it uses lips, a grimace, then a tongue tip on the palate, but who cares? She was still Helen on the dotted line, but in his arms she was always Nell. Helen Cynthia Parenteau. But everyone knew her as Nancy. Nell.

CHAPTER TEN

Ding Dong

The big, modern wrestling match is with puberty. Real scientists make it earlier and social scientists want to make it later. Any science that has the word "science" in it isn't a science. "Social science." "Computer science." If your field is so insecure about its place in science that your field has to sneak the word in, your field is probably not science. Nutrition makes puberty begin earlier and earlier, and do-gooders want it later and later. They say it's accelerated by pollution and hormones in the water, but the acceleration might just be access to a lot better food. Bunches of girls are hitting puberty at eight years old, and some parents want their kids in school until they're twenty-five. But we don't need those figures. Let's just go with hitting puberty at fourteen and the government trying to stop you from having sex until you're eighteen. That's a long four years. Okay, they *say* eighteen, but they *mean* sixteen. That's a long twenty-four months. They say we're young and we don't know.

The Little Fool was unusual in that he wasn't unusual and he knew it. He knew he had gone from hugging this monkey to slapping the other monkey overnight. His peers had grown up and had kids. And they started telling themselves they had got into sex too soon, much earlier than was right for their kids. Kids are yet another reason to lie to yourself. The Little Fool had no reason to lie to himself about this. He remained sexually active. It wasn't just his high school sweetheart, his wife, his co-worker, and one professional in Vegas. He was sexually active with real, single, sexually active women who were interested in a big guy who swam in raw sewage. Those women could have sex with him and not think about what critters were living in his gut. Those women thought about him saving kids who had fallen in the water. He had never saved a kid who had fallen in the water, but it was better than thinking of him digging through dirty water for corpses of ex-girlfriends. I'm looking through you, but you're not there.

The Little Fool had been sexually active through many sexual fashions. He'd seen those '70s porno, pubic-hair rain forests sticking out of underwear that covered the whole bottom. He'd seen the little shaved "landing strips" and "hitlers" and the bikini panties. He'd seen the fully shaved bikini wax gone wild with the g-strings that were there only to show above the back of the hip-huggers. Baby got back.

He'd also gone from no bras to white underwire bras to sports bras to water bras. He'd gone from nipples poking out of Danskins to hidden nipples, to pierced nipples, some pierced horizontally *and* vertically. He'd seen the pierced nipple with the crown around it. And he'd seen ink. Lots of ink. From the little heart on the ankle of the really bad girl in high school to Miss America types with jailhouse ink showing above their "God Bless the USA" shirts. He'd seen tongue piercing and genital piercing go from Jim Rose's Circus Sideshow to the local mall. The waters around you have grown.

In high school, he drove an ice cream truck. He washed dishes at Howard Johnson's and Famous Bill's restaurants. The Little Fool washed dishes at a hospital where he cleaned the food off sick people's plates. He had been disgusted the first week; he was eating off the plates by the second month. He was getting his gut ready for the dive team. But the only job that had mattered was ice cream delivering. He tells everyone he has worked on an "ice cream truck." But nobody ever referred to it as "an ice cream truck"; it was called "The Ding Dong Truck." This is Dickie you're listening to now, and Dickie is a sock monkey, and sock monkeys know the

real names of things. The Little Fool had been the Ding Dong
Man. He had been "Danny Ding Dong," and he had apprenticed
under "Irving Ding Dong." Those weren't the names on their driver's licenses, but those had been their true names when they were
in the truck. Ice cream man, reel and rock.

All the real education (outside of scuba) the Little Fool had ever
received had been in that ice cream truck. The Little Fool had
gone to a public school. "Better to be uneducated than educated
by your government." For a long time we believed Thomas Jefferson said that. But the Web says that's wrong. It seems no one said
that. So let's say I said that. A sock monkey said that. "Better to be
uneducated than educated by your government"—*Dickie, sock
monkey*. His public school had been in a hippie phase, so the Little
Fool had gone on "independent study" and had spent all day on
the Ding Dong truck. You study them hard and you're hoping to
pass.

Irving Ding Dong had long hair and a beard. And he had crippled hands. His hands were on his wrists, but they just hung there.
He couldn't move them. The Little Fool had been a customer and
they had started talking and soon the Little Fool became Danny
Ding Dong and was riding in the truck all the time. Irving was a
socialist. He was also a buddhist. He had been exactly twice the Little Fool's age when they met. They became friends of very different
ages. Irving became a mentor. This was the kind of mentoring the
government can't make happen. It was the kind of mentoring the
catholic church makes look bad. The Little Fool's Mom and Dad
had been a bit worried that the Little Fool's time was being spent
with an older man. But nothing sexual ever happened. Oh, it got
sexual, but it was always talking about girls. Irving talked openly
about sex. He was the only one who could be trusted. He was
very open about sex. He'd lost the use of his right hand because
of masturbation. That's what a priest had told him, and the timing sure had been right. When Irving had changed to his left
hand, that one went too. QED. He never knew what had really
killed his hands and had stopped him from playing the upright

bass with Herbie Hancock. It was just another symptom of a godless universe filled with random pain. So the religious blamed it on masturbation. That kind of anti-sex sickness takes a bit of work to get over. Irving had done that work and he was free. He wasn't going to pass it on. You must not act the way you were brought up.

Irving always called Danny "the callow youth." When you see the Little Fool, when you love the Little Fool, you want to call him something like the Little Fool. "Callow Youth" was what Irving chose. He was so close to the real sock monkey name. One quick consultation with the Sock and he would have changed to "the Little Fool." He's not little and he's not a fool, but he thinks of himself that way, and those who love him should use that true name. Irving had been very well educated. Liberal arts. He had a couple of master's degrees in things followed by the word "science." He knew everything. And he talked to Danny as if they were both adults. They could talk about art, sex, friendship, politics and the future. Really talk. Irving began assigning books to the Little Fool, and the Little Fool would gulp them down like Bomb Pops from the Ding Dong freezer, then talk about the books. The Little Fool read so fast he got intellectual brain freeze. Irving would shake his head in disgust at Danny missing the point. But Irving always told him the point. There had been no more schoolbooks; there had been only Irving books. There had been no classes; just riding in the Ding Dong Truck. He could have written a book: "Everything I Know I Learned on the Ding Dong Truck."

There was a private school for girls in the Little Fool's hometown. The school's purpose had been selective breeding. The girls were there for the mixers with the private school for boys. Both schools had gone co-ed while the Little Fool had been growing up, but the schools never let townies in. The schools would never become that co- in the -ed department. But the Ding Dong truck was a free ticket into the prep-land. You could drive with impunity on campus and ring your bells. I get on the bus that takes me to you.

Danny got to meet preppie girls. And he had the looks. He'd been young and strong and looked the way the boys' prep school kids weren't allowed to look. His hair was wrong. His clothes were wrong. He was a townie who looked more like a musician than the prep boys, and that's all that mattered. And he had Irving as a coach. Other adults wanted to stop kids from having sex. But Irving helped Danny. Irving wanted to thwart the selective breeding plan. Maybe it was about being a socialist. Maybe it was about being a buddhist. Or maybe it was the crippled hands, but Irving had helped. You were made to go out and get her.

Is there a difference between men and women? Male and female? Boys and girls? Yes, there is one difference. It's not covered in Rita Rudner's Vegas stand up act, but the difference *does* have to do with shopping. The Ding Dong Truck had many frozen confections. And these had been named to please young kids. The confections had stupid names. High school boys don't want to use stupid names. High school girls embrace stupid names. It's the only difference this bad monkey has ever found. Everything else is the same. Boys and girls even treat their monkeys the same. But in the names of frozen confections, the difference is pronounced. Here's how it goes:

Boy Transaction
Prep boy: Give me one of those chocolate things.
Danny: Which one?
Prep boy: The big chocolate one.
Danny: We have a lot of chocolate ones.
Prep boy: This one right here. (tapping)
Danny: I can't see through the truck.
Prep boy: You know, with the chocolate sprinkle shit on it.
Danny: What's the name?
Prep boy: The Chippity thing.
Danny: We don't have a "Chippity thing".
Prep boy: (mumbles)
Danny: Beg your pardon?

37

Prep boy: Chippity Chocolaty.
Danny: One Chippity Chocolaty coming right up.

Girl Transaction
Prep girl: Give me a Chippity Chocolaty.
Danny: Wanna go out tonight?

Vive la différence!
Irving Ding Dong had given the Little Fool the best advice of his life. Irving had said, "Ask the smart girls out. The mousey ones in the sweaters. The ones with glasses. The ones who are always reading. Get yourself into the advanced study groups and act like a punk. Check out what they're reading. It's Henry Miller and Anaïs Nin. The seduction has already been done by the best. Just go in and collect. The cheerleaders have to negotiate with the only commodity they'll ever have. The smart girls, they're waiting for you. Be a smart bad boy. And then just ask them. Make sure your looks will scare their parents, and then ask the smart girls. Don't play games. Just ask." How could all these others have won those Nobel Prizes and not Irving the year he had given that advice? It had changed the Little Fool's life. The popular kids had been dating; the Little Fool had been working his way through the *Kama Sutra*. Little red Corvette.

Irving had also preached, "Go with the fashion. Let your sexuality be led by fashion. When they're wearing short skirts, be a leg man. When they go braless, be a breast man. When they give you hip-huggers, be a crack man. Just follow, man. Don't you go trying to fight it. A word to the wise: Start getting into midriffs." Legs; she knows how to use them.

Nell's pubic area was shaved. She had one pierced nipple and she always showed her midriff. She was a woman of the times. And the Little Fool had Irving in the Little Fool's mind. When he'd first seen Nell, he'd been knocked out. He was living in his time. From the moment he met her, all he wanted to know was how shaved she was. He had needed to know that, even though it wouldn't have mattered if she had a bush out of time, '70s porno or turn-of-the-century bare.

He didn't care at all, but all he had wanted in the world was to know that. And he'd found out. But times had changed. Now he could see her pubic area only in the morgue. Now he wanted to know everything else. Tell me, momma, what is it?

CHAPTER ELEVEN

The Aristocrats

There's this joke, "The Aristocrats." Now, when you call it "The Aristocrats," you've just said, "Tell the one about 'to get to the other side.'" That's the punchline. And yet with "The Aristocrats," the people who want to hear it the most are the ones who know the joke. It's all in the telling. The journey is everything. You will read all about Nell. You will read more about the Little Fool. We will solve Nell's murder. But right now you need to read more about Irving Ding Dong. He would have approved. It's that zen fractal thing. The whole story is in every part. If you understand the Little Fool, then you'll understand what had happened to Nell and why it matters. If you understand Irving, you understand the Little Fool. I am he as you are he, as you are me.

Irving Ding Dong hadn't always been an ice cream man and mentor to the Little Fool. Irving had had a successful academic career somewhere in the Midwest. I believe he was an Iowa boy. He had that intense rebel quality that comes only to the corn-fed. If Jack Kerouac had been Johnny Carson, the revolution would have stuck. Corn-fed people keep a promise, and if the promise is to go bugnutty, they can do that, too. When Irving gave up on the vanilla straights, he didn't go back. To live outside the law you must be honest.

Everything happens to everyone. Irving could tell a story about driving a cab and a black blues guy beating him for a six-buck fare and leaving him a can of black cherry soda on the back seat, and

you'd be able to see all the truth in the world. To someone who's
not paying attention, it's just a lost six bucks. But this is a story.
This is a story that should be in a movie. This is a story that was in
a movie and was cut out. This is a story that works as fiction. It
doesn't need the "I swear this is true" crutch. The more time spent
convincing it's a true story, the weaker the content of the story. No
stories are true. Life is true. Stories are told. Listen to my story
'bout a man named Jed.

Irving, when he had had his non-Ding Dong name, had gotten
a job as a parole officer somewhere in Seattle. (The more details I
give, the less likely the story is to be true. And I don't care if you
believe it really happened.) Parole officer is a gig you can do with
crippled hands and a lot of degrees in phony subjects. It's a job a
sock monkey could do, except for the paperwork. I'm not going to
use a lot of details or respond to any of your plausibility questions.
I'll just give you the beats of the story, and you spend the time
thinking about it. If you need to, you can make it real.

Irving gets a call about one of his charges. One of his graduates
is holding a mother and her two kids hostage in their home. The
police have the house surrounded, and they're talking to the perp.
The police open communication, and he asks for Irving. The bad
guy wants to talk to his parole officer. The bad guy trusts Irving.
Billy, don't be a hero.

Irving doesn't legally have to go to the scene, but our narrative
demands it. He shows up. The movie version would have him walking in shirt open, to reveal he has no weapons. But he's got dead,
limp hands, so why bother? He goes into the house. A scared mom,
scared kids, a volatile perpetrator and our Irving. The two of them
talk while the other three tremble. Irving and the perp talk. The
cops outside have drawn a bead on the head of the scumbag who
has his gun pointed at the kids, finger on the trigger. Meanwhile,
Irving talks. He talks about trust. He talks about caring. He makes
eye contact. He lets the perp look into his heart. His gentle and
pure heart. He's David Carradine. Irving speaks for a long time (in
your telling of the story, you'll decide just how long). In a tearful

moment, a moment with more eye contact than anyone would want, the bad guy hands the loaded gun over to Irving. Irving is a hero. It's a movie moment. The sharpshooters relax a little. That's the way it's supposed to go. We are the champions.

But wait, there's more. If the story were to stop there, it wouldn't be a good story; it would be a Schwarzenegger vehicle. Our story continues . . .

Irving and the perp keep talking as Irving holds the gun, useless, between the wrists of his crippled hands. Psychopaths are very good at getting into your heart. Don't tell him anything about yourself, Clarice. Irving is a good man, living outside the law, working for the law. He knows he's working for The Man, but The Man doesn't own him. Irving doesn't run out to a cheering crowd, gun harmlessly dangling. He doesn't say, "That's how Irving does police work," then punch the police chief for something wimpy he does in the B story. No. Irving stays in the house. He stays with his charge. His sits and talks. The relieved Mom and the antsy kids watch and listen. Irving and the perp keep talking. The sharing doesn't stop when the gun moves from destructive to crippled hands. They talk more about trust. The perp talks more about caring. They make more eye contact. They speak for a long time. And in a tearful moment, a moment with more eye contact than anyone would want, the good guy hands the loaded gun over to the kidnapper. He holds it between his wrists, and offers it to the kidnapping psycho who, with a sincere, bittersweet, resigned smile, takes it and points it at one of the children. Once again, there's a working finger on the trigger. Ready to fire. In that second, Irving is finished. He's a loser. He'd been stupid. No one would do that. He'd done it. The law won.

The Little Fool's grandfather had asked at the end of every movie (except maybe *Dr. Strangelove*), "What happens next?" He always wanted to know. At the end of *The Graduate*: that sick smile, does that mean that mundane life comes flooding back, or are they happy ever after? Grampy always wanted to know. Grampy had picked me up from the floor a few times and pulled me out of the Little Fool's mouth when I was too soggy, but Grampy hadn't understood that life goes on, even if stories don't. That's why stories are so wonderful: they end. You can get your mind around them. You can enjoy the arc. Real life doesn't have closure. The real story ends with the gun being handed back. Life went on. No one had been hurt, the bad guy had given the gun back yet again, and Irving Ding Dong had been born. The real story has the perp's sad mental illness—too sad even for a tragedy. Irving had dropped out in a serious way, flown across the country, and never tried to work a real job again. He had driven an ice cream truck. Harry Callahan doesn't retire and drive an ice cream truck. But Dirty Harry is not half the hero Irving is. Irving is a true-story hero. Power to the people. Right on.

You could put that story in a movie to show how crazy Mel Gibson is. Mel could have pulled that off when he was young and good-looking. Mel could have pulled that off before christ. Mel's character could have gotten away with that at the beginning of the movie if he hurt bad guys enough by the end of the movie. But there's a more important Irving story. One more fractal piece before our journey continues. The Ding Dong route had included a stop at a nursing home. It was a hard stop for a teenaged Little Fool. It's hard to serve ice cream to that level of sadness. Old people are tough for punks. When you're a teenager, you want to see old people as evil; you don't want to see them as frail. Get on to a new one if you can't lend a hand.

Electroshock had taught Irving a lot about mental illness. He had the comfort of a cripple around human frailty. One old woman with a real smile would come to the Ding Dong truck. She had what Irving called "echolalia": she frequently just repeated the last thing she heard. Time had made her a more efficient parrot. Glossolalia is speaking in tongues. Zenolalia is speaking an unknown language. Echolalia is just repeating. It works for a lot of interaction: "Hello." "Hello." "How are you?" "How are you?" "Nice weather." You say, "Goodbye," and I say, "Hello." Hello. Hello.

Irving had had very specific directions for Danny. The old woman had known her part; Danny had had to learn the Ding Dong side of the interaction. When the old woman would come to the truck, she would hold out her hand and show her money to the man in the ice cream truck. Irving would say, "Hello." While she repeated, "Hello," he would silently count the money in her hand. He would calculate what she could buy with that much. Fifteen cents was a Popsicle, thirty-five cents was a Hoodsie cup, seventy-five cents was a Chippity Chocolaty. He would then look her in the eye and say the flavor and name of a Ding Dong product that was exactly the price she had. "You don't *ever* say 'Popsicle' to that wonderful woman. You say the flavor. People order a flavor; they don't just order a Popsicle. You say 'Chocolate Hoodsie cup,' not 'Hoodsie Cup.' Give the woman some dignity. Let her buy what we're trying to get rid of. Use every cent she has. Let her order what she wants." Gotta serve somebody.

Danny would choke back his tears, look the old woman in the eye, and say, "Lime Popsicle." And she would say, "Lime Popsicle," and Danny would take her money and give her the lime Popsicle. It was hard to get rid of the old lime Popsicles. And Danny would say, "Thanks." And she would say, "Thanks." And she would smile. Irving had known that when Danny could just smile back and feel happy and not fight back tears, then he was ready to graduate from the Ding Dong truck. The Little Fool had learned about love. Twist and shout. Twist and shout.

CHAPTER TWELVE

Attraction

Love at first sight is easy. The instant someone starts running for president, he has his highest approval rating. He hasn't alienated anyone. The longer he goes without stands on abortion, cloning, animal rights, and taxes in Alaska, the larger his group of supporters. Shut up. Just shut your mouth. People look good to other people. Smiles are nice; handshakes are nice. Ambition in its gentle form is very attractive. Some people respect opinionated, but very few are attracted to it. See that woman over there? The Little Fool loves her. What's not to love? Get to know her, and it's a whole different thing. The pupils dilate, the mouth waters, the nostrils flair for a whiff. When it's animal, it's easy; when it's human, it's hard. You know it's the way you walk.

Nell had been working at a strip club when the Little Fool met her, but he didn't meet her at work. Strippers at work don't give out information. They are running for the office of lapdancer. The sexual information floods all the various-sized fools' heads and the fools don't even consider it possible that this human being would have policies the fools wouldn't like. I'm speaking now of sane people. There are insane people who need to hate the people the insane people are sexually attracted to. Men and women who go to topless clubs feel the sexuality and believe the people who provide it are evil. We won't be dealing with that level of wrong in this story. We'll be dealing with decomposed dead bodies in raw sewage, huge puncture wounds, rage, pain and murder, but we won't touch upon the kind of hate that's contained in even the slightest anti-sex position. There are certain things a sock monkey can't stomach. In my story, there is no one sick enough to have negative thoughts towards a stripper. We're going to keep it clean and happy. Everything is beautiful.

For sane people at a strip club, every employee is a law student. Every employee is proud and happy about her body and open about her sexuality and loving. Every employee is sober, but loves to have a good time. The Little Fool has known a lot of sex workers and I got to meet many of them in his bedroom. When the Little Fool would go with male friends to strip clubs, he would ask his male friends one question: "If the men in this club were physically attracted to you the same way they are to these women, could you do *everything* these women are doing?" The Little Fool's friendship had this litmus test. If the things the women were doing was disgusting to these men, why were the men encouraging it? The Little Fool passes his own test with flying pink colors. He likes to think about doing the stripper's job. He likes to think about getting "denim burn" on his tight little rear. He likes the idea of being able to "dance" without having to study, or train, or even think about the music. He likes when another human being has a strong physical reaction to him. To his body. A reaction he'd be able to feel. Hear me roar.

All the "dancers" I met had no problem with the sexual parts of their job. But this was not a representative sample. If they were full of self-loathing and hangs-up, well, they never got to meet the monkey. All those women loved the idea of people looking at them in a purely sexual way. They all loved rubbing against jeans (or even gym shorts), and having strangers stare at their most private parts under bad lighting. All of them were fine with the gynecological poses. These are the strippers who get to meet me; they are the best of the best. But even they had trouble. Parents who don't want their daughters to be strippers don't understand why it's a bad job. It's a bad job only when it's *not* sexual, and that's most of the time. It gets bad when the dancers have to deal with loneliness. We

all know that we're in Norman Bates's "little cages." Scratching
and clawing. We all know that. We're sewn alone and we die alone.
But it hurts to have it thrown in our faces. Alone again, naturally.

The Little Fool's stripper dates talked with joy about the biker
who wore a miner's helmet to "get a little better look at the good
stuff." They were thrilled and proud about the guys who got "too
excited" during the dance and finished early. But the whole tone
changed when they talked about the sad guy who came in every
Tuesday and didn't want a "dance," he just wanted to talk. He'd tip
to talk. He wanted to know about the woman's parents. He wanted
to know where she went to school. He wanted to know what foods
she liked. He wanted to not be alone. He wanted to talk to her
about her hobbies. That'll destroy you. That'll hurt you wherever
you see it. It's hard to be paid enough to dance with that loneliness.
It's mostly what prostitutes are paid for. You're not safe even if you
step away from the sex industry. It's everywhere. Especially in showbiz. Situation comedies are for people who don't have witty friends,
or, more likely, never bother finding out if their friends are witty
and entertaining. Morning DJs talk with imaginary friendships to
real people. I'm the opposite: I'm imaginary, but the love is real.
Imaginary friendship is very sad. It's in diners and hardware stores.
Loneliness is like meteorite dust: it ends up everywhere. Knocking
me out with American thighs.

Many of the dancers see it as an acting job, which it is, but they
see acting as lying, which it is. So they make up "law school" and
parents in the Midwest and try to hustle another crotch rub out of
the John. The dancers don't give away too much. They just sell
the sex, and everything else they sell is fake and made up. Silicone
breasts are real breasts; strippers' lives are all fake. Nell hadn't done
that. She told the truth. She gave too much of herself for the
money. There's no way you can afford someone's heart, but Nell
had been generous. She argued with customers. Arguing is a gift
that most strippers won't give. Nell had reminded the lonely customers that there is no god. That truth should be expensive. It
should cost part of one's heart. She told them she didn't vote. She

told them, in a bar, that she didn't drink. They had gotten so much more than they paid for. Some of them didn't want to end the loneliness with a real person. Fine. There were plenty of other dancers, and if the customers had wanted to give her a visual pelvic exam, she was available for a reasonable price. If Nell had met the Little Fool at the club, the meeting would have been awkward. They would have fallen in love right there in the club. The Little Fool falls for truth. He's overwhelmed with the gift of heart to a stranger. Going home with a customer is frowned upon. Exchanging phone numbers has to be sneaky. Told me to come, but I was already there.

He met Nell in a bookstore. They had both run checklists: Atheist? Check. Sober? Check. Not obviously crazy? Check. Bob Dylan? Check. Freedom of disgusting, evil, hateful speech? Check. But that was just checking their work. All the real work had already been done at that point. They were on their way. They had seen each other. That doesn't give you too much information. They had gotten close enough to smell each other. This tells you a lot more. And then eye contact. The rest is just making sure you aren't being snowed by a creep. Women always know if they want to have sex with a guy the instant they meet him. The Little Fool had done a lot of debriefing on this subject. The Little Fool loves sex, but he likes the debriefing more. I have nothing to do with the sex, but I'm always there for the debriefing. After sex, before getting dressed, there's a chance to get information. "What did you think when you first saw me?" The information is always the same. Your partners always decide in the first five minutes. After that, the only change can be in the negative direction. After you win, you can only lose. Married. Killer. Kenny G. Smells bad. Kisses badly. Democrat. Bye, bye love.

Women decide in the first five minutes. It seems likely that men would be the same, but the Little Fool didn't do enough debriefing on that. I just don't have the information. It is possible to have sex with a woman who, in the first five minutes, didn't want to have sex with you. You can do that. You can become her friend. You can become her good friend. You can be charming, and loving, and open and caring. She'll get to the point where she'll say to her friends, "What's wrong with me? Am I looking for men to hurt me? Am I insane? I go to bed with all these guys who treat me like shit, and then I go to the movies with Rich. And he's so nice, and polite, and I can talk to him about anything. What's wrong with me?" And then she'll have sex one night with you because you're her nice friend; her friend who didn't get her animal going in the first five minutes. And it'll be mercy sex, pity sex. And that sex *can* ruin the friendship. It's sad to have sex with someone who doesn't treat you well, but it's sadder to have sex with someone *because* he treats you well. I'm just waiting on a friend.

Sex brings the Little Fool so much of what he wants. Sex is a backstage pass. Loud, sweaty, aggressive, nasty sex is a laminate. Once he's had his penis everywhere on and in her, he gets to run around inside her head. He gets to see things he can't see with her clothes on. Before sex, the Little Fool can't stare at his date. Oh, he can glance down at her cleavage, at her hard nipples poking through the girly fabric. He can watch when she walks away from the restaurant table. The women you want walking towards you are the ones that look best walking away. You want to get caught a little. She has to know that you want to look, but if you're caught staring, well, you don't respect her, or maybe you're a perv. If she's busty, don't look at her breasts very much. If she's flat-chested, you can get caught staring a little more, but you have to do it right. You can't let her watch you look. But after sex, you have that backstage pass. After sex, if you *don't* stare you're a creep. Being able to stare, being able to own her body with his eyes, is better for the Little Fool than the sex itself. The sex isn't the end; the sex is the permission slip. But the sex is really just the gate. It's the ticket. Breakfast with a new sex partner is the greatest time. Even better if it's in public. At dinner, the eyes have to lock in eye contact; at breakfast, the eyes can wander. They can do more than wander: they can land right on the money. The Little Fool often tries to make that deal with a woman he hasn't gone to bed with: "May I look at you like we've had sex?" I'm not there for that. It's too much for a monkey. My eyes adored you.

Most of the time the Little Fool was with Nell they'd been

living in the city: cabs, subways, buses. That's how the Little Fool and Nell got around. But—once—they had rented a car. It was in FLA. I hadn't been there. It was kind of a work trip for her, and kind of a vacation for both of them. Nell had had to stop in a pharmacy. Witch hazel? Who knows? Something. And the Little Fool had waited in the car. Waited in the car, playing the radio. Waited in the car like waiting for Mom. Waited in the car with a breeze blowing through the rented windows. Waited in the car really taking that time to smell the air and watch the FLA old couples help each other silently to their Caddies. He saw an older Mom with a Down's syndrome kid. They were holding hands and looking in the window of the pharmacy. Mom had dressed him in a striped shirt that was too bright; it called attention to him. They were holding hands and looking in the window. The Little Fool's Mother had been too old when the Little Fool had been born. He had had a high risk for that forty-seventh chromosome. The Little Fool doesn't like to look away when he sees kids like that. He likes to force himself to look at what he could have been. He doesn't like to look, but looking is the right thing to do. He wants to see that kind of love. That's the kind of love his Mother had for him. It had been the love that had been holding that twenty-nine-year-old child's hand and pointing to the treats in the window. The love that had cleaned the ice cream stain out of that bright striped shirt he had been wearing. Where do you buy shirts like that? Is there a retard store? No one else wears shirts like that. Maybe you have to be loved more than anything in the world to wear a shirt like that. The old Mom had been tired. She had been so tired from caring for her baby who would have been a man if his chromosomes had lined up right. It had been a pure love. And when the Little Fool sees pure love, he always cries. Just a little. He can cry. He's a real tough guy. He swims in sewage; he can cry. And he wants to be loved like that. All he wants is to love like that. Nature boy.

The Mom and her burden of love disappeared from the Little Fool's view. The Mom's car must have been parked around the corner. The Little Fool had turned the radio up: "It's the time of the season." Zombies were singing. The air was heavy with the smell of some flower mystery writers can identify. The Little Fool's eyes were still moist from Mom and her not-right kid. It had been a perfect moment. And in his rearview mirror, he saw the figure of a woman. Her face was reflected, he could see it—but he hadn't processed it. He'd gone right to her body. Perv. Letch. He looked at the woman's gently bouncing breasts, the most beautiful standing wave he'd ever seen. The breeze was pushing her summer dress against her breasts. He wanted her so badly. He wanted her so much. He wanted to get out of the car and leave his car for her. Leave his life for her. He wanted to rape her like a pig and love her like a Down's syndrome child. The Little Fool wanted all of her. *Give it to me easy and let me try with pleasured hands.*

It was his chance at love. It was his chance to do the right thing. He knew that she would get into her car, with her little bag from the pharmacy, maybe a bottle of water, some nail-care products, and some sort of good-smelling cream, and she'd be gone forever. *Carpe diem*, Little Fool, make your move. And she became bigger in the mirror. She came toward his car. She was going to talk to him. She was going to ask to save his life. Wait, she was going to the passenger side of the car. It was Nell. He'd fallen instantly in love with Nell without knowing it was Nell. There's no better feeling in the world than not recognizing your date and wanting her more than you've ever wanted anyone. But the Little Fool had wanted her too much. And when she got in the car, he hadn't been able to put it all together. It had been too perfect, too intense. How could he realize that quickly that she had been his pure sexual fantasy, and his best friend, and his lead shield against red kryptonite, and his Down's syndrome son? She was everything. If she had just been the woman in his rearview, he could have left with her for Mexico and never looked back, but she was more than that, and he had smiled and kissed her, and the world had started up again. Time started passing again, and then it was too late. Things had been too good to be dramatic. He'd been too happy with the woman he was with to leave everything behind to run off with her. It was a tragedy that he loved her too much in too many ways to end his life as he had known it. When I say she was cool, she was red hot. I mean she was steaming.

CHAPTER THIRTEEN

Disney Dead End

The Little Fool, true to his nature, hadn't been willing to throw away the life he had for a new life with Nell. After his wasted epiphany at the pharmacy, they had gone out for another four months and then he dropped out of law school and out of her life. They hadn't even had a fight. They just faded away because the Little Fool had been too full of emotion and too full of thoughts, and they hadn't talked to each other. "They" is not the Little Fool and Nell. The Little Fool and Nell had talked to each other enough. But the Little Fool's emotions and the Little Fool's thoughts hadn't talked to each other. How else can you explain that they had wanted the exact same thing and hadn't gotten it? Turn off your mind.

The Little Fool was now on the Manhattan deuce that used to belong to Damon Runyon and the Beastie Boys and now belonged to Disney: A big Disney Store on the corner where runaway girls used their bodies to bargain for street drugs. Talk about a wash. Talk about six of one. Talk about sadness. Couldn't we replace the sleazy horror with . . . well, anything but Disney? Anything at all. Nell usually danced out in Jersey; she was still dancing out in Jersey when the Little Fool lost her. Once in a while, she would dance at Show World on 42nd Street: when she was feeling like a nasty girl, a bad girl; when she hadn't even wanted to pretend to dance; when she had just wanted to sit in a phone booth and help guys masturbate on the other side of a slippery glass wall. She was always at her best after that. After she had twenty guys pay her money to show them "everything," after she watched twenty guys masturbate, she'd be really nasty. After she and the Little Fool broke up, she twice called the Little Fool just for sex after a shift at Show World. "Don't talk to me. Just use me. Anything you want. Please, please, please do something I don't want. Just rip me to pieces." The Little Fool wasn't sure it had been the best idea, but how do you say no? I think I love you, so what am I so afraid of?

He was now on 42nd Street. He tried to block out Disney and the duodeciplex theaters the way tourists used to try to block out the drug dealers. Even if you swim in sewage, that doesn't mean you can take Jiminy Cricket dead on. To get into Show World, the Little Fool had to buy a one-dollar token. He bought five. He was no piker. Show World had to use most of its space for kung fu and Abbott and Costello. The stairway to upstairs was chained off. The only sex was video peeps, and he had his five tokens. No live girls. The mayor and the police—the guys with the guns—had decided what percent of the floor space had to be nonsexual, so there was a lot of Amos and Andy. No live girls. No life. I'm all lost in the supermarket.

The Little Fool found a guy who looked properly sleazy dispensing tokens and preparing for the rush on Abbott and Costello Betamax tapes. The sleazy guy was pretty perfect, except he wasn't smoking. They probably even made smoking illegal. It wasn't really Show World anymore, but maybe this guy had been there long enough to know Nell. "Hey. Did you know a woman that used to work here named 'Rogue'? She also danced under the name 'Celine.' Her real name is Nell."

"I don't know."

"Did you work here when they had live girls?"

"Just for, like, the last week. I didn't know anyone by that name."

"I'm not a cop. Well, I am a cop, but this is not for a case. Okay, it is for a case, but not a case anyone cares about. You can't get in trouble, and you can't get her in trouble. She's dead. I was her friend, and I need to find out more about her.

"You don't know me. I can get in trouble talking to anyone. Talk to anyone who knows me. I can get in serious trouble sitting alone and watching TV. With a cop around, it's almost too easy for me to get in trouble. But don't worry, I'm telling you the truth, I didn't know many of the live girls here, and at the end, it was mostly chicks with dicks. Did Nell have a cock?"

"No."

"Then I didn't know her. I mostly knew the chicks with dicks. You need more tokens?"

"I still have five left."

You can't change the tokens back in for real money, but that was okay, the Little Fool wanted to watch some porno anyway. He went into the Clorox-smelling booth (it's not really bleach you're smelling; semen's PH is base, and Clorox is the most common base smell, so we believe we're smelling Clorox) and watched porno in one-minute chunks at a dollar a minute. He should have gotten more tokens. The time goes by fast. If they were to feature *Apocalypse Redux* in the video peeps, it would cost $197.00 even if you missed the last few credits. He spent five dollars and went home melancholy—the way you're supposed to when you walk by a big Disney Store where sleaze used to be. The horror. The horror.

CHAPTER FOURTEEN

Time for a Pedicure

"C'mon, baby, you're man enough to get a pedicure. Are we a little insecure about our masculinity? Red glitter toenails gonna shrink up your manhood? It's pretty hot to think about you walking around the diving-pig locker room with oh-so-pretty toes. Keep the other cops guessing. What are you afraid of? You afraid some of your tough-guy buddies might think about date-raping your toes?"

Nell's friend gives pedicures. When Nell and the Little Fool were dating, they used to get pedicures together once a month. Once a month, on a Monday afternoon, Nell and the Little Fool had a "Girls' Day Out." Nell always had Tommy do the Little Fool's toenails. The cat has chops. Tommy is the John Coltrane of pedicures. The Little Fool had gone to prove, with a giggle, that he was enough of a man to be effeminate. Once he'd started going, it felt so good. Tommy would dig out all the ingrown toenails, shave the calluses, and make the Little Fool's feet smell great. Tommy used extra Barbasol on his tools after his danger-diving customer so some poor second wife wouldn't end up going in for a day of beauty, only to find out three months later she had some exotic extra-disgusting sort of pedal parasite. Guilty feet ain't got no rhythm.

Tommy had always known everything about Nell. He might even already know she was dead. Tommy is gossip at its best. Gossip is as much a part of his job as his scrubbing glove wet with essential oils. He listens and he cares, and, if you have nothing to say, he talks. He can talk. He has lots to talk about. Imagination being fired by girl talk.

Tommy had lived as a girl for three years after leaving home at seventeen. He'd been little and very pretty. He was a club kid. Tommy "borrowed" his cousin Lynda's birth certificate and got his own ID complete with a very cute picture and an *"F"* next to *"sex."* The second Lynda, formerly known as Tommy, moved to New Jack. She was a street kid. She watched the hookers' rooms and tidied up a bit. She wore little tight jeans, and even did a little bit of the kind of hooking where you aren't apt to surprise a john in a way that could end up being unpleasant. She was good-looking enough as a girl to do some modeling—just local background for catalog shoots, but real modeling as a real girl all the same. Hormones gave her a full B and kept the chin tweezing to under twenty minutes. She was careful about dosage and regularity, but these were still street drugs and they made her cry when making the bed or putting Bounce in the dryer. But some say nature's own girly hormones do that too. Lynda landed herself a butch mechanic boyfriend who adjusted just fine when third base had to be carefully negotiated instead of stolen. Lynda and the butch lived happily until some of the mechanic's friends got to groping, and Tommy started to grow. She'd gotten bigger, and the tweezing took longer, the jeans didn't fit the same. It was time to taper off the hormones and live as a gay man. "The way," I'm sure some psycho would say, "god had intended." God only knows.

"I wasn't going to turn into some sloppy drag queen. If I couldn't look perfectly fish, I would just stay home and watch TV, girlfriend. I took too much pride in the scene."

Except for context, the Little Fool wouldn't have known what "fish" meant, and if the Little Fool doesn't understand something, I don't either. Tommy has stories. Tommy can talk to the girls. I used to feel so uninspired.

Tommy helped the Little Fool into the big pedicure chair. Tommy "helped" the way he always had: by holding the Little Fool's ass.

"You've put on a few pounds, but the tushy is still tight, tight, tight, and the shoulders are working."

"Thanks."

Nell had so wanted to see Tommy and the Little Fool together sexually. If the Little Fool and Nell had stayed together, it would have happened. The Little Fool isn't homophobic, and sex between the Little Fool and Tommy would have made Nell so happy. Tommy didn't seem against it. And the Little Fool had no reason to believe he wouldn't have fun. Gotta make way for the homo superior.

"She's dead you know, Tommy."

"That's not true, my big Romeo. There's plenty of life for her after water cop."

"No, Tommy, I dragged her body out of the river myself. With my own hands. She was killed, Tommy. Murdered. It was just co-incidence, but I was the one who found the body."

Tommy was pushing the cuticles back from the Little Fool's toenails. Tommy seemed to be ignoring the Little Fool, but tears were dripping onto the towel on the edge of the footbath. It was the first time we realized that Nell's death would hurt someone other than us. Until that moment, we had owned her death. Now it was public. It would explode and ripple through the drag queen/exotic dancer community. Her death would go Goth, and then through the lawyer dropouts. Whatever the Little Fool said to Tommy now would become the official story. The news today. Oh, boy.

"She was murdered. She's dead. I want to find out who killed her. I want to find out what happened. She was stabbed, Tommy. She was stabbed a lot. She was stabbed too much. She was stabbed a lot more than was needed to kill her. He didn't just kill her, Tommy. He ruined her. And he threw her in the water. She died young and didn't leave a beautiful corpse. She lost on every front. Tommy, I need to know what she was up to since we broke up."

"She loved you, asshole, but she got over you. You're not all that."

"Yeah, I know. I realized that in the past couple days. I know that, but I want to know who killed her, so I have to know what she was doing before she died. C'mon, Tommy, you know every-thing. Tommy, help me. I need you. I really need you."

"You're not going to find that psycho, rough-trade boyfriend she had after you that you can go and beat to death in some homo-erotic closure, Rambo. I'm not going to help you vent that macho shit. Everyone she dated after you was very nice. All of them nicer than you. She was over you, dude. She had her life together. We didn't need you. Your feet are a fucking mess, baby."

Tommy, the Little Fool and I would solve this crime together. Memories longer than the road that stretches out ahead.

CHAPTER FIFTEEN

Hairdresser, Scuba Diver: Cops

An empirical argument against bureaucracy. Tommy was the right partner for us, but the system could never know that. Only people can find the right people. Systems can't. But he was dead on. He covered our faults. He didn't think like us. The police force was weaker for not having hairdressers, but Tommy could never have made it through cop training. He couldn't have made it through the application. He's smart (not necessarily a plus in a cop, but you know what I mean) and physically fit. He does sit-ups as methodically as he used to take hormones. But cop departments have no place for him. They have no way to recruit him. Tommy isn't some flaming queen. He can pass for straight. Maybe. Kinda. Sorta. Okay, he can't pass for a breeder, but his sexuality isn't overt enough to make anyone but hardcore christards uncomfortable. He has the standard-issue male hairdresser's ponytail and is always growing a goat. It's never really there, and it's never gone, but he's always just starting to grow hair on his chin. He has facials in both senses more often than the average hockey goalie, but you have to look closely and think about it a bit to realize that. He has become too big to be a girl, but he still looks small next to the Little Fool. The Little Fool and Tommy had both loved Nell, and because of that, the Little Fool and Tommy knew each other really well. Because of that, they loved each other. When Tommy joined us, we were less alone. We were going to find the killer. I met her in a club down in North Soho.

"I'll hold your hand if you want, baby." They were about to
meet one of Nell's last boyfriends. After the Little Fool, Nell had a
lot of sex partners. No real boyfriends or girlfriends. She hadn't been
so much promiscuous as random. She hadn't had sex more often
than before, but her choices of partners would lack any pattern
to the casual observer. It might have seemed random to Nell, but
at the end of her life she seemed to have been little more than a casual observer of her own life. This was a good starting point. The
last time Tommy had seen Nell, which was around the day she'd
been stabbed to death, she'd been on her way to see M.J. If you're
a character in a book or a movie, having initials for a name is really
cool. If you're a friend of a friend whom someone is telling stories
about, having initials for a name is pretty cool. If you actually have
to meet people in the real world, if you have to really be someone
we're going to meet, have a name that's a name, okay? If you're going to be sexually involved with the dead woman the Little Fool
loved, you'd be so much better off going with "Mitchell" or
"Morris." Oh, oh, this little girl is mine.

"Did she meet him at work—at the club?"

"It's none of your business, and no. It was some book club and
it doesn't matter. You broke up with her and she's dead. Don't get
all hetero on me on our first interview."

M.J. was an architect or something. He had money. He had a big
loft in SoHo. Architects don't need big loft spaces. It wasn't as if he
was building his Howard Roark buildings right there in his studio.
Who was he kidding? Knock on the door. Deep breath. Oh, man,
eye to eye with the Little Fool. Nell sure had had a type. Blue eyes.
But this guy was a goon. He was wearing a leather jacket. It was one
of those leather jackets that isn't really a leather jacket. It's like a car
coat or something. Lou Reed could wear it, but Lou, hey, wherever
he goes, he's slumming. M.J., who we're now sure is "Morris," was
wearing this leather jacket in his own apartment. The jacket wasn't
a leather jacket; it was a black leather car coat, and not Samuel L.
Jackson-style either. M.J. wasn't pimpin'. He wasn't stylin'. He was
wearing a new, black leather car coat alone in his room. Does that

inspire him to draw better liquor stores? Isn't that what commercial architects do? Make models of 7-Elevens out of cardboard? Well, it was time to explain to him who we were. Who's a sex machine for all the chicks?

"Hi, M.J., you've never met me, but I'm Tommy. I was Nell's manicurist and roommate for a while. She must have mentioned me. I sure heard about you. We want to ask you some questions."

Tommy went on, giving the Little Fool's name and explaining that he was a cop but this wasn't really official business, but he was still a cop and Tommy was helping out. Tommy should have said the sentence. The sentence M.J. was waiting for. Tommy should have. But he wasn't going to. It was up to us. The Little Fool looked M.J. straight in the eye. The Little Fool tried to be a real man like his Dad. The Little Fool tried to say it like a real man would say it. The Little Fool wanted the gentle strength that his Dad had. The Little Fool's Dad had been a deputy sheriff for a while. Dad had to do things like this. Dad had never cried. Dad never cried in the line of duty. Dad cried at home. Like a real man, Dad cried at any movie where a dog is lost and finds its way home to the family. Dad hadn't cried to a sexual rival while on cop duty. Dad hadn't cried. The Little Fool drew himself up to full height and interrupted Tommy's Little Fool appositive. "She's dead, M.J. Nell's dead. Someone killed her. If you're in her phone book, other cops will be calling soon. If you were on her speed dial, they would have already called."

That last part hadn't been necessary. Three men in a doorway. Three men. Two men trying so hard not to cry that they were squeezing out tears of exertion. And one man very comfortable crying in front of anyone, and strong enough to not have to fight tears. Tommy is strong. Tommy is going on with, "We'd like to ask you a few questions." M.J. went to a drawer and pulled out a pack of cigarettes. They were an ex-smoker's old emergency cigarettes. When a lovely flames dies, smoke.

It's the *Columbo* problem. How do innocent people act? Everyone looks guilty. Everything. What was M.J. supposed to do? If he had said, "Why are you asking me all these questions?" Guilty. If he cooperated fully? Guilty. If he tried to help? Guilty. What do innocent people do? Are they indignant? Are they angry? Are they submissive? Well, in this case, they light up a cigarette, fight back tears, and try to find out more about how she died. M.J. was innocent. He was a good guy. He was smart and sexy and cool. Nell would have had fun with him. If this was a peer, the Little Fool was doing okay. Was M.J. going to decide that Nell had been his true love? The Little Fool and Tommy had to get out of there before that happened. The Little Fool lied about how Nell had looked when he dragged her out of the drink. There was no reason to put that real image into M.J.'s nightmare vocabulary. They were all starting to bond. They were talking about Nell. Oh, goodness, don't tell me there are going to be three of them running around NYC looking for the bad guy. Starsky, Hutch, and Baretta? Crocket, Tubbs, and Kojak? Book 'em, Dano. I'm so bored with the U.S.A.

M.J. hadn't killed her, but his genetic material would be found somewhere in her body. And the Little Fool was okay with that. If he could just have her back, he'd be thrilled to watch M.J. deposit that material directly into Nell. It was a sexy thought. A sexy group-sex thought about a dead lover. That's a stage after denial, anger, and acceptance. Tommy was taking notes on everything M.J. said. Tommy had a little notebook like a '70s TV cop. The notebook had a picture of Farrah Fawcett-Majors with big hair on the cover. Now that I think about it, just like a '70s TV cop. Tommy was writing down everything M.J. remembered. Nell had been in an intellectual mood that last night. She was asking a lot of heavy questions. Not about relationship and marriage. She was talking philosophy and art. They had talked a lot about *Moby-Dick*. M.J. had spent Nell's last evening with her having sex and talking literature, and then she'd left. She'd never slept over. Score! She always slept over at our place. She even held me once. At the time, the Little Fool hadn't liked it. He made excuses: He wanted to sleep alone. Now he was glad that Nell had insisted. He was glad she'd held his monkey. He'd been more important to Nell than M.J. ever was.

Now we really liked M.J. Maybe his name was really "Mike." M.J. was okay. With initials for a name, that rhymes. Tommy had pages of real police notes; we had memories of Nell waking up in the morning with hair that later in the day would need a product to look that way. It was okay that M.J. hadn't done it; we no longer needed to beat him senseless. It was a nice black leather coat. It looked good on him. Maybe the Little Fool should get one. Fur is murder.

CHAPTER SIXTEEN

Droppin' Like Flies

Tommy and the Little Fool were apart only to work and sleep, and even that wasn't going to last. Job seniority had given the Little Fool the weekends off, but that was Tommy's prime work time so the Little Fool hung around the salon on weekends. Tommy had a private business working out of the salon, and he had a lot of hairdos and tint jobs. "Fabric is dyed, hair is tinted, scuba boy." Tommy would do fancy nails for important dates on Saturday and full makeup for weddings on Sunday morning. "Chickens are plucked—we tweeze eyebrows." Hey, little girl, comb that hair, fix that makeup.

While Tommy cut, soaked, tinted, washed, and waxed, they would read over Tommy's notes and talk about the case. They would talk about Nell all day, and then over dinner, and then into the night. When Tommy had to talk to the customers to keep them happy, the Little Fool would make phone calls to everyone in Nell's address book. Nell had left her address book at Tommy's right before she died. It was originally Tommy's address book. It also had Farrah on the cover, and Nell had "borrowed" the book from him. Tommy figured it was okay to look at her address book because it was his address book. I just got out my little red book. I wasn't going to sit and cry.

Grade school morality is helpful to a cop. Tommy was getting to be a good cop. It was Tommy's address book, so they could use it. The information in that book had belonged to Nell, but being dead, she didn't have the power to give the Little Fool and Tommy permission to look through the book. That's the definition of dead: You no longer have a vote. The Little Fool wasn't as good a cop. He took the truth too seriously. When you take truth seriously, you have to admit you're lying, pig. The Little Fool had a morality test: Say you're a married man in a stated monogamous relationship. (He believed this was a nutty thing to get into unless you're going back in time and marrying a woman who's already dead.) While in this rather traditional marriage, you start having a sexual relationship with . . . oh, let's say, a male hairdresser. You're having sex with a queer, and your wife picks up a vibe. She feels you're being "untrue" and confronts you. She looks you in the eye and asks, "Are you seeing another woman?" This is the test: Would you say "no" and feel you were telling the truth? Tommy, the cop, believed it was easy. "Of course that would be 'no.' " And then Tommy asked his own sexy, hypothetical ethics question to his hypothetical, breeder buddy: "If you were out alone in the wilderness with a male friend, and you woke up with your tight little asshole all sore and covered with lube, would you tell anyone?" Before the Little Fool could answer, Tommy jumped in with, "Hey, wanna go camping?"

Any lawyer will tell you the answer in that situation, when asked "Are you seeing another woman?" is "No." Any politician will tell you the answer is "No," even under oath. That's not perjury. All that matters is what "is" is. Any third grader will tell you the answer to the equivalent question, "Did you hit your sister with a toy truck?" would be "No" if, in fact, you'd hit your sister with a toy airplane. But the Little Fool knows the answer to all these questions is "Yes." He knows that truth is the answer to the question the person would be asking if she knew what you know. It's not the letter; it's the spirit. The monogamy question isn't, "Are you seeing another woman?" it's, "Are you having sex with someone else?" Or, "Are you feeling a lot of affection for someone else?" This will drive you crazy, because the real question could also be, "Are you putting our relationship in jeopardy?" Maybe the answer would come back around, "No." You say goodbye, I say hello.

The Little Fool liked to use the strictest definition of "truth" and then admit he was a liar. He had a carnival morality. It's okay to lie to the marks, but don't lie to your monkey. Make sure you know what the truth is, then lie your butt off. In suspension. You're a liar. You're a lie.

Tommy was in the right, and the Little Fool was stealing information from the book, and he made the phone calls. He took notes on every phone call, but all he was really doing was telling anyone who'd ever had sex or planned to have sex with Nell that she was dead. Since he was there all the time, he also started to help Tommy with his cosmetology. The Little Fool dipped the little cotton balls. "Cotton Balls" became Tommy's in-shop nickname for the Little Fool. (You know, that's a fine nickname for me, too, isn't it?) He dipped them in a mixture of water, acetone, amyl acetate, castor oil, and D&C green number 6, and a few organic essential oils that Tommy put in to make the potion special. Cotton Balls would then place the moist cotton on the fingernails and toenails of Tommy's customers. Cotton Balls kept Tommy on time and increased the tips. Cotton Balls was helping. Working nine-to-five, what a way to make a living.

Illegally, without a proper salon license, Cotton Balls was starting to learn how to give a proper salon shampoo. He was getting to really like it when he decided he was losing focus. He made a formal request to his sergeant to switch to the weekend shift. It was easy to make that change. Soon both Tommy and Cotton Balls had Tuesdays and Wednesdays off together. I got you, babe.

The first weekend morning swimming in the Hudson instead of dipping into beautician's chemicals, the Little Fool's dive partner, Big Bob, stayed under water a bit longer than Cotton Balls. The Little Fool was about to go back in and make sure his dive buddy was okay when Big Bob came back up. "We got some meat down here." They pulled out the sinkers: two women chained together. They had been stabbed. Not just like Nell, but the same idea. Dead

dead dead. "Same m.o.," as Tommy the cop would say. There was
going to be all that pain. Cotton Balls got flooded with pain. He
was flooded with grief and despair. He needed to talk to Tommy.
Cotton Balls needed to get to a cell phone and call Tommy. We
couldn't do this alone. Do you really want to make me cry?

Back when Mom and Dad had been alive, the Little Fool had
been talking to an old carny friend, Stank. Stank had been a real
fuckling—he was born and raised in the carny. Had never gone to
school. He was illiterate. He kept it pretty quiet. If you gave him
something important to read overnight, he'd hire a hooker who
could read, and come in the next morning relaxed with all the material memorized. Stank's Dad was a patch, squaring any beefs the
straights had with those who were "with it" in the carny. Stank's
Mom ran the High Striker, that thing you hit with a hammer and
win a cigar after spending fifty dollars to perfect the technique.
Stank's Mom also did some hooking, and Stank's Dad rolled the
occasional john. To live outside the law you must be honest.

The Little Fool had been telling Stank stories about the Little
Fool's Mom and Dad. Wonderful stories. Funny stories. Stank didn't
laugh. He had kept wincing and looking away. Stank explained that
he couldn't bear to hear people with living, loving parents tell stories of that love. Stank could look into the eyes of filial love and see
the future pain the parents' deaths would cause his friends. Stank
said it with a lot of carny ejaculations and slang, but that's what he
said. The Little Fool believed Stank was crazy and, well, Stank was
indeed crazy, but he hadn't been wrong. After Mom and Dad died,
the Little Fool felt the same way. The Little Fool couldn't stand people who had their parents, and loved them, talking about them. The
embryonic pain living right below the surface, waiting to cause
pain, was too much to take. Future bereavement for a loved one is a
benign tumor that grows with love and gets malignant with death.
Since Nell's death, the Little Fool could see those tumors growing
everywhere, in every couple. Every happy couple, laughing, nuz-
zling, holding hands, was just a few stopped heartbeats from pain

bursting through one of their skulls. Bone-hard tumors of woe ready to burst through like the Elephant Man. The Little Fool looked at beautiful young women and knew that when they lost their biker boys in motorcycle accidents, those girls would be disfigured and drooling. I'm not an animal. I'm a man.

There were these two bloated dead women. They weren't as beautiful as Nell had been. The two new women meant nothing to us. But they were dead. Their pain was over. They, too, had been knifed to pieces slowly. It looked as if they'd been alive and conscious for much of the carving. It was torture. Who cares about that pain? The Little Fool had no more fear of being tortured and killed. That was kid's stuff. Those were sexy Disney nightmares. Torture is movie fear. The Little Fool had flipped; he had the real, hopeless fear of other people dying. That's the real deal. That's grown-up angst. When he was a kid, he'd been afraid of the dark, and he held me. When he got a little older, he'd been afraid of going to prison. He was afraid of being humiliated and raped. I was no help to him then; it wouldn't have helped the humiliation and pain of rape to be holding a sock monkey. For a while he'd been afraid of being found dead on a toilet. He outgrew it all. Now he isn't afraid of prison. He isn't afraid of death. He isn't afraid of getting sick. He isn't afraid of pain or humiliation. He is afraid of other people dying. He lost his Mom and Dad, and he lost Nell. There's only one way to hurt the Little Fool now, and that is the easiest way of all. All you have to do is hurt other people. The Little Fool doesn't stand a chance. If you're afraid of prison, there are measures you can take to make jail less likely. If you're afraid of death, you can't avoid it, but you can be careful, and once it happens it's over forever. If you're afraid of loved ones dying, you can work on protecting them and you can fool yourself into thinking you can make them safer. But, when you get to being afraid of anyone dying, you're skiing down a very slippery slope. You're greased Speed Racer on ice. The speed is going to pull your face into a contortion. Faster, pussycat. Kill! Kill!

He isn't really afraid of other people dying. He's afraid of the pain of those who remain alive. He lost everyone he loved except Tommy, and that made the Little Fool afraid of woe. Woe without a qualifier. Not his woe. Not a loved one's woe. Just plain woe with no limiter. Grief minus zero. No limit.

The Little Fool had a friend who'd finally found a beautiful girlfriend who loved him more than anything. She'd do anything for him sexually, of course, and would even make him a grilled cheese sandwich when she was making one for herself. He finally had a good job. Not his dream job, but a fine job. This friend had been over the hump. He'd made it. One day, after going to visit his alcoholic Mother, he called the Little Fool and left a message. It was one question: "Why do we want to watch people we love grow old and die?" That question had been on our answering machine. Why? Now the friend's Mom was clean and sober, his girlfriend was pregnant (from one of the less kinky adventures), the powers that be had put him on some antidepressant that's named after the imperial ruler of one of the moons of Jupiter, and the Little Fool was digging fresh, bloated meat out of the drink. Meat that would break hearts. Meat that would bring woe that the Little Fool could already feel. He felt all of the future grief of the loved ones as he looked at the meat. I can tell you anyhow I'd rather be than see one.

These two women were just the first of the weekend. The divers had hit the motherload of the dead. The perp must have dumped the new corpses at the same time, and they'd all gotten stuck in the same junk underwater. The divers pulled out five corpses that day. Five smelly old houses for five random lives that would now cause pain that was, to the Little Fool, easily imagined and felt. All the love that they had had in their lives, all the fun they had caused, all the joy, the warmth, all that love, would now change directly into pain. And that pain would visit the very ones they loved most. Those five ended lives would ruin at least fifteen lives, some of them until their own deaths ended their pain while spreading it to others. Death is a big Amway party. Death is a virus that doesn't need contact or even email. Pain is the only pyramid scheme that works. The Little Fool didn't take off his rubber gloves to touch these sinkers. He did that just for Nell. No glove, no love.

CHAPTER SEVENTEEN

It's Not a Job.
It's an Adventure.

Imagine my portrait done by a woman in her late fifties. She has three young grandchildren. She isn't really of the right generation to have been "just" a Mom and a homemaker, so she went to college and was always working, but really she only cares about her kids. If she had taken the job she really wanted to get her out of the house, the job would have been babysitting her own kids. Now her children are grown. Her three grandchildren don't live in town. They're about 1,200 miles away, in Phoenix. Her husband will retire in two years, and they will move closer to the grandkids. The woman and her husband have plenty of money. She has twenty-two months to kill. She'll fly to see her grandkids every chance she gets. She'll call them. She'll send them gifts. She'll log on to the Web five times a day to see any pictures her daughter may have put up. It's hard to spoil the grandkids when they're all the way in the desert, but she'll try. She'll send them a package for any occasion at all. Her daughter sent her a computer digital video of the kids with their sock monkeys that she sewed. She's very happy with that. Time passes slowly.

She takes an art class. She always wanted to paint, and now she has the time. The class is just a community college class, but she still takes notes and does all the homework. She doesn't want to change the world; she wants to pass the time. Her teacher is, of course, a loser, like all teachers figure they must be, but he's good-hearted and he knows a bit. She does all her assignments right by the book.

The nursery is now her studio, and she plays way too much Carole King. It's time for the woman to paint anything she wants. That's the assignment: anything. She needs a subject; a subject for a still life. A bowl of apples? No. Maybe the project could be something her grandkids would like. She goes into the closet and grabs her son's old sock monkey. He's a little heavier than I am, a few extra nylons around the stomach. His tail has a large hole that's been mended into a smaller hole right where the white hits the dickie-color of the tail. But he looks a lot like me, especially around the eyes. She starts painting. She does a study, just as she was taught. She works on it every night, right after she calls her daughter and gossips and tries to get a grandkid on the phone. Between the phone calls and getting in bed with her husband (they can finally have loud sex), she works on the monkey. Starry, starry night. Portraits hung in empty frames.

Okay, you got that? Now imagine she gets to see her grandkids. She and her husband move five miles away from their daughter. The woman is the best mother-in-law in the world, and an even better grandmother. Once she's closer, she gives her grandkids enough space to live and grow. Her daughter decides to have a yard sale, and our artist helps her get the stuff ready. "Oh, dear, there's that stupid sock monkey painting I did during my Whistler's Mother phase. So embarrassing. No one is ever going to look at that. Let's put it out and see if some fool wants to give us a dollar for it." Up comes a retro-punk with very large breasts stuffed behind suspenders that look more Bay City Rollers than Sex Pistols, and blue hair in a Mohawk. "I have to have this. Look at this! Oh, oh, oh, it's my little Fluff Fluff, but now he's from HELL! Look at those eyes! Look at those eyes! This is insane. It's nuts. It's five bucks. It's mine."

Grammy wasn't being arch. She wasn't trying to be scary, and there's more love in that one painting of my sibling than there is in all of Spielberg's films, and that's not saying enough, so throw in one George Romero while you're at it. There's love. There's passion. She understood her subject perfectly. There's just a lack of skill. And love plus obsession plus passion plus time minus skill is true. When you don't have the skill, you can't cheat. And the busty, temporary punk made the painting even more real. She moved the soup can from the supermarket to the Warhol museum. The painting is hanging in her living room. People sit on the dirty community couch, shoo the cat away, and look at the picture. I can see clearly. The rain is gone.

The woman couldn't even draw the straight line across the red heel for the mouth. The eyelashes look like surprise lines. I guess the teacher didn't cover perspective in that class. The painting looks as if you could peel the whole sock monkey like a sticker right off the background. The monkey is a little scary. Its creepiness is what makes the punk girl—who really just wants a sock to hug—able to put the painting up with the circle-A-anarchy signs all over the wall. The painting is really perfect. There's nothing mean-spirited. The punk and the grandma had a hearty laugh together when the punk bought the painting. Grammy said her son used to have a Mohawk, and she'd taken him to see the Buzzcocks reunion when he was fourteen. I want to be your dog.

The murder investigation Tommy and the Little Fool were working on is exactly that painting. They had time, love, passion, and an understanding of the subject. They had everything except skill. They also lacked legal authority. Grammy didn't have to worry about that. Look at that portrait of that monkey. Think of Grammy loving those grandkids. Think of the Little Fool and Tommy loving Nell. It was going to be sloppy, but that scumbag perp didn't stand a chance. Just look into that painting's eyes. Look deep into the lack of depth. Look at the anarchy symbols on the wall around the painting. Look at all that, and then just thank yourself that you weren't the one who flipped out and killed Nell. I'm gonna take you down to Chinatown.

CHAPTER EIGHTEEN

FuckMeHard13

"It's an abortionist who covers up the mistakes with murder. It's a member of the royal family. It's someone who knew the victims and could get close enough to them. It's someone they wouldn't have suspected. It's a woman. It's an abortionist woman from the royal family." Tommy had read one book on Jack the Ripper. The Little Fool gave Tommy a little help: "Abortion is legal, we have no royalty in this country, and one of the victims was a man."

"Good point."

Grace Banks, Renée Garland, Carol Gomes, Phyllis Meltzer, and Ron Nathanson were dead. The Little Fool had been fishing dead bodies out of the drink for more than a decade, but now he knew that the meat had once had life. His two-word titles—crack whore, suicide jumper, mob hit, very unlucky—no longer dismissed the pain. Nell had changed all that. Now every dead body had life in it. He had to know all about these dead. He was falling in love and making friends. His new friends and loves were all dead, but they were a start. He was growing. They were my friends, and they died.

The Little Fool was technically a cop, but he wasn't assigned to this case. He wasn't assigned to any case, ever. He wasn't a detective. He fished things out of sewage. Tommy picked up more police training from watching DVDs than the Little Fool had from the academy. But as a cop, the Little Fool had a cop ID number, he had a password, and he could get on the precinct LAN, and that got him to the NYPD database. He'd come in an hour before work, sit at his desk, find facts on the case, and email everything to Tommy's computer. The Little Fool's procedure probably wasn't legal. It might not have even been ethical. He'd stay an hour later at night and send off more. He didn't have to hurry home to meet Tommy. Without the Little Fool, Tommy had to take the polish off all the fingernails by himself, so he was running behind at the salon again. Tommy understood real emergencies, and he'd be there for his fish. He'd often fix a broken nail or touch up a tint job after hours to save someone's beauty life. She's got it coming, but she gets it while she can.

When Tommy would get home, the Little Fool would be sitting at Tommy's computer. Tommy had a faster computer connection, but that wasn't the reason. The reason was Tommy's place was cleaner and had better food. Tommy's place had food. The Little Fool had keys to Tommy's, and the Little Fool would be sitting there, typing, printing and snacking. Tommy would cook them dinner. It was comfort-food time—lots of meatloaf and macaroni and very sharp cheddar cheese. Then the Little Fool and Tommy would work all evening on the case. It made the Little Fool feel the way he'd felt doing jigsaw puzzles with his Mom. It's the existentialist's dream: a jigsaw puzzle that matters. Very nice. The more we talk about it, it only makes it worse to live without it. But let's talk about it.

They'd finished eating. The Little Fool cleared away the dishes and finished washing up. Tommy was continuing the Web searches of nearly every phrase in every relevant police report. Tomorrow they would hit the streets for interviews, but tonight it was all police reports, email from the private investigator, and web searches. Tommy's six-CD changer (three chosen by Tommy—Babs, Bette and Badfinger [Tommy was in his alphabetical phase]—and three chosen by the Little Fool—AC/DC, Plasmatics, and Sonny Rollins [the Little Fool was in . . . a phase]) was blaring. Tommy was pulling up maps of Midtown and marking where the victims had lived and worked. The Little Fool finished up, took off his Playtex gloves (he never trusted his hands to be clean enough for Tommy's dishes) and walked back into the dining/war room to get back to work. You light the fire. I'll place the flowers in the vase.

Grace Banks, Renée Garland, Carol Gomes, Phyllis Meltzer, and Ron Nathanson had been killed. Their throats had been slit. They had been knifed to pieces and dumped in the river. They had been tortured. They were dead. Tommy and the Little Fool spent a week going through every police report. They dropped a few hundred bucks getting a computer private detective to turn over everything a Social Security number, an address from the police, and experience would give you. That's a lot. That's everything. The Little Fool and Tommy had all of Renée's email from the past year. (Here's a hint: Don't use "fuckmehard13" as your password. Any hacker will guess it before "fuckmehard1.") Carol had used her Mom's birthdate as a password, so we had all of Carol's mail from the last four months before she had changed ISPs. Tommy felt no guilt. "If they didn't want this stuff read, they would have picked better passwords."

"Okay, Tommy, what's your password? 'TYO9PTKHL3'?"

"No, it's '#1cocksucker', same as my address. I want everyone to read my mail, Mr. Balls. That's my point. I want it published. I want everyone to jerk off to it. I want dangerous men and women to regret not raping me. I want the world to know what a cunt I thought you were. I only used the tic-tac-toe sign for number because the machine forced me to use non-letters. Renée wanted us reading her mail, darling. She wanted this, honey."

As Lenny Bruce would say, "A ten-letter word for a very bad man or a very good woman." Well, Tommy was a very good man, but he was very skilled at changing his ethics to fit the situation. Maybe he wasn't doing that. Maybe his ethics never changed at all. He was very okay with invasions of privacy. The guilt of those same invasions woke the Little Fool up in the middle of the night. It was what Tommy would want, so he did it to others. Tommy was an Atheist (of course) and he'd tossed off all that fag-hating religious propaganda completely by the time he was twelve, but some peripheral ideas stayed. He knew that Abrahamic religions are insane

and their stupid judeo-christian traditions still make us all crazy. If
you believe the bible, you're crazier than your monkey, but there
were other, more insidious ways to be ripped apart by the "teach-
ings" of those political, hallucinating, ignorant, death-dealing, starv-
ing jews. A lot of people lean toward Atheism but still say the bible
"has some good stories and some good ideas." The Little Fool had
read the bible twice and he must have missed those good ideas.
Where are they, exactly? Around Deuteronomy where the father is
instructed to disown his daughter who is now unclean because she
had been raped while protecting an angel? Is it around there?
When pressed, the only "ideas" the religious apologists push for are
"Thou shalt not kill," which is negated by the entire Old Testament
(the root of "testament" is "testacies"—balls to you, Daddy, you
know), and "Do unto others." Ah-hah-unh. And I'll do unto you
what you do to me.

Tommy still took the Golden Rule fairly literally. That's insane
and evil. And if you interpret it broadly, it means nothing. Not
a thing. When our Dad was sick, he wanted to be pampered. He
wanted to be taken care of. He wanted to be constantly asked how
he was. He wanted you to adjust his pillows and make him soup.
When our Mom was sick, she wanted to be left alone. She wanted
to crawl under the porch and eat grass like a dog. Do unto others
as they would do unto you would have had our Dad irritating our
Mom and our Mom leaving our Dad to suffer, alone and sad. Taken
literally, that one sentence of nonsense that starts "Do unto others"
is the worst kind of solipsism. But if you take it figuratively so it
means "treat people the way they'd like to be treated because you'd
want them to treat you the way you'd like to be treated," it says
nothing. The Golden Rule is evil, but it worked for Tommy. It
worked for their investigation. He wanted everyone to invade his
privacy after he was dead, so it was fine to invade away on these
strangers. He felt good about it, and the Little Fool felt sick. You say
"potato" and I say "potahto."

Even when the Little Fool was getting hot reading the e-sex
messages to and from Renée, he felt his behavior was really wrong.

That's how ethics are changed and grown. I was proud of the Little Fool. A woman writing about anal sex to a man she'd never met seems totally immoral to those who are living in the past, but to the Little Fool it was just a question of whether or not she'd wanted him to see it. Well, maybe she would have wanted to help him to catch the killer. Or at least stop him from hurting anyone else. It seems likely she would have wanted that. Hello, I love you.

He read everything. The last few messages had a lot of stuff about a book she was reading on Watson, Crick, DNA, and the double helix. She wrote long emails about the real motivations for solving that riddle. Was it existential? Was it fame? It seemed Watson did it just to get laid. She became obsessed with Barbara McClintock. Did Watson and Crick really *steal* important ideas from her? What did it mean to be part of the most important discoveries in history and not get credit during your lifetime? The Little Fool didn't give Babs credit until he did a Web search while reading Renée's private emails. The Little Fool started to really dig Renée. She was sexy, and as time went on, she was getting heavier and heavier. He loved her jumping around from anal sex to the double helix, to Hemingway, then talking about that Three Dog Night cover of the Randy Newman tune. Reading through the emails, he got hot and he learned a lot. What more could you want from a woman? Our hostess she ain't lasting.

"Okay, I'm going to call Ron Nathanson's roommate. It's nine P.M. That's not too late. It's not dinnertime. It's the perfect time. We have his number. I'm the one to make the call. He's a friend of Dorothy." Tommy reached for the phone.

"We have no evidence that Ron was and his roommate is gay. No evidence at all. I'd love to have you call, but what makes you think they were gay?"

"Because Jack the Ripper was only killing cocksuckers. That's what ties them together."

"No."

"Okay, because Ron was thirty-six years old, had a good job, and still had a roommate."

"Ron had been married."

"So what? You've had lots of girlfriends."

"Yeah, and I'm not queer."

"You're starting to peek out of the closet. Maybe Ron was still in the closet, too. Anyway, we have to interview his roommate. Remember, his roommate's name is Hector. I like to go south of the border now and again."

"The police talked to Hector. There's no mention of him being gay."

"It's just politically correct police reports."

Tommy called. He got Hector on the phone. It was hard for Tommy to understand Hector through all the tears. Tommy managed to set up a meeting with Hector without saying who Tommy and the Little Fool were. Tommy didn't say they were cops. He didn't say they weren't. He just kind of avoided the subject. Tommy's morality was more useful than all the computer records. Without Tommy's certainty that they were morally above all law, they wouldn't be getting anything done. The Little Fool was paralyzed and Tommy was pulling him along. Tommy hung up the phone. "You're right. They weren't queer."

"How do you know?"

"He didn't lisp and he didn't cry like a girl. But when we get over there tomorrow, we'll make him throw a baseball overhand, just to be sure."

"Fuck you."

"Hey, I am not going to do real police work without coffee and doughnuts. We have to have coffee and doughnuts. There's a Krispy Kreme in that neighborhood. Let's meet there at six A.M., okay, Cotton Balls?"

"Dunkin' Donuts is the cop's official donut of choice, and one other thing, *six* A.M.?! How fucking nuts are you?"

"Hey, I'm no longer a club kid. I'm a cop. We have to start early. We have a lot of real police work to do."

"We're not going door to door in the apartment buildings that

early in the morning, and you just set up our appointment with
Hector for ten-thirty."

"We'll talk in the Krispy Kreme. Now, kiss me good-night and
go home for a change. We don't want the neighbors to gossip about
us. If you get killed, I don't want some fake cops assuming I'm a
queer just because you're over here all the time."

The Little Fool kissed Tommy on the cheek and walked out the
door. Don't you know it's gonna be—shoo-be-do—alright.

CHAPTER NINETEEN

Hard Candy Hector

The body strives to be alive after the death of a loved one. You look for anything. Any sign of life going on. They should rent kids out for funerals. But not well-behaved kids being solemn. They should rent out hellions. It's one of those times you need a really bad kid. Another time you need really bad kids is around clowns. If you're at a circus, you better hope there's a clown-hurting, swearing, ridiculing, spitting kid nearby. Most people can't handle clowns. No adult can handle clowns. But the right rotten kid without a parent nearby is a gift. If parents leave kids unattended in a restaurant and they start raising hell, some very nice man or woman—usually over sixty and parked in the RV section of the parking lot—will say something like, "Listen, sonny, simmer down." But if there's clown harassment involved, even the most dedicated Good Sam Club member with stickers from all forty-nine states (I suppose someone has flown a Winnebago over to Hawaii for a sticker, but the news didn't get back to this nylon head) will sit quietly and watch the battle. Chewing gum in little girl's hair. Now, Junior, behave yourself.

That was something the Little Fool and Tommy were missing. They didn't have children. They weren't even trying. They lacked children to scream and holler and throw things and remind them of life. Well-behaved kids may bring a certain kind of joy, but they don't reaffirm life the way a really rotten kid does. A kid with no manners. A kid allowed to watch *T-2* as many times as he wanted

82

when he was three. A kid who watched just a little too much pro wrestling. If the death rituals of religion were really designed to give the living some hope, the rituals ought to include an unpleasant-looking kid with chocolate ice cream residue like feces all over his face jumping off the coffin while screaming, "And it's a brutal, flying-head bash kung fu style." Fuck you, asshole.

If you don't have kids around—if it's just a queer and a couple of failed breeders dancing with the newly dead—you have to make do with laughing. That's the *second*-best sign of life. Hector was talking to Tommy and the Little Fool. Why Tommy and the Little Fool were asking questions never came up. Hector didn't ask to see badges. He asked for nothing. He was so happy to talk about Ron to anyone. Hector would have talked to the KGB about Ron. Tommy was scribbling in his Farrah notebook (okay, maybe they *were* being up front enough about not being real cops). Hector wasn't Latin/Hispanic/whatever; he was just a regular American mutt named Hector. A man called "Cotton Balls" had nothing to say about a man called "Hector." I grew up quick and I grew up mean.

It seems Ron had been a little nutty before he died. He was read-ing everything Kurt Vonnegut wrote and eating a lot of candy. Hector was laughing really hard now talking about how Ron had eaten nothing but candy. Really nothing but candy. For the last six months, he ate nothing but candy: not a French fry, not a grape. Hector had the kind of laugh going that only comes out of crying and grief. The deep, rich, beautiful laugh of pain. Maybe it wasn't his stories that were hysterical; maybe Hector himself was hysterical, for real. But Tommy and the Little Fool didn't care. They were laughing right along with him. Laugh, laugh, I thought I'd die.

"Ron moved in with me," Hector turned around to find the re-mote control to turn down CNN so he wouldn't have to compete with the meat puppets, "right after he broke up with Michelle, the woman he'd been living with for six years."

"Told you so!" Tommy and the Little Fool mouthed to each other simultaneously.

"We were friends from college. Man, he was really funny. He could always make me laugh. But the candy thing was insane."

Ron had been a regular guy. He was a recording engineer. He had run a recording studio called "Ears 'r' Us" on 45th Street. They did mostly radio commercials. He had a receptionist, a businessperson, and three other engineers. He had big ears. Even more important, he had the patience to listen to clients say, "Put more space between the words and make it shorter." He'd been in love with Michelle, but couldn't bring himself to marry her. He couldn't take that step. She started having an affair with some public-access-cable producer-guy. Ron found out about it and proposed. Say it with me: timing. He'd lost her. He could have become a slut. He could have become a stalker. He could have turned to jesus. He could have gone to a therapist. He could have renewed old loves and friendships, but instead he ate candy and read Vonnegut. Nothing but candy and Kurt. Candy: The Breakfast of Champions.

First he stopped eating fruit and meat (if Tommy and the Little Fool had had an act, that would have been their stage name). Carrots had been the last to go. He ate carrots and candy for a few weeks, and then just candy. Nothing but candy. Candy and water. He didn't even drink soda. At first it was all kinds of candy, then chocolate fell away. After that, it was all Brach's and Jolly Ranchers. He bought pounds at a time. Then it was just Jolly Ranchers. He ate candy and obsessively brushed his teeth. Oral hygiene.

You buy an apple. You buy a Granny Smith, a nice, tart apple from Australia (people buy so few American apples nowadays, Johnny Appleseed weeps), you pick up a good, fresh apple, and you eat it. The skin gives just enough fight to your teeth, and when it finally gives way and bursts, there are those little squirts from all over the fleshy bite mark of the apple. If you had the sun behind you, the bite would look like a backwards sneeze: little pieces of apple sputum flying into your mouth. And the taste would be just barely on the sweet side of hurting your saliva glands. The texture is perfect and all you can think is, "I should eat apples all the time." And the next day you reach into the exact same bowl. The *exact* same bowl. And you grab an apple that looks *exactly* the same as the apple of the day before. And your sense memory comes flying back as you smell that apple smell. You remember the apple experience perfectly. You're ready for it. And you bite—but it's not the same. The flesh has just a little too much give. Just a little, like your wife's ass at thirty-five: still great, but a little bit different. Maybe even better, but a little different. It wouldn't be mushy or mealy; mushy or mealy would have telegraphed a hint before the disappointing bite. Not mushy or mealy, just not exactly the same. Maybe even better. That's not the point. It's just not the same. Not the exact right backwards-sneeze apple explosion. Not the exact same fresh taste. And what of the apple the third day? What about that same bowl again? Now, the reach for pleasure. The reach into the bowl for a memory of a crisp day at a New England county fair in the middle of September (okay, so maybe a county fair in the middle of whenever their fall is in Australia, mate). You're now filled with worry. Which apple taste would it be? Another unique apple experience? Who needs it? Lover and friends aren't the same from day to day. Work isn't the same. TV shows vary in quality. Man, you hear Beck's "Where It's At" on the oldies radio, and it's not quite right, the bass is adjusted wrong in the rental car or something, or they talk over the fade. Everything changes.

Ron couldn't take variation in food anymore. It had made him sick. Steak! No idea how that steak was going to taste and feel. More variation steak to steak than live bull to live bull. He couldn't take it. Chocolate wasn't right, either. Temperature makes a big difference in chocolate mouth feel. Who can handle that? How much character are we expected to have in this life? How strong do we have to be just to eat? Ron had found Jolly Ranchers. Thank you, Hershey's, Inc. You deserve a whole town, even if it's in Pennsylvania. Open a Jolly Rancher apple hard candy and you know what you're getting. It might not pop those memories the way the Granny Smith does. The Jolly Rancher might not feel healthy, but it feels right. You could eat hundreds and hundreds of them and there would be no variation. Not a bit. Day to day, season to season, location to location. For days Ron would eat just Jolly Rancher apple, and every one was perfect. Nature didn't have quality control. All the gene splicing and storage barns of pure CO_2 that can kill a worker in four minutes but keep apples fresh can't give the consistency of Beatrice Foods. Those Beatrice people can't do it with other products. You can't make Pop Tarts perfect. But the Beatrice people have Jolly Ranchers hard candy nailed. Hey, Ron, you should have varied your diet a little. Okay, this week, watermelon. True like ice; like fire.

Tommy and the Little Fool were sold. They had to pick up some Ranchers on the way home. If Hector could have explained that in less than a minute, it would have been the greatest radio spot ever. They could have recorded it at Ears 'r' Us. Jolly Ranchers would have had to buy the whole of whatever country they're made in. They aren't made in the USA, right? There have to be Jolly Rancher sweatshops somewhere. That one commercial could have pulled the whole Third World into the twenty-first century. Hector explained that eating nothing but candy had hurt Ron's health. "But you said he brushed his teeth," Tommy weakly argued. "There's vitamin C, so he wouldn't get scurvy. I bet he had a lot of energy."

Ron had also slept with all the lights on full and the TV on loud. He read with the TV on. He'd been lucky that Hector was a good, tolerant friend and a sound sleeper. "I could hear it all night coming from the next room."

"That doesn't prove they weren't gay," Tommy mouthed to the Little Fool's smug smile when Hector turned for a moment to turn CNN all the way off.

Ron had awakened screaming and crying several times a night. We know that a lot of the anti-sugar hype is just hippie hype, but maybe it was related. Ron had been eating nothing but candy, and reading that weird heavy comedy sci-fi. He'd been in bad shape. He'd been doing really badly. You gotta walk the darkness of Candy's hall.

Hector talked for a couple hours. He laughed so hard during the candy story. He cried so hard. Hector missed his friend. They were talking about books all the time, high school brooding stuff. Hector wasn't forty years old yet. That's too young to lose a friend in modern America. He would lose his Mom and his Dad and lots of friends in the future, but the pain would always center around Ron's death. Hector's life would never be the same. Movie funeral scenes with people crying would seem like what people who have never watched porno believe porno is. It would seem tawdry; exploitative in the worst way. Hector was in for a hell of a ride. The Little Fool wanted to invite him back to Tommy's. Hector could eat leftover macaroni and extra-sharp Vermont cheddar cheese while the Little Fool and Tommy ate Jolly Ranchers. But that wasn't right. They were cops, kinda, sorta. They were *like* cops. They had to keep working on the case. They had to find the killer. Tommy's Farrah notebook was filled with much too much information on the Jolly Rancher company, but maybe there were clues somewhere. The Little Fool and Tommy had to talk to some other victims' families and friends. Maybe all the victims had been eating too much candy. Maybe the killer was a greengrocer. Hector was thanking the Little Fool and Tommy and shaking their hands like crazy. Hector never found out who the Little Fool and Tommy were or why they had been there. Hector had just been happy not to be alone. The Little Fool and Tommy should have sent a rotten kid over: He could have helped Hector and gotten lots of free Jolly Ranchers. Jolly Ranchers. One Texas death row inmate had Jolly Ranchers for his last meal. Good thinking. I'll make you mine, and I'll have Candy all the time.

CHAPTER TWENTY

Falling in Love Again

Grace Banks, Renée Garland, Carol Gomes, Phyllis Meltzer hadn't eaten candy all the time. None of them had been strippers taking the bar exam. They all knew how to read. Big deal. They all more or less lived in midtown Manhattan. There were no bridge-and-tunnel commuters. The Little Fool kept tabs on what the real police were doing. They weren't finding much. The Little Fool knew that most of what they were finding out wouldn't be on the computer where he could get to it. Most of what they were finding would be in little notebooks (not Farrah notebooks; more likely McGruff the Crime Dog notebooks). But all the really important ideas were only in the detectives' heads. The Little Fool had expected their talk with Hector to be awful. He'd planned on Hector busting them for not being cops. Or busting them for being cops. The Little Fool expected to be humiliated and reprimanded. We learned that people in mourning don't check credentials. That's how psychics work. They sashay in right after a death when hearts are open and hurt, and the psychics strike. Karma, karma, karma, karma, karma chameleon.

The Little Fool read so many of Renée's emails over and over. He had read all the Barbara McClintock fan sites he could find. Renée had saved both in- and out- in neat little mailboxes. The Little Fool still made Tommy type the password. The Little Fool couldn't do it himself. There was nothing in Renée's private mail that could help the case, but fortunately, one can never be really sure of that. One has to read everything. Get all the clues. Her sexual m.o. had been a bit backwards. She hadn't met people on-line and worked out a time and place to have sex with them. She had met people in person and then exchanged addresses to have cybersex. She was very hot. The Little Fool was really starting to fall for Renée. He was digging her. He started to feel as if he were cheating on Nell. Was it okay to be seriously in love with more than one dead woman? You gotta keep 'em separated.

Renée could really write dirty. This wasn't, "Oh, baby, I have on a sexy nightie and I crave your touch" fake, HBO sexy. This was really sexy. Really dirty. Dirty-sexy enough that some people wouldn't be able to find it sexy at all. If you aren't grossing out some people with your sexual wishes, you might as well be Nicole Kidman fake sexy. You don't have to put out the red light.

Renée had been no e-sex dilettante. No virtual virgin. She had pictures in her mailbox all ready to click. Not too much flesh showing. Less than you'd think. Just a little bit. Lingerie. Nothing extreme. Nothing really to see. Nothing you wouldn't see in a music video. Except you wouldn't see Renée in a music video. She had been a good-sized girl. Our Mom had one home-care person who was from some Scandinavian country. (Is there more than one?) The Scandinavian had said about one of her coworkers, "The wind wouldn't blow her off the road." She had thought it was a cliché that existed outside of language. We'd never heard it before, but the poetry rang true. It made our Mom laugh. It made her laugh a lot. Mom laughing had been good. The Little Fool would have never shown these Renée pictures to his Mom or her home-care person, but if he had, one of them would have said, "The wind wouldn't blow her off the road." Feel the beat from the tambourine.

The Little Fool knows a suicidal Mexican. A beautiful woman he'd met when she was buying sleeping pills to kill herself. He'd helped her through a very bad day. She got in touch eight years after he had saved her to thank him for saving her life. He was thinking a small sexual favor might be in order, but she'd repaid with philosophy. "There's an old Mexican expression—how would you say it in English? 'That which does not kill us makes us stronger.'" *Mexican* expression? What? Imagine being a good enough writer that you write an aphorism that gets picked up by an entirely different culture and passed on as its own. What did that expression have to do with her attempted suicide? That which didn't kill her in this case would have put her in a coma. Maybe she had meant "mentally stronger." If she'd gone through with her suicide and it hadn't killed her, it would have made her a vegetable. How good of a writer do you have to be to write an aphorism that gets picked up by another culture *and* isn't true? Call any vegetable.

Yeah, Renee had been a little heavy. But oh, she had looked good. It hadn't been her body. She didn't have a girl-sexy body. That's the kind of body that heterosexual women see and say to their dates, "She has a nice body." Thin, rich, tastefully dressed. No, this had been boy-sexy. The kind of body a guy sees at a county fair. The kind of body that's built for one thing. Built for comfort and not speed. Girl-sexy is Isabella Rossellini in those old Revlon ads. Boy-sexy is Isabella Rossellini in *Blue Velvet*. Isabella is the only one on record as being both. She didn't get Henry Ford's memo on division of labor. The Little Fool remembered the state fair Harley girl perfectly. With a Harley baby-doll top struggling to do part of its job and giving up on the other part. Her midriff had been too big, but still sexy. Sloppy, floppy, all over. Big hair, bad teeth, and the beautiful date sees her guy looking. "You're looking at her? She's a bit fat, isn't she? And dirty? I mean, she's not even clean. I don't mean sex dirty. I mean hygiene dirty." Sometimes there are very few reasons to live. When everyone you loved is dead. When other people who love have lost people they love. But that county fair memory was always a reason to live.

It had been a crisp, fall, New England day. The Little Fool had been walking with the most beautiful woman he'd ever dated. The most girl-sexy, beautiful woman he'd ever seen in person, and he was dating her. He was having nasty sex with her whenever he wanted. It was hard to remember, but she was better looking than Nell.

The girl had been a real model. Everything about her was perfect. He'd taken her to a county fair, I guess just to show her how the other half lived, or at least how the other half ate things off sticks while walking around on dirt. So, the Little Fool was walking with a woman who was professionally beautiful. You could have taken her anywhere. She'd been sexy, but Mom had loved her. Believed she had a "cute little body." Jackie Kennedy-pillbox-hat-wearing face. Perfect. Clean. The Little Fool was walking with her. She was holding his hand. She'd eaten cotton candy and her hands weren't sticky. That's how perfect she was. She wasn't a prude; she was sexy. The Little Fool had gotten very nasty with her. But no matter what you did and how you did it, she came out of the event fresh and beautiful. Cover Girl's the one for clean makeup.

As they walked around the fair, the Little Fool had seen this biker woman ten years older than his date. Nowhere near as attractive. And he almost broke his neck looking at the biker chick. He'd been with a "10" and was turning around to stare at a "4." At the time, it seemed depressing. It was a depressing event. How could he ever be happy? How could anyone be happy? There was no one better than his date, and he still wasn't satisfied. He knew that if he'd been walking with Isabella Rossellini, he still would have turned for the Harley woman. The Little Fool read somewhere that whenever Walter Matthau saw a beautiful, sexy woman on the street he would say, "Well, someone is sick of fucking her." That's the depressing way to see it. When you're young, it's depressing to think that someone would not be satisfied with another person. Even another perfect person. But that isn't right. It has nothing to do with satisfaction. The Little Fool had gone beyond that now. He realized that the only hope for the world—the only hope for life—is the perfect optimism in that story. As long as you can be with the most beautiful woman in the world and still look at some skank, there's a reason to live. You can't be satisfied because you're alive; because you're an animal; because life goes on and it's all okay. You have to look around because time is passing. The fuse is burning. He was in love with Nell, but he was thinking nasty thoughts about Renée. It would have been the perfect affirmation of life, except both Renée and Nell were deader than doornails. I'm riding in my car and a man comes on the radio.

No matter who you were with, no matter how much perfect woman-flesh you were buried in, you'd have to give these pictures of Renée a second, third, and fourth look. It was in her eyes. She hadn't wanted the viewer to think she was pretty or sexy. She wanted the viewer to *use* those pictures. The Little Fool could see that she had four pictures and she used them as different attachments, depending on where the cybersex was going. They might as well have been labeled "ass man," "tit man," "whore lover," "virgin lover." They were all ready to go. And she had saved some pictures sent to her. These pictures might as well have been labeled "ass man," "tit man," "whore lover," "virgin lover." There is nothing sadder than how alike we are. The myth of fingerprints.

People know everything about us before we know it about ourselves. We're the last to know. Take a regular person—someone who's been around the block a few times—and line up all the kids in a high school class in front of him. Just in the clothes they happened to be in that day. And don't tell the kids why they're there. Just line them up and have our regular guy walk along and tell them the information they need. Give it to them straight out just to save some time: "You fifteen guys, you're gay. Don't worry about girls anymore. Now exchange phone numbers. And you six girls, you just go ahead and give sex with girls a try. It might work out for you. The rest of you are just straight vanilla, except you, you, you, you, you, and you. I have no idea about y'all. You'll have to find out for yourself." We are the champions.

That would save some time. "You girls who are all grouped over here together? You're peaking right now. You look the best you're ever going to look. Enjoy it. You might not want to waste time with 'hard to get.' The same with you guys standing around these girls. Get while the getting's good. You three girls with the braces and your hair in your faces? You'll peak in ten years. You have some time to read. You, kid, are going to be filthy rich. Don't sweat anything.

And that pimple on your face is really a malignant melanoma. Just kidding. You five are going to own your own companies. Just keep working hard. The rest of you, we have no idea, no way of knowing. Your whole life is ahead of you and you can surprise us. Now, all of you, drop out of school now." It would save a lot of time. You've got no choice. Making all that noise 'cause they've found new toys.

The Little Fool understood Renée. They would have gotten along very well. The Little Fool used to go out on dates. He used to bring women home to me. He didn't do that for a while after Nell died. He didn't feel like having sex or even dating. He was distracted being in love with Tommy and Nell. And Renée. He had a lot of love in his life, but less sex. He'd spend all evening working with Tommy on the Nell case, and then the Little Fool would come home with a few emails from Renée printed out. He would read them naked in bed. That was sex for him now. Even the double helix stuff started to work for him sexually. You know that woman's magazine cliché that all the good men are married or gay? In our world, all the good women were stabbed to death and thrown into the river. The Little Fool was reading one letter from Renée over and over. It was a letter to some breast-loving guy, describing Renée's perfect woman for a threesome. It was a perfect description of Nell. Just perfect. It had nothing to do with Nell until the Little Fool read it. It wasn't really a description of Nell at all. Not really. Renée never knew Nell. Renée never would know Nell. The letter meant nothing to the case. It wasn't good for police work, but it was very good for police recreation. Get it on. Bang a gong.

CHAPTER TWENTY-ONE

Who Are You Talking To?

Tommy is sitting at his manicure desk. He's sculpting product onto the ends of a second-wife's fingernails. She's talking about how Tommy should do bikini waxes because the Koreans are too brutal and "you're just one of the girls." Behind Tommy there is a wall phone. It's also an intercom. And one of the features this phone system's salesman boasted about is that you can play music over the phones. You don't need a bunch of radios. You can use your phones for Muzak. No other business in NYC that bought the phone system would ever use that feature. It's like the ruler on your Swiss Army knife. But Tommy's salon uses every feature. It isn't even CDs they play. It's a radio station. So some '80s station is always playing over the speakerphone. On the hour there are breaks for news. Just the top stories. Just three items read off AP. We go by faster miles an hour. If our story were being told in a movie (and all this monkey ever really wanted to do was direct), one of those news stories on the salon phone-radio would be about the case Tommy and the Little Fool were working on. And we'd come in close on Tommy's face as he sculpted nails. It would show the audience that they're really supposed to care about these deaths because the whole city cares. The whole nation is shocked. That's a lot of murdered people; it can't be just Tommy and the Little Fool who care. Maybe we'd see a shot of a couple in Japan seeing the story on TV and hugging their little child. Even the Japanese love their kids enough to be scared of death. You have to do that in movies. They would make you. You have to make the story breathe. The story can't be just Tommy and the Little Fool. It can't be a story of how they loved Nell and each other and tried to solve a case. It has to be really important. If these deaths matter, why aren't they on TV? The story can't just take place in apartments and a salon. Can't we go to the river more? Can't we see more of our guy on the job? You know, the dive-team guy, not the gay guy. Why are we at the salon? What is this? *Shampoo II?* We want to see the divers, and the butch stuff, and the equipment they use. Those police divers are our money. That's our movie. And the city is panicked. Can we see the divers working? Can we see them in the locker room? It can't be a "rug show." It can't be all inside apartments. Let's get outside. Let's get in the streets and in the river. I want them both diving in the river. Let's get the gay guy in the river. There's comedy there because he's fastidious and the water is so dirty. And hey, it's a big, beautiful city. It's gritty and it looks good on screen. Let's see more of NYC. I think the city is a character. Don't you see it that way? And we have to know what's happening in the world. We have to see that. You oughta be in pictures.

After the shot of Tommy doing the nails while the radio news is on, we have to have the Little Fool and Tommy walking by an NYC electronics store with a stack of TVs in the window all showing a picture of Nell. We need newspapers spinning in and freezing on headlines about "Hudson Jack." That's the way you're supposed to make things important. But I'm not telling the story that way. Maybe those news stories really *were* on the radio and maybe Tommy heard them and thought about them. Maybe the city was freaked about these murders. Maybe the Little Fool and Tommy did walk by "Exposition Electronics" in midtown and see some other details that would be important later. But I have no way of knowing that. I have no idea about anything that happened to Tommy when he was alone. I have no way of knowing what went on outside of the Little Fool's focus. I'm a monkey. I know nothing from what I read in the papers. Nothing. I read the news today. Oh, boy.

I'm trying to tell you the story of the Little Fool. I'm trying to tell you how the Little Fool sees the world. I'm trying to write about what's in his heart. Sometimes I want you to say, "Yeah, I know how he feels," and sometimes you have to say, "What a nut." Another human being—compare and contrast. Give you a little glimpse of which particular used nylon stockings make up his guts. That's our goal. I'll tell you all about the Little Fool, I'll bare his heart to you, and I'll tell you the story, but that's all I'll do. I'm not going to talk to you about you as if you're not you. I won't do that. I'm not going to write to you about what other people like you are feeling. That would be cheating. That's not right. That's what many radios, TV, newspapers, and magazines do. They address the people about the people. Not just of, by, and for, but also about. Who are they talking to? They sing while you slave and I just get bored.

Maybe you can't see this. Maybe you have to be a crazy monkey to see this, but it's insane. There's some election. Let's say it's for president. And the third-party candidate gets enough percentage points in some poll so that the meat puppets have to deal with her. This is hypothetical, so let's make it a woman. It doesn't do any harm to be progressive and fair in fiction. So they say, "Nancy Lord has to convince the electorate that she's a viable candidate. She has to show them that she can really win." Who are they talking to? Who is "they"? Who is "the electorate"? That's us, right? (By "us," I mean "y'all." They're not counting sock monkeys.) So, it's saying, "She has to convince you that she has a chance to win with you." Well, if *we* want her, *we* vote for her and she wins. Her "chances" don't matter. The media don't want you to "waste your vote" by voting for a loser. But you can't waste your vote voting for a loser you want. You can waste your vote only by voting for someone you don't want. You don't want the winner. Don't waste your vote on someone who's going to win. He doesn't need your vote; he's going to win. Keep voting for the lesser of two evils and things will just keep getting more evil. That's game theory that even this monkey understands. Who are they talking to? Meet the new boss same as the old boss.

If they just did it with politics, that would be forgivable. Maybe politics don't matter at all. We don't pay too much attention to politics. The Little Fool still voted, Tommy still didn't, and I'm a sock monkey. But they also do it with art, and that's unforgivable. They do it about Steve Martin. The TV states "People say he was the first comedian who was treated by the people as a rock star." Okay, then, what are you saying? Yeah, you, the guy on TV, what are you saying? Was Steve Martin the first comedian-rock star? Is that what you think? And I'm not being a stupid monkey. I know the guy on TV doesn't think anything. I know that guy is just reading prompter. I know he's a meat puppet, but *someone* is writing the copy, right? Someone is writing what the guy on TV is reading. What does that person think? What is he saying about Steve Martin? Married to a donkey, funky Tut.

Polls are not news. Don't talk about people to people. Talk to people. Tell me something real. You can't keep taking polls and talking to us about us. You can't do that. Once again, I don't mean "us"—I'm a monkey; I don't have a vote—but they shouldn't do that for you. You see, I could do that. I could talk about people as though I were outside of them, because I really am. Imaginary friends don't get to vote. But never forget, we have power. Awesome power. Dangerous power. We're still mentioned and trusted on the money. All others pay cash.

Politics can't be watched like sports. The media got confused because both events happen in real time, so the coverage seems similar. But in sports you're trying to accomplish a task better than other people can. And sometimes those others are trying to stop you. And it happens in real time. No one knows what's going to happen, so you make guesses. You do handicapping. You talk about which past and present events may give us a clue as to what's going to happen. You place your bets. TV is perfect for sports. TV is a sports technology. Make that puck look bigger, put a camera overhead. Video killed the radio star.

Now politics looks the same, at first. The politicians are trying to get votes. Some people are trying to stop them. It's happening in real time. But the playing field is the hearts of the people watching.

So you can't handicap. You can't guess. When the goal is to get the people to trust, to believe, to agree, then you can't do that by reporting how much the people trust, believe, and agree. They need real information. The public must stop caring about the public. So, that's why I'm not going to tell you how NYC was reacting to these murders. That's why I'm not going to make this breathe. Our Dad used to say, "What do I care what movie most people want to see? I want to know what I want to see." If you don't care about Nell and Renée and Ron, if you don't care about the Little Fool and Tommy, if you don't care about Dickie the sock monkey, there's nothing more I can do. If I tell you that all of NYC cared and was crying and locking themselves in their homes in fear, that would be cheating. So you want to be a rock and roll star.

CHAPTER TWENTY-TWO

Wounds

The killer wasn't making a girl suit. He wasn't a surgeon. There was no surgical precision. There was no evidence of rape. There was no pattern. There was no hobby to discern, other than making people dead. Nell had something very big stabbed in her while she was still alive. Some of the others had flesh cut off while they were alive. But if there was a ritual, it wasn't explained. Movies are about the bad guys. *Snow White* is good because of the evil queen. *Psycho* is all Norman Bates. We don't care at all about Marion Crane or Janet Leigh. She's dead before it gets going. She's out of the picture. Good guys don't matter in a plot. Hannibal Lecter makes Jodie Foster interesting; so interesting that she doesn't even have to stay Jodie Foster for the sequel. What makes *our* bad guy tick? You're going to find out at the end of the story. There is an answer to this mystery. You're going to hear Hannibal Lecter talk. And our bad guy can really talk. He'll go pages without a breath. He'll talk until you really understand. That's where the fun is. You'll understand our killer at the end of this story. You're learning a lot about him as we go along. I'll give you a hint right here: How he kills them doesn't matter. It isn't sexual. It wouldn't even be considered crazy to most people. But you won't really meet him formally until the end of the story. Don't touch the glass.

The perp beat the victims, cut them, even stabbed them with a blunt object. The Little Fool and Tommy wanted so badly to know what that blunt object was. They were sure it would help. Did he

stab her with the handle end of a hoe? Was he the Killer Farmer?
A hoe would have been too random, and a crucifix too dead on.
She might as well have been stabbed with a wild goose. They
thought it was an important clue, but they didn't find the answer
until after they found the killer, and then it didn't matter. I guess
they could find out now, but they don't care now. It became unimp-
ortant. Tommy, the Little Fool, and the police worked so hard on
figuring out what weapons were used, and the bad guy didn't even
remember. It wasn't his focus. The police report talked about how
much strength was involved in stabbing with this blunt object, but
they confused strength with passion. The bad guy really believed
these people needed to be dead. He didn't want to rape them or
skin them, but he wanted them dead. He might have wanted them
dead slowly, but he wanted them dead more than he'd ever wanted
anything. He wanted them dead so much that he found whatever it
took to make them dead. It's the point of every Broadway musical.
The point of this truly American art form is that you can do whatever you want if you put your mind to it. The "think system"
works for the American marching band. Pull yourselves up by your
bootstraps. It's not true, of course. Broadway musicals aren't true.
After bike racer Lance Armstrong wins the Tour de France, he has
the luxury of saying it was because he had faith in himself and knew
he was going to win. The loser doesn't get the mic. The loser may
have wanted to win much more than the winner, but the loser didn't
win, so he doesn't get the forum to express his pure desire. The loser
just lost. Sometimes it seems like you and me against the world.

Gene Pitney sings, "The man who shot Liberty Valance, he was
the bravest of them all." It may be true, but the two parts of the
sentence are not related. He may have been the bravest, but shooting Liberty Valance is no evidence of that. Don't you have to be
braver to go up against sharpshooter Liberty with less skill? Didn't
the man who shot Liberty Valance have a good amount of skill?
But maybe Hal David, who wrote the lyrics, told Gene that it was
known from another source that the man who shot Liberty was the
bravest. Maybe there was other evidence. I never saw the movie;

maybe they explain it in the movie. I just heard the song on the oldies station. What a town without pity can do.

It's the problem with all these "attitude can save you" do-gooder medicine things. When the poor ex-junkie dies of AIDS anyway, as he's slipping away he knows that not only is it his fault for using a dirty needle, it's his fault for not thinking positively enough. Double bummer. He didn't have a bright enough outlook. He didn't want to live enough. Houdini said he was tired of fighting, and died. It's your fault for dying. You didn't laugh heartily enough at the unfunny, scratchy, mono, b&w, boring Laurel and Hardy bootleg videos this scumbag, quack therapist recommended to you. "You can do anything you want." No, no, no. The last train to Clarksville.

The Little Fool was talking to a woman who was good-looking enough that the checks and balances of public conversation were no longer in play. She had large breasts, a firm behind, and those big sock-monkey lips, and because of that people didn't argue with her. There was always the slight chance she'd give you an opportunity to have sex with those big, fat, wet lips. Why make those minuscule chances even lower by saying, "Actually, I don't think there's any evidence that plastic Evian bottles cause cancer"? It was her punishment for being good-looking. Average-looking-and-below society hates sexy people and punishes them by smiling and nodding when sexy people talk crazy. Society rolls its eyes at ugly people. Society lets the attractive go mad. It's the fastest way for society to manufacture a nut: Take away peer review. So, the Little Fool was talking to one of those unchecked, pretty wackjobs, and she said, "I believe if you visualize something you want enough, it will happen." The Little Fool decided to help her. He closed his eyes. He visualized perfectly, exactly, with all his heart, with all his mind and points down below, what he wanted. He did what NASA (a real acronym) did for Einstein: ran a test. And all the wackjob's clothes stayed on and her mouth stayed as empty as her head. The Little Fool said, "Nope, you can visualize things perfectly, and they won't happen." She knew what experiment had failed. She knew what he was visualizing, and she just alibied it. She said that he must not have really wanted it badly enough. The Little Fool didn't argue after that. Hey, why ruin what little chance is left? I want you so bad, it's driving me mad.

But with killers, the Broadway musical thing is kinda, sorta true. Killing is almost always within your power. What you're trying to do isn't that hard. Killing people is pretty easy. It doesn't take superhuman strength. It takes exactly human strength. Anyone can do it. Really. You can do it. C'mon kid, all you have to do is really want it. Visualize it and "go for it." Put on your Nikes, and kill. That's all it takes. Hey, now. Really. Anyone. A little sock monkey can't kill. Well, maybe I could get lucky. If I hate my owner (which I don't), maybe I could wish for him to roll face down on top of me and smother. Choke on my tail. But I never wished that. Not that it matters. The great thing about wishing and hoping is you don't have to think at all about what you wish and hope for because wishing and hoping don't work. But killing works. You can do it. You can really do it. One day the Little Fool thought it would be funny to catch a pigeon. Just pluck one out of the air as it took off. They're fast, they're wary. Pigeons are New York City. They're no one's little fools. Fast, crafty, flying rats. The Little Fool went to a bunch of them, he moved quietly and patiently, and he reached for one as it flew away. He missed. He realized that he just hadn't wanted it enough. He tried again. This time he didn't worry about technique. He just kept wanting it. He really wanted to grab that piece of flying filth. And he did. In a flash, in an instant, he was holding the bird right in his hands. It wasn't that gross—this is a guy who swims in sewage looking for dead bodies; a city pigeon can't gross him out. It had little scabs from the mites. The animal went into that animal-panic mode. All it wanted, all it visualized, all it wished and prayed for, was to get away. Pure prayer from an innocent animal. And to the bird brain, the power of prayer works. The Little Fool had accomplished his goal, so he granted the bird its wish. He didn't want to kill the bird; he just wanted to grab it, and he had done that. But he could have killed it. He had the power to kill many, many living things. He had the power to kill most living things. He had the power to kill his own kind. All he had to do was want it enough. All you have to do is want it. Everything's coming up roses.

Tommy and the Little Fool had JPEGs of the autopsies. The Little Fool and Tommy let the JPEGs run in slide show mode on their computers. The pictures moved up and down the body. The lighting changed a little with each shot. The sheet was pulled back for each body part, modestly. The wounds gaped immodestly. A police doctor had determined which wounds had killed the victims, but it didn't matter. It was six-blows-to-the-head, half-a-dozen-stabs-to-the-torso. Show them how funky and strong is your fight.

The pictures had been taken by a forensic photographer. They had been downloaded from a digital camera to the precinct computer. The Little Fool copped them off the network and downloaded them onto his work computer. He then moved them to his buddy's computer that had a CD burner, and the Little Fool burned them onto disks. He carried them home to Tommy's, where the Little Fool loaded them onto Tommy's computer. Tommy and the Little Fool downloaded the pictures from the computer screen right into their heads. They didn't need backup. That slideshow ran in their heads all the time. Especially at night. In their dreams. They knew every wound. Every matted hair. In dreams, sometimes they were the killer, sometimes the victim, sometimes omniscient, but never omnipotent. They couldn't stop the killer. They couldn't even stop the pictures. I close my eyes, I see blood.

The Little Fool and Tommy interviewed all the people who knew the victims. The Little Fool and Tommy went out interviewing in the evenings, and all day Tuesdays and Wednesdays. Tommy filled up a lot of notebooks. The Little Fool was trying to read some of the zillion books that were mentioned, learning about some of the heroes of the dead. All three of his Farrah books were chock-a-block. Obsessive, careful little writing. Thousands of details that didn't matter to the case. Who the hell is Norman Bourloug? What poems of Tuli Kupferberg? Thousands of little details that were all that mattered in life, and life didn't matter in death. They were thinking about all the little questions, while the murderer and the victims had been obsessed by the biggest questions. By the time he got to the *A-Team* notebook, there was a system for the minutiae. The order of the questions was established. By the time Tommy got to the *Scooby-Doo* notebook, he'd have most of the answers filled in before he and the Little Fool even got to the interview. Should the teacher stand so near, my love?

The Little Fool grew pubic hair in the days before VCRs. He didn't see dirty pictures moving in the privacy of his home. The kids today have it easy. His dirty pictures were still pictures. There was a picture of Marilyn Monroe that his father kept hidden. Very pink. Very red. Lily, oh Lily.

The first full porno movie the Little Fool ever saw was at a real movie theater. He was either still in high school, or right after. He went with a girlfriend. She just walked in with him. She was the best girl ever. She was cool. She didn't hide her face (bad). She didn't even giggle (worse). She didn't comment on how dirty it was. She was the best girl ever.

The Little Fool never went to porno alone. He never went without a girlfriend or a hooker. Nothing embarrasses the Little Fool, but loneliness scares him. He never wants to see it. He never wants to have to admit he's lonely. Loneliness lives in sexual entertainment. If you go with a girlfriend to a dirty movie theater, you don't have to look at the men sitting alone and know you're just like them. You're different; you're there for a goof. If you're there with a love, the porno movie really is a marital aid. When Nadine Strossen was the president of the ACLU (an initialism, not an acronym—she said it stood for "All Criminals Love Us"), she floated in front of her board the idea that they could take the position that censorship of pornography is discrimination against the ugly. "Why should only good-looking people be able to see beautiful people naked?" It was genius. It was ahead of her time. It didn't fly. Although he's not a man some girls would think of as handsome.

The first time the Little Fool went to see porno, he got very depressed. It wasn't that he felt the actors were exploited, that's crazy talk—they all seemed to be there more voluntarily than Bobcat Goldthwait in *Police Academy* 3. The Little Fool was depressed because it all looked just like when Cindy (the girlfriend he went to the movie with) and he had sex. It's tough to see how alike we are. It hurts to see that your most intimate moments aren't special. When he was kissing and licking and moaning, it seemed unique. It seemed like he and Cindy had invented it. It was her idea to lick his testicles. That was her original idea. They invented anal sex together. And yet there it was on the screen. The actors even said the same things. They even did all the same things in the same order. Sock monkeys are pretty much the same, too. Our mouths, our eyes, our tails. We're loved the same, hugged the same. People read poetry to celebrate how alike they are, and porno breaks their hearts with how alike they are. If you call phone sex right now, they'll have scripts that'll work for you. It was even worse for the Little Fool. The Little Fool actually thought he invented masturbation. He really did. He was in the bathtub, and he was playing with his penis. It felt funny and he wanted to see how much he could take that particular stroke before he couldn't stand it anymore. He persevered. He'd taken it. He was able to stand it longer than ever before, and his penis exploded. Wow. He invented that. It didn't exactly feel like pleasure, but he wanted to do it again. He'd invented something very dramatic. He was the Louis Pasteur of bathing. When he put two and two together on a Ritz and realized that what he was doing had been done by all humans, he was very sad. He hadn't found something special about his body. No one wants to be alone, but everyone wants to be a little more special. Gonna use my my my imagination.

In that first porno movie, the actor had the idea of having an orgasm right in the actress's face. The Little Fool and Cindy both wanted to scream, "Hey wait a minute! That's our idea!" But they hadn't. They just went back to her dorm room and didn't get any semen on her face. They made out while saying things they hadn't heard in the movie: "Oh, baby, there's a clown in the refrigerator. Put your honey badger in my comb." It made them laugh and that was good: The people in the movie hadn't laughed. It shouldn't really have bothered them. They had a romantic restaurant and other couples went there and it hadn't bothered them—but this was different. Points of her own, way up firm and high.

Cindy left the Little Fool. Her Dad had broken them up. Dad hadn't been a redneck worried about his daughter having sex; he was an NPR liberal worried about his daughter dating a guy who didn't want to go to college and, even worse, who wanted to be a cop. It was easier to be upset about that than the fact that the Little Fool was banging his little girl. When she left, we believed he would never have sex again. He had to find something else to do with women. He couldn't ever do the same things he'd done with Cindy; they had invented that together. He'd never invent anything else. His best work had been in his youth. It's like the Fields Medal. The Little Fool did get over it. He can now have an orgasm in someone's face without feeling pedestrian. He's gotten better. I guess it saves time. You don't want to waste time inventing new tricks every time you get into bed with someone new. It's good to speak the language. I'm special, so special.

Homosexuality was even worse for the Little Fool. In high school, when the Little Fool had been a dietary aid (dishwasher) at the hospital, he worked with a cook who was very gay. The Little Fool talked to the cook about music. The cook, Charles, had given him Bette Midler and Yma Sumac records. Charles and the Little Fool became very close. Charles cooked special lunches for them to eat together in the walk-in refrigerator just to be wild. They talked about everything together. The Little Fool finally got up the nerve and asked Charles what homosexuals do. The Little Fool knew what heterosexuals do. He believed that homos had some real perversions. Charles went down the list of everything gays do, and there was *nothing* on the list the Little Fool couldn't do some version of with a girl. Nothing. That was when the Little Fool decided not to be gay. If anything, gays had one *less* option. It was depressing. Even Tommy only had one or two tricks of his own. In the Navy.

Sex is true. Sex is human. And so in sex, people are most alike.

It digs down deep into the lizard brain. There really isn't going to be much variation. What is the variation going to be? High heels? There's nothing there. And grief is almost the same as sex, but grief is even worse. The primal howl of pain. Everyone the Little Fool and Tommy talked to told the same story. The story of love and loss. All summed up with some little detail. The loved ones all had one little detail. And the detail always made the griever laugh. Always a deep laugh of joy and pain. The survival instinct trying to give its host some reason to live. Nothing special about the Little Fool's love for Nell. Nell was everything: she was the funny story that made the Little Fool laugh and gave him reason to live, and she was a face that he'd had many orgasms all over. Write that down in your notebook. I pity the fool.

CHAPTER TWENTY-THREE

Oh My Goodness

The Little Fool saw Uma Thurman in *Baron Münchausen*. He came out of the theater and said, "You know that woman that came out of the water on the shell? I thought she was really attractive." Reverse solipsism. "I'm crazy, I like ice cream. I'm such a nut, I like to get paid a lot of money." The Little Fool lost his love for Uma right away. He wasn't discovering her at a DQ outside of Austin; she was in a Hollywood movie on a screen. You go to see Elvis Costello in concert and everyone sings Elvis's early songs of alienation. We all share those lonely feelings, but it's weird to celebrate the sharing of those lonely feelings. This was happening on the Nell case. It wasn't even the Nell case anymore; it was the "Hudson Ripper" case. We couldn't really play detective anymore, because now we were competing with CNN for the interviews. The Little Fool wasn't the only one stealing the police files and pictures. The *New York Times* had published stuff that no one was supposed to have seen. The Little Fool loved finding Tommy and sharing grief with him, but the Little Fool didn't want to share grief with the whole world. On TV they had all the victims' pictures, and there was Nell right along with them. It wasn't okay. This was his grief. They didn't have a right to mourn. It's my party and I'll cry if I want to. Cry if I want to.

The Little Fool hated TV, but he was watching. Watching the news all the time. Watching the interviews. If you're going to interview someone on TV, and you get "good TV" of them crying, and you don't cry yourself, you're a pig. It's as easy as that. If you're a TV person and you're not blubbering when you throw to commercial, if you can keep track of the fifteen seconds that are left in the spot, you're a pig. When Tommy did his interviews, he always ended up crying. But Tommy and the Little Fool weren't making good TV. Just what were Tommy and the Little Fool doing? Two questions: What were they doing and what did they believe they were doing? They weren't working on a case; that wasn't their job. They weren't vigilantes. They weren't giving comfort to the grieving; there was no comfort to give. What were they doing? Were they just enjoying the live stage show of the good TV? Did they just want better seats? Did they want to see the grief and panic up close? Were they ratcheting up from reality TV to reality reality? The longer it went on, the more it seemed they were just dating while sharing a hobby. Tommy and the Little Fool were seeing each other all the time, and the case was what they talked about. Two people who meet each other at a *Star Trek* convention and flirt, and date, and feel safe while talking about things that don't really matter while wearing rubber, pointy ears. Did the murder matter? Should they have taken up bowling together? Live long and prosper.

Two wrongs don't make a right. Sure, but no one seems to believe it. Oliver Stone lied his eyes out in *JFK*, but that's okay because the Warren Commission was all jive. Nixon says it best in his book, *RN*. In *RN*, Tricky Dick writes about all the mistakes Woodward and Bernstein made in *All the President's Men*. Some of the mistakes were made on purpose. Nixon writes about the lying, cheating and bad journalism. And then Nixon says he understands that evil. Woodward and Bernstein believed the end justifies the means, and that's the mistake Nixon made. Nixon says that. He gets it. He says Woodward and Bernstein did what they did because they believed that getting Nixon out of office was so important. He made his mistakes because he believed that staying in office was more important. It seems that everyone believes the end justifies the means. Isn't that the plot of every cop movie? The Little Fool is about to do something wrong. I'm sure I could blow that by you. I could just tell you this part of the story, and you'd be fine with it. He's about to do this bad thing because he and Tommy loved Nell. You might not even notice it's a bad thing. Hey, it's just a book. But what he's about to do is wrong. It moves our plot along, it gives us some excitement, and it will, eventually, help them find the killer, but it's wrong. And it eats away at me. The Little Fool was raised better than that. We took good care of him. We taught him right from wrong. The end doesn't justify the means. Ever. The Little Fool knows that. You know that. And now, all together now, we will do wrong. Tommy, the Little Fool, you and me will take that step. Sail the ship. Chop the tree. Skip the rope.

They were all working double shifts in the dive squad. The NYPD, the mayor and the media all wanted any new bodies to be found fast. They wanted every body found. The Little Fool wanted to find the new bodies himself. It was the only way he'd have special access to more clues. He was working double shifts like everyone else, but he was really working them. He wasn't using any of the tricks to do less work. He was the first one in and the last one out and he was swimming fast. He knew where the body dumps had been and he was figuring the current. Bingo, he comes up with the newest freshest body, and that's when he brings some action to our story. It was a whole different feeling for him. He was happy to have found the dead body. Very happy. He was winning! That's where he turns this story into his story so it can be told from the POV of this diver's sock monkey instead of the lead detective's sock monkey. The Little Fool found the newest body. He dragged it up. But this time he didn't think about all the grief the body would cause. He didn't think about the pain or the suffering. All he could think about was what clues he could get off the body before anyone else got them. This is the moment in our story where we doubt the nobility of our hero. I still love him. I don't have a choice. I'm going to try to get you to love him again by the end of the story. But this is a moment of weakness. At this point he wants to win. At this point, he's going to hold back clues from the detectives so he and Tommy can work on the case. What has this got to do with his love of Nell? What has this got to do with his love of his sock monkey? What has this got to do with his love of Tommy? Nothing. Now he wants to win. Now he wants to find the killer before anyone else. Now he's a bad guy. Behind blue eyes.

Are you disgusted with the Little Fool? Would you be above it? Would you be sucked into the game? It really doesn't matter what the clue is, does it? It doesn't matter at all. It's still wrong. But, get this, the clue is a note. A note written by the killer to the Little Fool. Remember, to have a good story we need a really interesting villain, and I think we're about to have one. An interesting villain will make this a much better story. And now we have a hero who is flawed. I guess as you've been reading, you may have found some other flaws in him. He's not perfect. But up until now in our story, he hasn't done anything really wrong. All of a sudden, though, it's renegade-cop time. We're undermining the system. We're not a team player. We're unethical. I know what you're thinking, punk.

Pinned to the corpse's clothes was a note. It was printed in waterproof ink. It was written on a piece of plastic. It was rolled up and pinned in a pocket of the corpse. I could tell you all the gory details of the wounds (same as all the others). I could tell you the sex of the corpse (same as one of the others). Yeah, yeah, yeah, this corpse had suffered and had people who had loved him and was going to cause a lot of pain and blah blah blah. But there was also a note. The other real police detective people should have had this note. The forensic chemists should have had this note. Maybe they could have traced it back to a particular printer at a particular Kinko's. A forensic psychiatrist could have studied it and concluded that it had been written by a middle-aged, white man (as all villains in all stories must now be). But they won't see it. Not now, at least, because we have the note. And we have a story. Hey, wanna know what it says? Lonely days are gone, I'm a-goin' home.

CHAPTER TWENTY-FOUR

(A Note—Not by Dickie)

There are some things I want to help you all to understand. But these things are not facts or philosophies. They will not solve our crime. "What," "when," "how," and "where"—you don't need my help with those. You will figure all those out. Working together, like good humans, you will find answers. As far as "why": If you're looking for a "why," a prosaic "why," a "why" that you can understand, a "why" that you can afford, a "why" that makes you safe, a "why" that reassures that it won't happen to you or anyone you love, a "why" you can print in the newspaper, a "why" you can parrot on the news, a "why" that Stern can speechify to Robin about—you shan't find it here. And "who"—I sincerely hope you will not find "who" here. I'm trying to keep "who" to myself.

Don't bother underlining 'shan't' and 'speechify,' pigs. Those are dead ends. Yeah, it's regional usage, but that ain't (underline that) gonna (that, too) help ya (now we're cooking). As you read the following work of fiction, you're going to think that my heart is in it, and because you're looking at my heart, open, bleeding, and all red on the inside like my so-called "victims"—just because you will see my heart does not mean you can find my heart. I am giving you my emotional heart in this piece of art, in my writing. My emotional heart is in the following story, but my physical heart, the heart that 72% of the population will want to legally stop from beating, the heart that 100% of the population will want to lock up forever, that heart is going to be harder to find. I'm keeping that heart to myself. I won't give you that heart on a platter. You'll have to work for that real, fucking, beating heart. The 72% figure is made up; I didn't do any research, so that won't help you. You can't find anything about me from the sources I use.

The waterproof ink on acetate I'm pretty sure won't give you much. I'm pretty sure that'll give you nothing. I'm very sure. Hey, I'm betting my life on it. All Kinko's use pretty much the same machines, and all their ink is "waterproof," and they buy it in bulk. "Pretty much" might give you hope, but it shouldn't give you too much. You're fucked on that front. I'm writing this document in Word with the default fonts. That makes it tough. Blame Bill Gates's monopoly for making this so hard to trace. "Well, at least we know the letter writer uses Microsoft products. Get me a list of everyone that uses Office Suite." Good luck, you stupid cocksuckers. The sentence structure—the run-on sentences (so far the letter writer has written almost no run-on sentences, so mark that down), the smug quality, the parallel constructions, the half-assed erudition, the nearly random cunt obscenity— what's that going to tell you? Are you going to be able to figure from this that I'm a little odd? Do I write like a crazy motherfucker? Is that new information? What about the fucking corpses, assholes? Don't you think that shows a bit of my eccentricity? How many of you are nuts enough to kill? I don't mean kill the way some pussy cop kills, shooting some twelve-year-old black kid in the back a dozen times for reaching for a cell phone. I'm talking about the kind of killing real men, real artists do. The kind of killing that's now in your dreams every fucking night. When you do it yourself, the dreams go away. When you're really killing. Killing like a craftsman. Killing like a carpenter. Doing it right, like Sam, the dog, told me to. (I'm just fucking with you, Five-oh-oh-oh.)

You have to pass this note around to everyone. You have to rip it apart word by word and ink molecule by ink molecule looking for clues. Smell the acetate. Stare at the big, giant blowup of my words. Memorize this. Add it to your dreams. Recite it like the opening 'graph of Lolita. *I can't write like Nabokov (hint: I pronounce it right), but he couldn't kill like me, tripping off the tongue. The smart friends and families of the victims won't read this. The stupid ones will feel it's part of the healing. But dead people don't heal, you dopey motherfuckers, and neither do dead hearts. The press will all have big hard-ons dripping with pre-cum to print this note on the front page. (The pig-shrinks will go nuts with that big sex image because I* didn't fuck the broads I killed or even the dudes [underscore—two different generations of slang]. I'm sexually all over the place, repressed and acting out, all at once.) This is going to look good in the papers with all the fucking expletives fucking deleted. "Big [expletive] dripping with [expletive]." You know, it's fucking sexier that way. Who's going to be the first to print the whole thing? It'll be on the Web instantly, and then the fucking, bullshit Voice will print it, right? Or fucking Hustler? That cocksucking cripple, Larry Flynt, will find nude pictures of the dead girls and print those. Did any of them do nude modeling before I met them (oh, he's admitting he knew them—no shit, Sherlock)? I guess you'll find out. The free market will parade my corpses naked. Go go go. Go, you fucking, money-sucking pigs.

Here's a work of fiction for you. The following story is a fantasy. It'll show some knowledge of our country's blood-donating and bone-marrow-typing system. Does that mean I worked at one of those places? Does it mean that I'm an apheresis donor? Is my bone marrow type on file? You'll have to follow all those leads. You have to do that. You have to take all the obvious routes. No tern unstoned. I can't tell you not to bother. Who would listen to me, anyway? Who am I? I mean, besides the only one who fucking knows what you fucking want to know, you stupid cunts.

I was going to ask you a favor. I was going to ask you all to give the following piece of fiction one read-through, without looking for clues. One read just as fiction. One read where the ideas just flow over you. One read as the lie that tells the greater truth. One read for the answers to the real important questions. The questions that don't start with a "w" and can't be asked in one word. Then, after that, go through and destroy the art with scrutiny. I understand you have to solve the crime. But you wouldn't want to do me any favors. "If we do what he says, the terrorists have won." Well, you know, the terrorists always win. Always. Everywhere. It works. Killing always works. Killing always sends a message loud and clear. If you want to scare people, killing people is a damn effective way to do it. It always works. But my message is just a red cunt hair too complicated to be delivered by stiffs alone. The death will do more than underscore. The death is the truth; the following story is the appendix. My message needs an appendix. (I got to see and *touch a few real, physical appendixes. I'm telling you, to the lay observer it does seem like a useless hunk of flesh.)*

My story uses the literary device of a conversation. A phone conversation. I hope you like it.

CHAPTER TWENTY-FIVE

(A Piece of Art, a Poem, Some Truth—Not by Dickie)

"Hello."

"Hello, is this the Jenkins residence? Mr. and Mrs. Jenkins? Tom Jenkins and Tina Jenkins? And do you have a little son, a son named William? You probably call him 'Billy.' Or 'Bill.' Or maybe 'Will.' I hope you don't call him 'Willy.'"

"This is Tom Jenkins. Who is this?"

"My name is Parker. Parker Davis. Like the pens. You're in Toronto, right?"

"Who is this?"

"I just told you."

"What do you want?"

"How is your son doing?"

"I'm sorry, but if you don't tell me what this is about, I'm going to have to hang up."

"This is about your son's leukemia. It's gone now, right?"

"Well, yes. It looks good. We're hopeful."

"Are you thanking God?"

"We're very grateful. What do you want?"

"How did God help?"

"God answered our prayers."

"Little Willy is going to be okay?"

"We don't call him 'Willy.'"

"Maybe you should. Think about that. I want to run that up the flag-pole and see who salutes it."

"*I think I need to hang up now.*"

"*You're going to hang up on the man who saved your son's life? The man who took that needle deep into his hip? The man who had his marrow sucked out and gave that marrow to your son? The man who took the blood cancer out of your life?*"

"*The donor has no contact with the recipient or the families.*"

"*Do you know why? Do you know why they keep that information secret? Why they don't tell? Do you know why?*"

"*It's a privacy issue.*"

"*Only if it's a stranger. If it's a family member or a neighbor or someone else from the bullshit local drives that they always do around dying people to get everyone typed, they tell them. If they find a hit in the family or among friends (they never do), they let everyone know. If it's a family member or a friend, you know who it is. But your donor was a stranger.*"

"*That's correct.*"

"*And they don't tell you who it is when it's a stranger. Do you know why they don't tell?*"

"*Privacy.*"

"*That's not an answer. The reason is because too much thanks is irritating as all fuck. Have you heard of Lenny Bruce? He was a funny junkie who died at the toilet. Like Elvis. The way real heroes die.*"

"*Yes, I've heard of Lenny Bruce.*"

"*Have you heard, 'Thank you, Masked Man?' It was a cartoon, too.*"

"*I think I need to hang up. I don't like your tone.*"

"*I saved Willy's life, you ungrateful prick. Listen to me. Lenny's routine is about why the Lone Ranger doesn't wait around for 'thank you.' Because it's addictive. Because it's irritating. It's a very funny routine. Dated, but funny. It uses the word 'fag' for shock value, and now the shock value is in the other direction. Now, it's not being a fag that's shocking; it's saying the word 'fag.' It used to be the thing that was wrong. Now it's the word. Tom? Are you a fag, Tom?*"

"*No.*"

"*Ever try it, Tom? Even once, Tom?*"

"*No.*"

"*College? Boy Scouts?*"

117

"No."

"C'mon, really? Boy Scouts?"

"No."

"Catholic school?"

"No. I'm going to hang up now."

"Me, neither. I've never tried it. I've never touched another man's penis, and no man other than a doctor has ever touched mine. I'm not queer. There's nothing wrong with being gay, but I ain't no queer. Do you think there's anything wrong with it?"

"No."

"But you're not a dick smoker yourself, right?"

"No. But it's none of your business, and I'm going to hang up."

"They don't give out the names of the donors because the families have no way to show enough gratitude. There isn't enough gratitude. But they try, and it's irritating. It drives the donor crazy. Every single fucking birthday the little bastard has, the donor would get a card and a picture and a long, teary letter about all the joy his marrow gave. It would get on a person's nerves."

"I don't believe you."

"You don't believe it would get on your nerves? Oh, I think it would get—"

"I don't believe you are the marrow donor that saved our son."

"Type O negative is not just a band, brother. It's the type of your son. It's also the type of me. I didn't have that virus that ninety-five percent of the people have. That made it easier. A better chance of it taking. Remember that? I was a lucky hit. Do you have all your paperwork? Do you remember the case number? Go look at it. Look at the case number. You published his blood type all over, so I could know that. When you were begging for anyone to do what I ended up doing for you, you published the blood type everywhere. You went on local TV telling people to sign up, but you didn't publish the case number. Why would you publish that? Who cares? The number is on your insurance form. It's on mine, too. The hospital computers all have the numbers and names encrypted, but you have the number and I have the number. Go get the forms. Go find them. Now! I'll wait."

"*I'm not going to play this game.*"

"*How can it hurt you to look at the form? C'mon, be a sport.*"

[Pause]

"*Okay, I have the form.*"

"*I have mine, too. Put your finger on the case number and read along with me: seven three four dash nine nine seven six dash five dash zero one zero three six three nine eight dash nine zero one zero two zero three. That's a lot of numbers, huh? Huh? And you have the same numbers, right? Am I right? Hey, Skippy, am I right?*"

"*That's the number on this form.*"

"*Do I have your attention, sport? Las Vegas. Thirty-four-year-old male. Perfect match. Nice, clean blood. That's me, brother.*"

"*I'm still not convinced.*"

"*You don't have to be convinced. You'll be convinced later. I just want your attention now. It's your job to get convinced. When I hang up, hire a private investigator to get into the records. It'll cost you under a grand. Get the phone number of the donor. Get the home phone and the office numbers. Call those numbers. My secretary will put you through. You'll get me. It's not super-secret information. They just don't make it too easy. They don't want you to annoy the donor. But this donor wants to talk to you. There's a good enough chance that I'm the donor that I think you should listen. May I have a little more of your phone time?*"

"*Okay, speak your piece, but, I swear, if this is a sick, prank call, I'll report it to the police.*"

"*It is a sick, prank call, but I hope you won't report it to the police. I hope you're grateful enough to not report it to the police. I like Lenny Bruce. Lenny also said that the only real anonymous donor was the guy who knocked your sister up in a taxicab. Have you heard that bit?*"

"*No.*"

"*Well, it's a good bit. Again, a little dated, but the idea is right. I'm no longer anonymous. You know my name and soon you'll know my phone number and where I work. As a matter of fact, if you have Caller ID you have my home phone number now. It popped up. I'm calling you from home. I'm on my personal line. This is a personal call. I'm not ashamed of who I am or this call. I want you to know exactly who I am. Is your wife*" around? I want to talk to you privately. I don't want her to know about this phone call."

"She's out, with Billy."

"Showing off your healthy child?"

"I suppose."

"Okay, you'll find out later that I'm really the donor. You'll get proof. But let's just take as a given, just for the sake of discussion, that you're really talking to the real-deal donor. Will you do that? What harm will it do? Just do that for me, okay?"

"Go ahead."

"Remember you prayed to God. When Billy was diagnosed, you prayed to God. You weren't very religious before that. I mean, you weren't not religious, but you never really thought much about it, did you? And then Billy, who you should call 'Willy,' was diagnosed and you got really religious. You prayed to God. You begged God. You tried to make deals with God. You said you'd do anything. You begged for God to take you instead, just to save Willy. You prayed, didn't you?

"Of course."

"You promised anything. Anything."

"Anyone would. That's not hard to guess."

"And you were never bone-marrow typed before that, were you? You didn't even give blood. You didn't give a fuck until disease came a-knockin' at your family door, and then you were all high and mighty. Everyone should get typed. You shamed everyone you knew and many you didn't know into getting typed."

"We were very active in getting people to register."

"You want to know something else weird about me? As strange as this phone call? Here's the weird thing: I've never known anyone with leukemia. I've never known anyone that needed bone marrow. I went and got typed to help strangers. I wasn't shamed into it. I wasn't scared into it. I just wanted to help, so I went in and got typed. You didn't do that, did you?"

"I'm typed now, and I would love to help anyone. I would give my marrow to anyone, no questions asked."

"But not until you tasted personal fear. Family fear. Not many people are like me. I'm a good man, don't you think?"

"You're making me very uncomfortable. You don't seem like a good man."

"Right, but you're going to take as a given that I'm the one who saved your son. If that's true, I'm a good man."

"If that's true, you saved my son's life. You're a very good man."

"Yeah, I gave your son his life, didn't I? And it is your actual biological son, right? You're the one who knocked your wife up, right? You found that out during all this testing?"

"I knew that before the testing."

"But now you're sure, right?"

"I always was sure."

"Okay, sure. So no one you knew matched. And you prayed and you said you'd do anything. Anything to have your son safe and healthy. Didn't you? Didn't you say you'd do anything? Didn't you?"

"Are you calling me to get money?"

"I'm rich."

"Why are you calling?"

"If you'll shut the fuck up, I'll tell you. So, you didn't care at all about other people's children, but you wanted everyone to care about yours. You and your wife and all your relatives were not close enough to a match, right? So, they went through the registry of strangers. It's mostly white people, you know, there's a crisis in the Black and Asian populations. It's mostly white people, but, even so . . . Do you know what the chances are of a stranger matching?"

"One in a million."

"Do you know the chances of something's chances being exactly one in a million? Well, it's one in a million. The chances of the chances of any random thing being one in a million is one in a million. But the chances of a stranger hitting for a marrow transplant really is around one in a million. That's the ballpark. And you prayed. You begged God. You would do anything."

"Yes. What do you want?"

"I didn't want anything. You weren't allowed to pay me legally. You can't pay for my marrow. I have to give it freely to you, and I did. I even paid for all my hospital expenses. I wanted to give. You didn't have to beg me. *I didn't even sign up because of you. I didn't want to help Willy at all. I just wanted to help anyone. Anyone at all. And I ended up helping little Willy. I saved his life."*

"Yes, and if that's really you, thank you."

"If I had asked you before, if I had snuck around the bureaucrats and asked you what you'd give for my precious marrow, for the inside of my bones that would save your son, what would you have given?"

"Anything."

"Of course. And I gave that gift. I gave the priceless gift for no price. For free. God gave that gift to you and expected nothing. Not a thing in return. Your prayers were answered. Answered by God and me, right?"

"If that's you, yes."

"And I didn't ask for anything."

"Not at the time, no."

"But now I'm going to ask, because now it's interesting. It's very interesting. I have no bargaining power. What's interesting to me is my lack of leverage. You have the biggest gift you will ever get and you have it free. I am not *threatening* your child or your family in any way. I will not hurt anyone! *Do you understand that?"*

"I hope you're telling the truth on that."

"Oh, I am. There is nothing I will do to you. You have my marrow inside your son. You have that. Your son is living because of me and I will not take that back. And I will never call you again. And I will never ask for anything after this phone call. Never. I will not contact you again in any way. Do you understand?"

"Yes."

"You are home, safe and sound. My gift had no price. You know it hurts a lot to donate marrow. You saw the size of that needle, right? They tell you when you're signing the papers that it's going to hurt as much as 'yard work.' They say it's going to be 'a little stiff.' You know they're lying. I knew they were lying. You knew they were lying. It hurts liked a greased bitch. You know that, right?"

"Thank you."

"You're very welcome. It's all free and clear. You have all the power. You have your son all healthy. You have your family. The insurance covered it.

I'm never going to call you again, and, if I do, you will have my name and address and you can call the cops. You can get a restraining order. You can lie and say that I threatened you. You can talk to your friends about what a creep I am and how helping someone else should be enough thanks. They'll ask what kind of monster I am. You are in the right. I am a creep. But your son is alive because of me."

"What do you want from me?"

"I'm rich, asshole. You don't have anything I want. Well, you don't own anything I want. But I was thinking as that needle was going into the bone of my hip about all your prayers and deals and how those deals that desperate people make with God are never collected. How 'I'll do anything' never means anything. 'I'll do anything' always means nothing. It means jack shit. I thought about that a lot. I got a bit obsessed. So, this is an ex-periment. Maybe it's a performance art piece."

"What do you want?"

"I want you to tell me the truth. You answered this before, but now I want the real, deep truth. Have you ever had any homosexual experience at all? Ever?"

"No."

"Okay, here's what I want. I want you to suck my cock until I cum in your mouth. I want you to check to make sure I am the man who saved your son's life, and then I want you to buy me an airplane ticket, first class, from McCarran airport to whatever the bullshit airport in Toronto is called. Fly me there and book me a room. A nice hotel room. We'll set up a time that's convenient for both of us. You'll come to the room. You'll get on your knees and you'll suck my cock. You'll do a good job. You'll do a great job. You'll do it for your son. It'll be the first blowjob I've gotten from a man. It'll be the first one you've given. Once. That's it. I want to shoot hot cum down your faggot throat. You'd said you'd do anything—'anything.' This is one blowjob. Your wife does it to you all the time, and she did it to other guys before you were married. She's probably done it once or twice to other guys while you were married. What the fuck do I know? You know I'm safe. You've seen my blood work. I'm not HIV positive. I don't even have herpes. If my marrow is good enough to save your son's life, my cum should be good enough for you to drink! Drink my sperm like a whore. There's no

harm *in this at all. I just want one deal with God to be paid off. And it's paid off cheap. I just want to shoot a load of cum in your mouth and have you swallow every drop. I won't touch your precious cock. I won't fuck your tender asshole. I won't give you a reach around. I don't want to kiss you. I won't even know if your cock gets hard while you're sucking. I just want to see if you'll pay up. I want to see if you're good for the deal you made with God. That's all I want. I have to know that. I need to know about human nature. I don't want you to answer me now. Please, don't answer. I'm going to hang up before you can answer. I want you to think about it. That's what I want. I guess you can call the police on me and say this was an obscene call and get me in trouble. I guess you can just hang up and shake your head and say that I couldn't really be the guy who saved your son's life. You can hang up and say that, even if I am the guy, you don't owe me anything. But I think you owe God something. And I think you owe yourself something. And I think you owe me a blowjob. So, I'll be waiting. Write down my name. Write down my Caller ID number. Think about it. And if you're a man, you'll hire a private dick (pardon me) and you'll find out that I'm for real. And if you're a man, I'll get a call from you. And if you're a real man, I'll get a plane ticket and a room. And if you're what a real man should be, you'll suck my cock. If you're a man who loves your son, loves your family, loves truth and justice and God—you'll swallow my cum. For God. Lick it up, lick it up, yum, yum, yum. So long, Sport. Ta ta."*

[Click]

CHAPTER TWENTY-SIX

Out of the Italics

"That's the sexiest thing I've ever heard. Now I have two reasons to find that guy."

Tommy liked the story.

"We are in so far over our heads. So far." The Little Fool was freaked. They were dealing with a really bad guy, and, even worse, they were kinda bad guys themselves. Tommy was okay, but the Little Fool had done something pretty bad. The real police hadn't seen this note. The Little Fool had stolen a piece of evidence. The line between vigilante and accomplice had become wafer thin. Day becomes the night. Try to run. Try to hide.

It's the *Death Wish/Dirty Harry* problem. It's the reason we have society. Society doesn't need to stop most of us from being judge, jury, and executioner. The last thing most people want is to be judge, jury, and executioner. So few want to be those three things, ever. We usually avoid being even one of those things. What have you done to get out of jury duty? It's yet another reason not to register to vote. Checks and balances exist not only to distribute power, but also because nobody really wants that power. It wasn't the judge's fault; the jury did it. It's not the executioner's fault; he's just doing a job. It allows us to get unpleasant work done without it being anyone's responsibility. Tin soldiers and Nixon coming.

"Judge, jury, and executioner" would be a much cooler phrase if there were a "j" word for "executioner." A "j-u" word would be even better. If there were a "j-u" word ending in "e-r," like "juggler" or "juicer," that means "a guy who kills people," "judge, jury, and executioner" would be a phrase that got used a lot more on talk radio. Those wild talkers sure like alliteration. Let's say "juggler" means "executioner." I would like that, and radio would love that. It's not that hard. "Executioner" could then mean "one who performs entertaining demonstrations of great dexterity." It wouldn't mess up the language that much. It would just make talking and writing about vigilantes a little more musical. Help along our love affair with our mother tongue. Let's do it for G. Gordon Liddy's sake. I don't want to get greedy, but if we're going to make that change, there's another word change that's even more important than "executioner/juggler." This one for the sake of country-western artists. If "drinking" and "thinking" didn't rhyme, C&W guys would never write about their thoughts. And C&W guys shouldn't be writing about any thoughts. "Ramblin'" rhyming with "gamblin'" is perfect; that's a gimme. If you wear a hat on stage, you're gonna wanna talk about wandering and taking chances in the same couplet. But "thinking" just gets thrown in there at random. The Little Fool once wrote a country song. Just strum an E chord and sing these words to whatever tune you want: "I've been ramblin' / and gamblin' / and drinkin' / and thinkin' / I had an orange." Country guys don't want to sing about thinking. Now, imagine if the word "thinking" meant the idea of bowling, or, more precisely, the idea of bowlin'. And "bowlin'" could mean "to do some serious pondering." That one little change would revolutionize country music. I guess it's going to be hard to get the ball rolling. (Ball rollin', as when you're out thinking in your Thursday Night Thinking League. Of course, the ideas of rollin' and bowlin' would no longer rhyme, but even C&W artists don't use that rhyme much.) Those two word changes sure would be nice. Just those two changes and we'd have a better language. Just execute that around in your head. I bowl I love you.

It's the *Death Wish/Dirty Harry* problem. It's the reason we have society. Society doesn't need to stop most of us from being judge, jury, and juggler. The last thing most people want is to be judge, jury, and juggler.

The Little Fool had taken on the obsession of finding Nell's killer. The Little Fool had dragged Tommy in with him. They were working parallel with the police department. They had violated some privacy, but they hadn't crossed any big moral line until now. No reader was going to hate our lead characters before the note. But now they were really getting in the way of police work. They were in the way of justice. They had the biggest clue in the case, and that meant the police department didn't have the biggest clue. Some readers are going to turn on the Little Fool and Tommy. Some readers are feeling the Little Fool and Tommy crossed a line. In stories, the ends justify the means, so I'll tell you right now the Little Fool and Tommy are going to find the killer. If I didn't harp on it, you'd hardly wonder whether the real police might have found the killer sooner. So you don't have to feel too creepy about the Little Fool. Cut us some slack. To tell you the truth, in all the excitement, I've kind of lost track myself. Do you feel lucky? Well, do ya, punk?

Don't feel too creepy about Tommy digging the killer's story. And please don't feel we have Tommy thinking that because he's gay or something. The Little Fool believes the killer's story is sexy; the Little Fool is just busy worrying that he's gonna get caught for withholding evidence. If he had Tommy's clear conscience, the Little Fool would have rolled that sex-for-marrow idea around in his head a bit more. He's planning on rolling that idea around in his head a little later tonight, but right now he has to feel guilty. Yeah, the killer's little story is creepy, but sometimes creepy is very sexy. One, two, princes stand before you. Just go ahead now.

The Little Fool really wants to give the acetate to the real police, especially now that he's read it. He and Tommy handled it very carefully, now the Little Fool should just copy it down and turn the acetate in. If he gives it to the police at this point, he wouldn't hurt the investigation very much. But it sure would hurt him. They would know he's been withholding evidence. He's an accessory after the fact. He would be off the police force. He would probably even go to jail. "Is this acetate important? I found it on the body. I brought it home accidentally." That wouldn't work. "I found this today diving near where that last body was found." Two-inch visibility. Yo-yo, I don't think so.

They have to find the killer and they have to find him soon. They can't take all the responsibility for long. They're altering the case. The killer expects the note to be talked about. He expects to hear about it in the media. The killer's going to freak when he hears nothing. He's really going to freak. But what could he do? Start killing people at random? This guy didn't have much headroom under the crazy beam. He was already banging his wacked-out head. The real police wouldn't really know much about what to do. They can't trace the note. No shrink is going to be able to find the guy by studying the note and his story. What reasons do you need to die?

There was a lot of mental executing to do. They needed some time to bowl.

"Hey, C.B., would you read that to me again? Slow."

CHAPTER TWENTY-SEVEN

Pretty Healthy Killer, All Things Considered

"He's not gay. You can tell he's not gay, because it's way too sexy. The whole gay-sex thing means a lot to him. It means too much to him. It's nothing to me. I couldn't write that story because I couldn't make a blowjob mean that much. I couldn't make it mean anything. He makes giving a blowjob mean a lot, and only a straight guy can do that."

"Doesn't he seem to have a pretty good attitude towards sex? In a weird way, it's a pretty healthy short story. He's not freaked out by sex. He doesn't seem to hate sex. He doesn't seem to hate women. He's not the kind of guy that dresses up like his Mom when he thinks a woman may be naked in the shower. There aren't really any major sex hang-ups. But it *is* a little odd that he doesn't fuck the victims."

"Did you just say that he seems too well-adjusted to not fuck people that he's just stabbed to death with a blunt object?"

The note and story gave them a burst of excitement, and they were all ready to get back into the groove. They were ready to sit together and pore over the case. Reading all the Farrah and *A-Team* notebooks over and over. Reading them to themselves and taking turns reading them aloud to each other.

"Blister in the Sun" played from the phone in the pocket of the Little Fool's shirt, which was draped over a chair. He never wore a shirt when we worked at Tommy's. He looked at the phone's Caller ID and hit the button. "Hey, Big Bob, what's up?" Every time the Little Fool used that name he realized that if his name had been a little more common, he too would have had "Big" in front of it. He thanked his Mom and Dad again. And everyone knew you didn't give no lip to Big John.

"Hey, man, I thought you'd want to know this. We dug up another victim. This one is really fresh, the detectives are all over it, but I know that you and your boyfriend are making this into some kind of hobby or something. This is a big deal corpse. There's a note on plastic with this one. And a story."

"Fuck!"

"Yeah, the detectives are going ape shit because the note mentions another note, and they didn't get that one. They took everything with them, but I took a couple quick pictures for you. They're not too clear, but you can read all the words."

"JPEGs?"

"Yeah. I thought you'd be interested. I mean, I'm betting it'll be in the paper tomorrow. No one could keep something like this under wraps. He wrote a story, man, and it's fucked up. This guy is really fucked up."

"What was your first hint?"

"Yeah, okay. The stiff is another woman, but she's a different age and shit. The letter says he whacked her just to get this message to us. It's fucked, man. You want to come down or you want me to send the JPEGs to you? Where are you?"

"I'm at Tommy's place, working on the case."

"Yeah, working on the case, sure. Want me to email them to your boyfriend's address? I'm right at my work computer right now, and I loaded the pictures in."

"Please."

"You're gonna owe me another one, brother."

"I owe you my ass and my life, man, but you can have whatever else you want. I owe you everything."

"What's his address?"

"It's, ah, yeah, 'number1cocksucker@nyccable.com.' "

"Hey, that's why I had to go with 'number two cocksucker' for my address. You ever going to hang out with the men again, Cotton Balls?"

"Fuck you. Hey, Bob, thanks a lot for sending the pictures, man. Thanks for helping me. I'm into this deep, brother."

"I don't understand what's going on, but I'll send you the pictures. I'll do what I can. Hey, man, let's hang sometime, okay?"

"Yeah, sure, I'd like that. Was she stabbed bluntly like some of the others?"

"No, he used just a knife this time. Or something sharp. He was in a hurry. Forensics said that this one didn't suffer much. This one was fast. The sick fuck explains it in the note."

"Thanks for sending the pictures, Bob. Thanks a lot."

The Little Fool hit the disconnect button on the phone. Tommy had been listening to the whole conversation. "They really make a lot of fun of you for hanging with me, don't they? I'm sorry. I'm really sorry. I wish I didn't embarrass you."

"You don't embarrass me, Tommy. I'm proud to know you. And Bob and the guys understand. They aren't homophobic breeder freaks or anything. They just joke around." He hugged Tommy. "You okay?"

"Yeah, I'm one tough little queer. I just don't want you going through all the shit I went through. I mean, you are so fucking straight it's disgusting."

"Tommy, Tommy, I'm really scared about this note. I think I did something really bad. This is really bad."

So, sock monkey fans, you ready for some more from our bad guy? You ready for this? Love letters in the sand.

CHAPTER TWENTY-EIGHT

(Once More into the Italics—Not by Dickie)

How many bitches and motherfuckers does a guy have to stab before he gets some attention? Who do you have to blow to get a drink around here? Did you decide to not release my last letter and short story to the press? Was that your needle-dick stupid thinking?

Were you trying to show you have power over the press by not releasing my last letter? Or were you trying to show me that you have power over me? Either is stupid. You know what Tom Jefferson said, "[W]ere it left to me to decide whether we should have newspapers without a killer, or a killer without newspapers, I should not hesitate a moment to prefer the latter."

DON'T YOU TRY TO ALPHA-MALE ME YOU FUCKS!

I want to see this printed and I want to see it printed soon. To you they're just dead bodies to fish out of the drink, to me they're a vanity publishing company.

How about you print this short story AND the other one RIGHT NOW.

This woman wasn't ready to die. She wasn't. It wasn't right. She hadn't decided. But it's for the greater good. Think of all the people my fiction will help.

You wouldn't want me to be Kafka, would you? You don't want me to be appreciated only after my death, do you?

I'm giving you the benefit of the doubt. Maybe my last note and story washed away. I didn't want to send this one. I really didn't. It's not my best work. It's my older work. But it makes the same point as the other story. It's the same idea as the other story. It's the same point. If you understood the other one, you'll get this one.

I wrote it over 10 years ago. It's not my best work, but it makes the point. The SAME fucking point I made with the last story. This woman died because the message didn't get delivered. That's not a reason to die. She didn't die right. She didn't. And it's your fucking fault. Don't fuck with me. Just print the fucking story. AND DON'T EDIT IT—IT'S PERFECT!

As fast as I can write, people can die, and I'm very prolific. C'mon, piggys, do the right thing.

CHAPTER TWENTY-NINE

(Another Story—Not by Dickie)

I Quit Smoking

"*If you can quit smoking and handle American cockroaches, you can do anything.*" *An entomology guy at the American Museum of Natural History said that to me. He had done both, and by the end of that week, three years ago last Tuesday, so had I.*

Today is my 31st birthday. They had a nice party for me and it was a balmy March night in New York, so I decided not to take a cab home. It's a twelve-block walk right through Times Square. I love Times Square. I like neon. I like being given Xeroxed ads for sex clubs, and I like hookers asking me for dates.

It wasn't a surprise party. I knew about it, so I wore a suit, a tie, a vest, the whole shebang. It was a good joke. I'm a slob. I wear the same pants for a week or two in a row even though I make a lot of money. It's a pretension that I always thought was a charming eccentricity. But tonight I wore a tailor-made suit and I looked like the successful man I am. It got a good laugh.

I'm walking home, and right in front of the Pussycat porno theater these two guys ask me for a light. I said, "Sorry, I quit."

The taller of the two in a black leather jacket—not a biker jacket or a punk jacket, but one of those long, belted, shiny, cheap, black leather coats— he sticks the point of a buck knife against my vest and says, "You say a word, asshole, and I'll stick this knife right into your fucking stomach."

"No problem."

"Oh, there's a problem, you stupid cocksucker, and you got it. Give me all your fucking money, asshole."

"I've got a couple hundred bucks and credit cards. Here. Take it. All of it."

"Don't worry, asshole, I'll take all of it. Now what else you got?"

"Nothing, man, that's it. Honest. You want my watch? It's just a digital, and I don't wear rings or bracelets."

"Any money hidden on you, asshole?"

"No." And then he stuck the knife into me. An ex-biker once told me that a knife is the worst. "If you have a choice, choose to be shot. A knife hurts going in, coming out, and all the time in between." I was amazed that I was still alive when the knife came out, it hurt so much. Then he stuck it in me again. I screamed and begged. He stuck it in again and again.

They ran away and I knew I wouldn't make it until the ambulance came. Jesus, no one had even called it yet. And as I lay there dying I had only one major regret. I wished I had never quit smoking. I never really minded the coughing in the morning and I loved rubbing the ash against the side of the flip-top on an almost empty Coke can. And I loved having the sole of one boot against the wall, and my head down, and smoke curling against the brim of my baseball hat. And I loved my silver Zippo.

And I would've had a light.

I guess you gotta play the odds.

CHAPTER THIRTY

Mamma Mia Culpa Maxima

"I'm responsible for the death of a human being. I stole a letter, and that got a woman killed."

"Yup."

Tommy paused for a while and then spoke again. "And if I had told you to give that to the police, you would have. You would have done the right thing if I had told you to. And I didn't. I'm responsible for her death, too."

I myself am also responsible for the death of Kelli McCormick. I am just a sock monkey, but I am a sock monkey who has the ear of this perp. I could have nagged his conscience and he would have brought the note to the police, and it and the story would have gone into the newspaper. How do we assign blame? The Little Fool hadn't known that the evil nut would kill if the note were stolen. The evil nut would have killed anyway. But the Little Fool had known that stealing the note was wrong. He was guilty of stealing the note. He was guilty of hiding evidence. Is he guilty of murder? No. Well, not murder one. He hadn't planned to kill, but he had planned to steal. So, here we are. We're a little more than halfway through the story and our protagonist has killed a woman. He's also about to lose his job. Do I even have to write up the part where he brings the note to work and they fire him and ask him to be thankful that they're not bringing him up on charges? I probably do, because his reaction was different than yours, and that's the stuff you need to know. You need to know there are other ways to live.

That's why you're reading. He killed a woman. He lost his job.
The only woman he ever loved has been dead since pretty much
when you came on board. He's still got Tommy and he's still got
his monkey. Nuttin's plenty fo' me.

How could the Little Fool have wanted the perp stopped more
than the Little Fool already did for killing Nell? Well, we just got
our answer. Now he wanted him so bad he could . . . Now he
wanted him so badly he could . . . Now he wanted him so bad he
could . . . Well, find him. Yeah, that's what he had to do. That's
what he had to do before. It's as if you're watching some cheesy
vigilante movie and you see the bad guys kill a bunch of people
and rape a bunch of people and then about halfway through the
movie the bad guy finds the vigilante cop's family and rapes and kills
them. "Now he's pissed," the audience screams in unison. "Now it's
personal," the ad taglines brag. The meters were already pinned.
There was no headroom on that "wanting to catch the killer" dial.
He wanted to catch the killer. Hey, ho, let's go.

I was wrong. Just as wrong as the Little Fool was to keep the
note, I was wrong about the Little Fool. There was headroom. His
whole face changed. He didn't hear Tommy trying to calm him
down. Before, the Little Fool had been trying to hold onto his job.
Before, he'd been trying to be some sort of normal human going
through a bad time. Before, he still opened his mail. Before, he'd
been a grandmother painting out of love and passion. He didn't go
Jackson Pollock. Before, the Little Fool was breaking guitars like
Pete Townshend on stage. Now the Little Fool could destroy every
guitar with no one watching. The time for histrionic passion was
over. People try to put us down just because we get around.

Ronnie Wallen had gone to grade school with us. He played basketball on the North Parish Bulldogs. The Little Fool played center
and Ronnie played one of the other positions. We don't know sports;
there are four others positions and Ronnie played one of them.
When the Little Fool missed a shot, he didn't really care. He was a
little hurt and humiliated, but he would just go on with his life. But
Ronnie showed his rage. He showed how much he hated himself.

He punished himself and yelled in his grade-school way. He would scream, "I stink!" His face would get red. He'd let us see his angst. The Little Fool bought it at first. Blame yourself before anyone else can blame you. But, as long as Ronnie knew someone could really hear Ronnie's suffering, his self-image tree wasn't really falling in the wilderness. Like silent raindrops fell and echoed in the well.

The Little Fool had been making it very clear he was obsessed with the case. He wasn't sleeping, and he let people know it. He wasn't eating right, and he let people know it. He wasn't dating because he loved Nell and had Tommy, and he told everyone he wasn't dating. When he worried, he furrowed his brow. When he thought, he stroked his chin. That ended. When he read the JPEG of the note, he threw away the junk food. He decided he needed to get some sleep. It wasn't time to show himself and the world how much he wanted to catch the killer. It was time to catch the killer. The Little Fool was no longer trying; now he was doing it. This wasn't grade-school basketball. This was life and death. This is the time and there is no time.

There used to be ads in NYC, posters up all over, for some comic who wanted to make it doing monologues in theater. ("What's the difference between stand-up and performance art?" "Ten bucks.") The posters said his name, which we've all forgotten, and then the poster said, "Only the truth is funny." This isn't true—even one elephant can't really fit in the glove compartment of a VW—but it's still a funny image. Sometimes the truth is so funny you can't laugh. From the gymnast yelling "Hey, everybody, watch this" to the same gymnast croaking to the paramedics "I don't want to die." That's all of life, isn't it? Life is what happens between those two declarations. Proudly yelling to the world, "Hey, everybody, watch this"—that's where we start a project, and "I don't want to die" is where we finish. Prologue and epilogue, and then the story is in the middle. The Little Fool has rocketed off the springboard. He's in the air. He has no regrets and nothing to lose. There is no more showboating. Other folks, we've got to work. Just watch me now!

When the Little Fool was in high school there was American

military action overseas. College students were protesting. There was a buddhist on a campus near the Little Fool's high school. The buddhist wasn't a real buddhist—he was a college student buddhist. If it's stupid to believe in a religion with a god who looks out for you, how stupid is it to believe in a religion that has *no god* watching over you? Buddhism is the slowest competitor in the Special Olympics that is religion. So, this kid, this white suburban college kid, had been calling himself a buddhist and was going to light himself on fire to protest the war. He had his real Asian robes on and he had his real American gasoline. He soaked his college student robes in college student gasoline and took his college student match and he lit his college student ass on fire. The Little Fool saw a picture of this in the paper. The picture stuck with us our whole lives. Is the horror that of a teenage life cut down for a war that was going to end anyway? Is the horror that of his passion and love that would lead to his death? Is the horror that of young healthy flesh burning and suffering? A permanent solution to a temporary problem? Is that the horror? No. None of those should break your heart. There's beauty in all of those. Here's the heartbreaker. He died. Well, of course he died. He lit himself on fire, the idea was to die. But he didn't die in the middle of the commons where he lit himself on fire after his prayer and his impotent cry to stop all war. No. He died in the fountain. He died in the decorative fountain, a gift from wealthy alumni. He died in the decorative fountain that was right off the commons. He died throwing himself into the water trying to put himself out. He no longer wanted to die. He couldn't stand the pain. He changed his mind. While he was on fire, he changed his mind. "Hey, everybody, watch this . . . I don't want to die." Now is the time for your tears.

The Little Fool didn't care who was watching. The Little Fool didn't care how much pain. He wasn't going to run to the fountain. He wasn't a grade-school kid who wanted people to know how hard he tried. The Little Fool was on fire. He was burning. The skin was peeling off his body and he felt nothing but pain and he was standing right where he was. He wasn't going to move a goddamn inch. Three-hundred-sixty-five degrees. My house.

CHAPTER THIRTY-ONE

Wake up and Smell
the Anal Sex

The Little Fool got to work on the case. He drank a glass of milk, brushed his teeth, took a bath, and slept for twelve hours. He slept the kind of sleep you can't wake up from. The kind of sleep that leaves you staggering. He dreamt he was having anal sex with a young girl in a fancy hotel room. Some magician he'd seen on TV led a walking tour through the room while the Little Fool and the young girl were having sex, and the magician opened all the curtains and yelled, "They're having sex." It was close to a real sex dream; it was the closest the Little Fool had come to sex since Nell died. Oh, just so you know, "young" in this dream, in this book, is twenty. Legal everywhere. Okay? And then he dreamed of a big candy shop and he was buying chocolate-covered apples. Like candy apples, except with chocolate. I guess that is a candy apple. He wasn't buying them as pedophilia bait; he was shopping for his own consumption. And he dreamed of that "honeycomb" candy stuff. It's like maple Styrofoam candy. It's hard when you bite it and then it just dissolves down to nothing. Some candy shops have it, but it's always covered with chocolate, which is wrong. An apple with chocolate, that's okay, but not this honeycomb stuff. That candy should be plain. I guess they have it like that in Australia, or maybe it's covered with chocolate there, too. He slept so hard he wasn't thinking about the murderer or Nell at all. He needed some time just to sleep. Sleep. I am tired, I am weary, I could sleep for a thousand years.

He'd fallen asleep in Tommy's bed. It was a very realistic dream. Hmmm. Tommy did have a little ass. Hmmm. Little breasts? Was that really a young girl? Hmmmm. Well, it was just a dream. The Little Fool looked very closely at his penis. He tried to smell it. If he'd ever been limber enough to smell his penis, he would never have left his room when he was in high school. He would have gone the other few inches and been self-sufficient. He would still be in that room. Mr. Infinity. His penis looked clean. He looked for a hint of real sex. The bed looked as if it hadn't been messed up by anything more than a deep sleep. He was still sleeping. He was dreaming he was waking up and wondering about having had sex with Tommy. The world got clearer. There were no signs of real sex with anyone. As the Little Fool woke up he realized it had all been a dream. There had been no sex with Tommy. There was no sex with Tommy to deal with. Everything had been a dream. He was disappointed there was no real candy. It was nice to do detective work about something that didn't matter. He had slept alone. There had been no new experiences. The excitement left; the sadness came back. Like disco lemonade.

Now he smelled pot roast. He remembered having a conversation with Tommy about pot roast. It's a New England thing. The Little Fool had talked about pot roast and Jell-O. After the JPEGs, he needed pot roast and his special Jell-O, and Tommy knew that. The Little Fool told Tommy enough about it. Orange Jell-O with crushed pineapple and grated carrots and some Miracle Whip with pineapple juice thinning it to pour over the top of the Jell-O. Our mother had a ring mold. Not a skin disorder, but a special Tupperware knock-off device for making Jell-O. You really needed that mold for potluck suppers. When the Little Fool was younger, our family attended the Church of the Covered-Dish Supper. It was New England church without passion. Church that didn't matter except as an excuse for Mom to wear a hat. Mom had made her Jell-O for church functions, but she always made enough for the Little Fool to have plenty at home. Sometimes Mom put food coloring in the Miracle Whip/pineapple juice and called it "The stuff that makes it good." The ring mold had a star-shaped place in the top to put in the stuff that makes it good, but the place hadn't been deep enough; you couldn't fit enough in the cavity for the amount of Jell-O. But Mom always had more in the refrigerator. Jell-O is better at home. The church suppers were held in the same room where the family bought me. It was comfort. Hot biscuits and sweet Marie.

That wasn't sex and candy he smelled; that was pot roast and Jell-O. Anyone could make that mistake. He didn't want to wash the sleep out of his eyes, but he did. He kept his hair really messed up because he believed that Tommy might believe it was cute. The Little Fool looked in a mirror. Now, after his dream, he really wanted to look good for Tommy. He tried to see a well-rested hero in the mirror. A man who would solve the case and stop the killing. He tried not to see a lonely man without a job. He tried not to see a boy whose best friend was his monkey. My shaving razor's cold and it stings.

Tommy had a fluffy bathrobe with fluffy cuffs. The Little Fool put it on for a joke. Tommy had bought the bathrobe as a joke, but wore the bathrobe for real. The joke fell away. The joke lasted on the Little Fool for the amount of time it took him to walk out of the bathroom. By the time Tommy saw him, the Little Fool was just a middle-aged ex-diver wearing a fluffy-cuffed bathrobe. The joke of the bathrobe and the cuteness of the tousled hair were no match for the joy of pot roast. Tommy was so happy at how happy he was going to make the Little Fool that nothing else could have touched him. It's just a restless feeling I have inside.

The Little Fool didn't know what time it was. He still didn't really know where he was. Reality was coming back slowly. He didn't know who he was. He wasn't a diver anymore. He wasn't really home with his Mom cooking his favorite meal. He wasn't really with his gay lover. But the Little Fool was with his friend. And there was pot roast. The Little Fool made a depression with his spoon in his mashed potatoes and spooned in the gravy. He salted without tasting and didn't get caught by Tommy. The Little Fool sniffed.

Deeply. He tried to pull the comfort from the food into his heart. He ate slowly. The pot roast melted in his mouth. Tommy brought out corn on the cob. Butter and salt. The Little Fool slowly loaded the comfort into his stomach and kept sucking the comfort into his lungs. Nell was gone. His job was gone. But his life wasn't gone. He had pot roast. And potatoes. And corn. And Jell-O. He was very close to crying into his dinner when Tommy said, "What, do I have to blow you for a 'thank you'?"

"Thanks."

CHAPTER THIRTY-TWO

Is It Literary in Here, or Is It Me?

"C.B., my little closeted friend, we haven't found the killer, but I sure feel smarter. This has been, I don't know, very literary. Very literary. I mean, I never read this much in my life. We've read those killer stories over and over and all these interviews with the friends and family talking about the victims talking about all these writers, Vonnegut and Jefferson and all those guys. Man, I never talked about great writers. I guess I'm just a superficial queer. I should have read more. I should read more."

"Hey, don't be beating yourself up. No one reads enough. People don't talk about books. When was the last time you were talking about books, authors, and real things to your friends? You and I only talk about this stuff because it keeps coming up in the case."

There was a long pause.

It was a longer pause than that.

Ed Wood is pure thought. Ed recorded the way humans really think. Remind yourself of these excerpts from Criswell's opening monologue in Ed Wood's *Plan 9 from Outer Space*: "We are all interested in the future, for that is where you and I are going to spend the rest of our lives. And, remember, my friend, future events such as these will affect you in the future . . . My friend, can your heart stand the shocking facts about grave robbers from outer space? . . . Can you prove that it didn't happen? . . . Many scientists believe that another world is watching us this moment."

The cultural literacy on Ed Wood is that he made the worst

movies ever made. Maybe you remember Johnny Depp as Ed
dressed in a fuzzy sweater. But the most important part of Ed
Wood is that he had no editor, so he recorded how people really
think. Lots of people don't have outside editors. As I write this, I
don't have an editor. I'm a sock monkey. Eventually someone will
check all the spelling and the grammar and punctuation. People
will check to make sure the character names stay the same and
there aren't any drifts in style where there shouldn't be. The Little
Fool's friends will make comments. He talks to friends. But even if
he puts out the very first draft with no changes, it would still be
heavily edited. A real editor will go over every word and she'll do
a few drafts, but that's not what I'm writing about here. Everyone
edits before they do anything. People start editing before they even
start to think. People like to believe that Lenny Bruce, Sam Kinison, and even Howard Stern never had internal editors, but Lenny,
Sam, and Howard are the worst examples. They were always going
for the joke, always trying to be interesting. The only real record in
art of real human thought is in the work of Ed Wood. Not the
perfect rambling thoughts of Nicholson Baker or the remembrances
of things that had happened before Proust sniffed a cake. That's not
the way any of you really think. Not really. Not deep thinking.
Before the editor in your brain makes the words make sense, there's
a flash. It isn't even really an image. It might be a word or a phrase.
It's not directly related to what's happening. It's never what you're
really working on. It could be a little snippet of anything. And
then smart people, careful people, artists, take that pure thought and
clean it up until it seems as if they're putting out a pure thought, a
glimpse into their hearts for others. But the original thought was
never recorded. The original pure thought would have sounded
like Ed Wood. Your stupid minds, your stupid, stupid minds.

Tommy and the Little Fool didn't know what they were thinking. Their brains were stumbling like Bela and Tor trying to dance
a ballet in rollerblades on a moving sidewalk full of marbles. Oh,
how I wish I could write like Ed Wood. Not all the time. Please: If
one wish gets granted, let's not have it be that one; I don't want to

write like him all the time. If I get one wish, well, let's go for about fourteen inches of stuffed monkey sock hanging between my legs or a vaccine against HIV with the patent in my name. But I'd like for just a paragraph or two to be able to write like Ed so you could see the process as Tommy and the Little Fool solved this case. "My friends, we have been worried, struggling, a case full of love for a girl, that, though beautiful, is long dead, cold, in the ground. And there is something about great writers, thinking about great writers of all time, and talking to someone, maybe a very bad, very bad, very, very bad man, a killer who talks of great authors and deep heavy thoughts before the death of the innocent whom we have grown to love." That's the best I can do. Pull the string. Pull the string!

The same person had been talking to all the victims about life and literature before they died. And that person had done it for a long enough period before they died that they had talked to their friends about it.

Finally Tommy spoke. "Fuck! Fuck! Fuck! Fuck! Motherfucker! Fuck! Fuckin' shit. Motherfucker. [You see? No one can write as clearly as Ed Wood.] Fuck. Motherfucker. Nell was talking shit the last time I saw her."

"What exactly did she say, Tommy?"

"Oh, thanks for asking. You know, if you hadn't asked me, I would have never thought to try to remember that."

"Sorry."

"Fuck. *Moby-Dick!* Was *Moby-Dick* more important to her life, to any life, than the evolution dude and his work, and whether an idea or a concept were more important?" Now we're sounding a little like Ed.

"Darwin?"

"The book."

"*Origin of Species?* The *Beagle* thing?"

"No, the guys."

"Darwin."

"And the other guy."

"Huxley?"

"No, the *Moby-Dick* guy."

"Melville?"

"Yeah. She had to pick one, Melville or Darwin, to be her hero or have dinner with or something, and then she was joking about which one she'd rather spend the night with. She was bummed there weren't any women on the list. She was trying to like the fat dyke, and then joked about spending the night with her."

"Gertrude Stein?"

"Or Frank Zappa. She talked about Zappa and Dylan and the *Geek Love* woman. Nell was a lot smarter than me. I got lost whenever she talked to me, but it was usually about law, or movies, or breeder sex or something. She didn't talk books around me. What the fuck do I know? But she was spacey. She was asking me questions. Heavy questions. What qualities I like most in myself. What I hate. It was weird."

"A lot of the relatives and friends mentioned having heavy talks with the victims before they were murdered. Fuck. What got her thinking that way? C'mon, Tommy, who got her thinking that way?"

"Fuck." Tommy was no longer thinking. Now Tommy was trying to prove to the Little Fool that Tommy was thinking. Now Tommy was Ronnie in grade school missing a lay-up shot. Tommy knew it was important, but he had nothing else. The Ed Wood moments were over and now it was acting. Now he just said "fuck" and waggled his head around. He squinted up. He even scratched his head and, if he had had a beard, he would have stroked it. He had to prove to the Little Fool that Tommy was thinking, but he was really just waiting for the Little Fool to let him off the hook. Counting flowers on the wall.

Tommy's thinking act worked.

"Hey, Tommy, stop beating yourself up. Maybe we should go down to the diner and get you a Greek salad. We're getting somewhere. We're on it. I can feel it."

"Okay, if you think that'll help."

They went down to the diner, but not before Tommy put on a clean pair of jeans. You had to look good to think in public. The Little Fool would have gone out in the fuzzy bathrobe if Tommy hadn't stopped him. Did you hear anything? I thought I did. I thought I did.

CHAPTER THIRTY-THREE

Know Thyself

Tommy got his Greek salad. The Little Fool was in full crime-fighter mode. He was eating an egg-white omelet and a dry, toasted bagel. He was wide awake and thinking hard. Who kills people who are starting to think about literature? How do you find people at the exact moment they start thinking about literature? Gertrude Stein, Melville, Darwin, Jefferson, Vonnegut, Randy Newman, Picasso, Watson, Crick, Zappa, Dylan, even Joan Baez. Okay, not all literature, but all thinkers. Okay, except Joan. Why had the victims mentioned all those names? Why had the victims been talking to their friends about those people, about those things? The victims hadn't been college students getting their heads together. They were grown-ups. It was admirable, I guess, to think about this stuff. But why think about this stuff and die? I guess if you knew you were going to die, you might start examining your life to make the rest of your life worth living. But these hadn't been suicides. There was no indication that these people knew they were going to be murdered. They hadn't known they were going to die. Time takes a cigarette, puts it in your mouth.

It's a creepy idea: People thinking heavy thoughts before they're killed. What could connect them? Was the killer killing everyone who joined some Book of the Month club? Could it be some book discussion group that he got the membership list for? Could it be some club you join where you talk about all the heavy parts of life, and then someone in the club whacks you? But if the killer were a leader of some cult, the others in the cult would notice the members dying. No one mentioned being scared or being in a creepy club. No one had said a word about that. The murdered people didn't seem to know what was coming. Were they all suicidal enough to know they were going to die and not tell anyone? People do that. Suicides do that. They plan and don't tell anyone. But could that be true for this many people? They all couldn't have known they were going to be tortured and brutally murdered and not hint about it to anyone, could they? Not all of them. I thought I heard her calling my name now. Hush, hush.

Tommy was just happy with his salad. The Little Fool kept looking at him. Tommy didn't examine life much; he just lived it. He spent his time examining every forkful of salad he ate and every jeansful of ass that walked by as the bars emptied out and the bountyless cruisers needed comfort food. The Little Fool had stopped examining life when he stopped liking what he found. This killer sure wasn't going to get either of them. They were as safe as milk. An unexamined life may not be worth living, but it'll keep you from killing yourself. And it seemed it would keep this nut from snuffing you. I want you to lick my decals off, baby.

None of the victims had been religious. Is that weird? Why didn't the cops talk about that? Why didn't the press talk about that? Is that normal? The Little Fool doesn't know anyone who really believes in god. He knows a few people who don't call themselves "Atheists." He knows a few people who were born into the jewish culture who still call themselves "jews." He knows some people who had weddings in churches, or went with their grandmothers to xmas masses, but he doesn't know anyone who really, actively believes in god. But when the Little Fool watches TV, it seems as if all the people in charge believe there are a lot of people who believe in god. Of course, on TV there are witches and talking dogs. Don't the majority of people believe in god? The meat puppets on TV don't say "goddamn," and don't they cater to the masses? The Little Fool had read that in the sciences, among real scientists, most people don't believe in god, but the victims hadn't

all been in the sciences. The victims hadn't been connected by
occupation. But, thinking about the Farrah and *A-Team* books of
notes, if the victims hadn't been Atheist, at least they had all been
non-theists. Why didn't the press pick up on that? Why weren't
these "The Atheist Murders" instead of "Hudson Ripper"? Wasn't
that a big deal? Yoko and me, and that's reality.

Tommy had stopped pretending he was trying to remember anything else Nell had said. He was all just feta and olives now. It was
nice to sit in the diner. The Little Fool felt a spark of life. A diner at
night contains all the hopeful sadness of romance. You could meet
the love of your life waiting tables in a diner. You could see an old
friend, you could hatch a plan for a multi-million dollar company,
you could scheme out a Tarantino crime. You could solve some
murders. Diners offer all of that. Diners are that lighting. That
coffee-shop wood on the walls. A diner is a place to drink sour orange juice in stupid little glasses and drink much too much coffee. A
diner is a place to smoke. She's a loner likes to mingle.

Tommy finished eating. "I think I might do better trying to remember other things that Nell said if I went home and laid in bed
for a while." Our hero just sat there. Crime fighters can eat jelly
and drink coffee, he figured. Maybe he was more of a Dirty Harry,
lots-of-sugar-in-the-coffee kind of crime fighter. He sat there eating the remains of his bagel with much too much "berry" jam
from those little tubs. He saved the grape jelly for last. He ripped
off the top, and there it was. Food as skating rink. So smooth, clear,
fresh, and full of sugar. He put two tubs of grape jelly on about 2.5
inches of burnt bagel, and he drank coffee. He wasn't really a coffee drinker, he didn't really like coffee, but he didn't smoke and he
was in a diner. He had to do something. He was Kinky Friedman's
"Sirhan Sirhan, party of one." There was a rumor about a tumor.

It didn't take much to get the Little Fool going. Just talking about
the people who had been killed contemplating the big picture reminded the Little Fool that he needed to read all of Dickens. The
Little Fool would start that. It was time to reread *Atlas Shrugged*. Why
wasn't Ayn Rand on any of those lists? I guess there are reasons not

to think about her right before you die. Tommy had said that he believed Nell had decided against Darwin. She'd been leaning toward
Melville. She'd rather have had dinner with Melville than Darwin.
Besides being an odd thing to think about, it was a very odd choice
for Nell. That must be a clue. Nell had loved *Moby-Dick,* but she
didn't love Melville. She always said that Melville hadn't known
what he had. The beauty of *Moby-Dick* is that Melville tapped into
things that he himself did not understand. Darwin knew what he
had. Watson and Crick's original paper on the double helix in 1953
has the big, swinging-dick line near the end, "It has not escaped our
notice that the specific pairing we have postulated immediately sug-
gests a possible copying mechanism for the genetic material." James
and Francis knew what they had and bragged about it. There's never
been a rapper who bragged more than they did. Of course, this is a
brag with the twisting, double, tiny bling bling helix to back it up.
And Darwin knew what he had, too. Charles didn't know his idea
was going to explain as much as it did, but he knew he had a very big
deal. He knew it meant no god. Nell always said that Darwin had
known that. The Little Fool had had the heavy talks with Nell. Nell
said that women's biggest shame was Emma Darwin, Darwin's wife.
Darwin had been Jerry Lee Lewis; he married his first cousin. Nell
said she pictured Darwin with long, greasy hair falling into his eyes
while he had banged at his writing desk like an out-of-tune, early-
Southern-rock grand piano, unleashing the fear of something so
much worse than Jerry Lee Lewis's balls of Satan's fire. What's scarier,
wilder, and more liberating than satan? No satan, no god, no nothing
but us! Emma had been the cousin having sex with the man who
had the origin of the tiger by the tail. You rattle my brain.

  Little cousin Emma was also heir to the Wedgwood china fortune.
China dishes had made her family rich. Dishes gave Darwin the time
to walk back and forth, back and forth, and think about things.
Wearing out the dirt above the earthworms that he had loved to
think about. Wallace, the vegetarian, women's-rights, tree-living,
psychic-nut-job seemed to have the "natural selection" idea first,
and Huxley was mean enough and loud enough to get everyone to

listen, but Darwin had the intellectual muscle. He did the work walking back and forth in his garden (what we Americans call the "backyard"). He was the man. The main man. Nell had always said that Darwin proved that there is no god, and his intellectual honesty was going to make him publish that proof, but the power of the pussy with the purse strings made him stop short of announcing that outright. Darwin's beloved daughter had died a miserable death and Charles was prepared to chuck the whole idea of god. It's no comfort *and* it isn't true. But he didn't go all the way. *Origin of Species* leaves room in the margins for god. Even catholics can weasel and embrace it like a twelve-year-old altar boy's hips. Nell was sure that was Mrs. Darwin's doing. And Nell was ashamed of that. It's a place in history where stand by your man overlaps intellectual truth. Where Tammy Wynette and Madame Curie are one and the same. And show the world you love him.

Why had Nell changed to Melville? Why baptizing the sword in fire in satan's name instead of the perfectly beautiful simplicity that creates all the complicated life in our world and any other? If the Little Fool could answer that, he would find the killer. It was all there. It was all there. Hey, Grandma.

CHAPTER THIRTY-FOUR

You Can't Quit Me. I'm Fired.

The Little Fool stayed up all night in the diner thinking about the big questions. He was contemplating the big picture. Down South that has to be done with liquor. In NYC, it should be done in a coffee shop in the wee Sinatra hours. The Little Fool was ready to die. And he was ready to go to work and lose his job. It was going to be an important day at work and he wanted to look and feel his best. He wanted them to feel good about firing him. When you never drink, it's hard work to look right to be fired. But a night of not sleeping and crying alone in a diner because Emma Darwin hadn't had the strength to not act the way she'd been brought up gave him the veiny eyes he needed. All the coffee in his non-druggy body gave him a nice shake and a twitch. Wearing the same clothes gave him a nice little funk, and his hair was just perfect. He was ready. He had killed a woman and knew it and there was no punishment that could hurt more than that knowledge. Bring it on. He loved his job more than anything, but love had been killed. He was now a true romantic. Realists see the world through rose-colored glasses; romantics see the world through sleepless eyes behind cheap sunglasses. Hit that street a-running and try to meet the masses.

He went upstairs and sneaked into Tommy's room, where it seemed Tommy thought snoring would help him remember the details of what Nell had said. The Little Fool quietly opened the top drawer next to Tommy's side of the bed. The Little Fool moved aside the crusted bottle of Astroglide and got the box of latex gloves. The box was a little less than sterile, so he dug down several gloves and grabbed a couple of really clean ones. He waited until he was out of the bedroom to make the sexy, rubber-snapping sound that, if done in the bedroom, would have made Tommy roll over Pavlov-style. With the latex gloves, the Little Fool picked up the note he'd stolen and dug down in the box of manila envelopes to find a clean one. He slipped in the acetate story. He would take the stolen evidence to work. It was 5 A.M. The Little Fool had to be at work at 8:30 A.M. He had time to go home. He held the envelope tightly in both hands like the valuable cargo it was and walked across town to his own apartment. I've got the world on a string.

Walking through Manhattan streets in the early morning when you've been out all night is one of the best feelings in the world. The Little Fool tried to be depressed and noir, he tried to feel like Jimmy Cagney, but the Little Fool kept sliding gracefully over to Fred Astaire. All the proletariats were just rolling out of bed to go to work, bleary eyed with a whole day ahead of them, and the Little Fool had been up all night and was heading in to get fired. It was a Fred Astaire dance challenge: The Little Fool had to create a dance featuring the manila envelope as the most important thing in the world. The envelope was the girl Fred had to design a dance around. The Little Fool held the envelope like a collapsed top hat in both hands in front of him. He started moving it around in front of his chest. With a hand on either side, he moved the evidence in a circle in front of his chest. He started dancing. Hey, he was definitely about to be fired from a job he loved more than anything. He would be arrested. He might go to prison. He had definitely killed a woman and his life was ruined. It was time to dance. He had his top-hat envelope and his eyes were hung over. He was dancing home from his special friend's apartment on a busy, industrious Manhattan morning. Top hat. Tails.

The Little Fool could hear Raymond Scott's "Powerhouse," the tune that's used in Warner Brothers cartoons to indicate busy, industrious, and modern. The cabs felt squatty and claymated like

Wallace and Gromit. Garmentos were carrying big packages like ants with breadcrumbs and the Little Fool was dancing. Dancing. He had his hate letters from a murderer as his top hat. He untucked his dirty button-up shirt to give him those folded-beetle-wing tails. The first big, honest smile in two weeks slid onto his face. Been down so long it looks like up to me. He hit the bottom like Orwell in London and Paris. The Little Fool was smiling. Deep. Alone. The lack-of-sleep sweat under his armpits was cooling in the breeze. He could smell himself, like an animal. Like Fred Astaire as an animal. Man, it was good to smell his own funk. It was good to be tired. He blinked his eyes and held them shut just to feel the sting. He was dancing to work to get fired. He'd lost all he'd worked for, lost all he had loved. It was time for fun. You must be at least this lowdown to ride this ride. It might be his last morning not in prison. It might be his last chance to hate himself full out without the cheesy defensiveness that would come when others hated him, too. It was a solitary, personal self-hatred that was liberating. He was free. He was dancing. He was dancing in morning Manhattan. He smelled exhaust, coffee, and his own overnight funk. In the serious moonlight.

He didn't take the elevator. He danced up the stairs to his apartment. He unlocked the door and spun in place before he went in. He had all the guilt of Michael Jackson dancing into Neverland. The Little Fool never looked or felt better. With exaggerated fastidiousness, like Oliver Hardy adjusting his tie, the Little Fool put down the envelope on the counter. He picked up an umbrella that was by the door (he never used umbrellas. Tall people hate umbrellas. They're tools for little Asian ladies to poke the big freaks' eyes out), opened it inside his apartment, and danced with it. Even bad luck would be a step up for him now. He needed to break the mirror to keep this feeling for seven years, but he had more looking to do. He walked into the bathroom and urinated. When he was finished, he didn't shake it at all, just flipped it right back through the fly and let the last few squirts of early morning coffee urine trickle into his pants. A pee stain would make him easier to fire. He even smelled crazy. He went into his closet and got the briefcase his Mom bought him on his first day of law school. She shouldn't have spent that much on him. It was real leather. It wasn't a briefcase he was ever going to use. When she died, there was no chance of ever getting rid of it. It sat on the shelf with its stupid little golden keys still in an envelope still in the leather business card pocket that had never been used. He rhumba'ed back into the kitchen and put the precious manila envelope in the virgin mother briefcase. He looked at himself in the mirror. He looked almost perfect. He felt like Jack Lemmon after a night of multiple-sex-partner confusion in some '60s screwball, leering sex comedy. Trying to be tidy. He looked at the pee stain on the front of his pants—abstract art. He smelled his armpits—love-in incense. He grinned ear to ear. He picked up the bottom of his shirt and blew his nose in it. He did a spin in front of the mirror and blew himself a kiss. He made that Little Richard/ Paul McCartney/Lee Michaels/Michael Jackson "woo" sound. He jumped straight in the air, dropped as near as he could get to a split, and left the briefcase on the floor while he ran into the bedroom. He had a bumper sticker that a biker friend had given him. It was in a file folder with lots of pictures of the past. The bumper sticker was a precious souvenir he'd been saving for the right time. He looked in the file cabinet and found the bumper sticker right away. He pulled it out of the envelope and walked into the other room. He peeled the back of the bumper sticker, did the W.C. Fields thing of it sticking to one finger and then another, and carefully stuck it across the brand-new, expensive, Mom briefcase. He looked at himself in the mirror: He had done pretty well in one night. His hair looked filthy, he had snot on his shirt, piss stain on his pants, armpit stains, and a brand-new briefcase with a bumper sticker that said in bright red letters: "Fuck Jesus Hard in the Handholes." He broke the mirror with his fist. In the movie the mirror'll break the first time, but it took him three tries. He danced out the door to be fired. Puttin' on the Ritz.

He walked out the door and froze. He didn't move. It had been a perfect exit from his apartment, but he needed one more thing.

One more thing that he hadn't ever been seen with in public in his adult life. The only thing that mattered to him. He was off to get fired and he didn't want to get fired alone. When being hired it's important to make an impression, but when being fired it's required to make an impression. He left the invaluable briefcase on the floor of the hall to reach back into his pocket and pull out his apartment key. He unlocked the door and walked in. He walked proudly to the bedroom and offered his bloody hand to me. Our hands touched. He pulled me up by my one arm into his arms. He slow-danced me around the room. He needed his monkey. I would go with him. Dancing, with Mr. D.

The Little Fool still had time, so he walked all the way to work. He was afraid his pee stain would fade, so just as he got to the station he relaxed and forced out another couple of squirts. He walked right by all the guys getting ready for work, right into the captain's office, holding his briefcase and his sock monkey. The captain doesn't matter at all. The office doesn't matter. We're slo-mo now. We're underwater. We're watching through a telephoto lens. There's only one character in this scene—a man with his monkey. Everybody's got something to hide except . . .

Still clutching me to his chest, he put the briefcase down on the captain's desk. "Open it up. In there you'll find a note and a story from our perp. They were stolen off Monday's floater. [C'mon, Little Fool, don't pull back with that pussy, passive voice. Blaze of glory. Blaze of glory.] I stole them off Monday's body. They should have gone right to the lab, they should have been leaked to the press, but they weren't because I stole them. I've been trying to solve the crime myself with my friend and my monkey. I loved Nell and thought I could help. I withheld evidence and obstructed justice. I'm the reason the last victim became a victim. I'm where the note went."

"Wah, wah, blah, blah, blah," like Charlie Brown's teacher. Who cares?

"Here's the key to my locker. My badge and my dress uniform are in there. Just throw away all the personal stuff. I won't need it.

While you're thinking about what to do, I'll go down the hall and lock myself in the holding cell. Here's my wallet, keys, and my pocket knife."

"Yadda yadda yadda yadda."

"You're right."

"Yip yip yippity yap."

"Absolutely."

"Doo wah diddy diddy dum diddy do."

"That's good. That's fine."

"In-a-gadda-da-vida."

"I understand. Get me that incompetent public defender, the one the cops always hope for, that black woman who straightens her hair and never goes to trial. I'm going to plead guilty to whatever you say."

The Little Fool freshened up with another little squirt into his pants, waited to make sure the chief was looking, and then looked me right in the eyes and said "I'm a bad boy" in that voice Lou Costello used after he'd forgotten what was funny about the first time he'd said it. He spun on his heel and walked to the cell, holding me tight. Since my wings have got rusted.

The Little Fool fell asleep the second he sat down in the cell. I was more a pillow than a comfort. It was a deep, peaceful sleep in his own funk. We slept together in jail. He slept the sitting-up-on-an-airplane sleep for almost two hours. The cell opened and he was shaken awake by an angry friend. "Just get out of here and get help. We'll cover everything else. If you get better, come back. Get help, man. Get help."

"If you need me, I'll be fighting crime." Take this job and shove it.

CHAPTER THIRTY-FIVE

Darkness

*In everyday life, you will find that your boss, your lover, or your gov-
ernment often try to manipulate you. They propose to you a "game"
in the form of a choice in which one of the alternatives appears definitely preferable. Having chosen this alternative, you are faced with a
new game, and very soon you find that your reasonable choices have
brought you to something you never wanted: you are trapped. To
avoid this, remember that acting a bit erratically may be the best strategy. What you lose by making some suboptimal choices you make up
for by keeping greater freedom.*

—David Ruelle, *Chance and Chaos*

The Little Fool had read that book on chaos theory. The book is a
math book for lay people. The Little Fool can get his mind around
it. Right in the middle of that book, the author throws in the
acting-erratically philosophy. Math-game theory for the macro
world. Day-to-day advice from the fringes of mathematical theory.
The Little Fool likes that passage and it stays with him. Well, he
made some serious "suboptimal choices" and found the greatest
freedom. He was there. He had no job. He had some money saved.
He could always go in and make some chump change washing hair
for Tommy. The Little Fool would get some tips. He worked on
the case all the time. The papers published the stolen notes as
though the reporters just found them. The Little Fool called a couple friends at his old job to see if he could get any more clues than

were in the paper, but his friends just said, "Get help." They said "get help" automatically like "bye bye." It meant nothing. Now he was one of those nuts who reads the papers, watches CNN, and tries to solve crimes. He wasn't a cop. He was just another nut. I'm crazy for trying and crazy for crying.

The days were all over the place. The Little Fool walked the streets. The "look" he had put together for his firing became his everyday look. He did stay clean; Tommy saw to that. Tommy made sure there were no pee stains and even gave the Little Fool's hair a cut that wouldn't need any maintenance, but the Little Fool still wandered around looking crazy. He typed up all of Tommy's notes from the Farrah and *A-Team* booklets and memorized most of them. The Little Fool walked the streets, reciting the notes. He wasn't thinking; he was just reciting. Eyeing little girls with bad intent.

The nights hadn't changed much. Tommy kept the Little Fool okay. He still trusted Tommy. Tommy came home from work and cooked them dinner. When Tommy came home, it all got okay. They ate macaroni and cheese and worked on the case. Tommy never said, "Get help." Tommy was help. He'd pore over the notes and make the Little Fool good food. Tommy, can you hear me?

The Little Fool had just come in from walking the streets. He'd spent the day walking from one apartment of a victim to another apartment of a victim. It was the "Traveling Salesmen" math problem. He was finding every route, finding what they had in common. Walking where they might have walked.

Tommy and the Little Fool were sitting at home when suddenly all the lights went out. The computer screen went dark. Tommy and the Little Fool looked out the window. The neighboring buildings were dark, too. It was a blackout. The Little Fool was still enough of a cop to know that if something that's happening to you is happening to a dozen other people, you don't have to complain to anyone. Some other squeaky wheel will get all the wheels oiled. This is the backbone of pure capitalism. The blackout didn't feel like an emergency. Tommy and the Little Fool weren't worried. Tommy's six-CD changer (three chosen by Tommy: Sonny Rollins, Sonic

Youth, and Streisand [he was still in his alphabetical phase], and three chosen by the Little Fool: Phil Ochs, Boy George, and Sun Ra [he was in some sort of protest phase]) went silent. Their eyes adjusted. A calm came over the room. There was peace. As a kid, the Little Fool loved blackouts. He and his Mom and Dad would do jigsaw puzzles by candlelight. Blackouts were snowdays at night. The same peace. The same feeling of family. All the Little Fool needed now was his monkey to hug, but I was back in the Little Fool's bedroom across town—Tommy's orders. The blackout continued. Tommy didn't jump up to get his tastefully scented fuck candles from the bedroom. Tommy and the Little Fool didn't stumble to the drawer to get a flashlight. They just sat there, waiting for each other's eyes to adjust enough to share their gentle smiles. And Massachusetts is one place I have seen.

Modern Luddites are wrong and evil. The "good old days" had an infant mortality rate of 500/1000, and half the Moms died in childbirth. People worked more hours just for food and suffered more pain. There was more rape and more violence. Nature is the enemy. Nature wants us dead at twenty-three years old. Nature wants us HIV+. Nature wants spinal meningitis. Electric lights and computers are good. Just plain good, no qualifier on that. I won't start the next sentence with "but." I won't take it back. Just plain good. Tommy and the Little Fool just didn't know themselves well enough to know that this happened to be the right time to turn off the computer and sit quietly and work on the case that way. There was no synchronicity, there was no serendipity, there was no luck, none of that Sting garbage. If any of those things existed, they would have kept Nell alive. But there is life. And there is what you do with every event and every moment. Tommy and the Little Fool were using the blackout. They were thinking in the dark. You can't start a fire sitting 'round crying over a broken heart.

The Little Fool was crying. It was safe crying. It was crying with your family. Tommy was there, the facts were all there. I was with him. I was in his heart. He was okay. "Tommy, you know, I really needed you. I really needed someone, Tommy, and you were there. You helped me."

"You're gonna say something like 'hold me' or 'back rub,' one of those other things breeders say when they want a blowjob from a queer right? I mean, say, 'Hey, pansy, wanna suck my cock?' and your chances would be about the same. You don't need to seduce. But I'm not telling you my answer until you grow a dick and ask me like a man."

"I'll make a note of that. What if you weren't there for me, Tommy? What if I wasn't lucky enough to have you? What would I have done?"

"Found a manicurist, a cook, and maybe eventually a hooker?"

"What do people do when they're lonely, fucked up and empty?"

"Dye their hair?"

"Tint."

"You're learning."

"All the people that died were really fucked up, Tommy. Nell wasn't happy with M.J., she wasn't happy with her career, she wasn't happy with her life."

"So, your point is she should have settled down with Prince Charming of the sewer swimmers?"

"None of them were happy, love. All the people we fished out of the drink were at bad times in their lives. They were walking around looking for some answers."

"They were prime candidates for a personality test from L. Ron Hubbard."

"Yes! Right and double right, my cocksucking Watson."

"I thought *I* was Shylock."

"Sherlock."

CHAPTER THIRTY-SIX

Any Place but Starbucks

"None of the victims went to church. They weren't churchgoers, and they weren't drunks—they didn't go to bars. There's only one place left: Starbucks. People who are alone go to Starbucks and drink overpriced coffee from well-treated, indigenous people. The connection is a bulletin board at Starbucks. I know it. I can feel it. Let's go."

"You said it. You just said, 'let's go.' You hate movies that say 'let's go.' You said you could tell a bad movie because someone in it says, 'let's go.' You said no one in the real world ever says, 'let's go,' and you just said it. You just jumped up with a revelation, explained something in terms I couldn't quite understand, and then said, 'let's go.' Is this just a bad movie?"

"Yeah, and we're about to cut to Starbucks."

The Little Fool and Tommy were standing in the nearest Starbucks (which is, as you know, at the corner of Tommy's street). It was almost closing time, right after a neighborhood blackout. It was busier than the employees wanted while they were trying to clean up. Starbucks have their industrial coffee machines right out there in plain view, so the workers have to be very sneaky when spitting in the drinks. The Little Fool butted ahead of some nose-rings and asked the goatee behind the counter where the Starbucks bulletin board was.

"Sorry, man, we don't have a bulletin board."

"Where is the nearest Starbucks that does?"

"None of them do. I think it's part of the bullshit, pig-power-structure corporate strategy, but, hey, I'm happy to be a team member."

The Little Fool turned back to Tommy: "So, there are no bulletin boards in any Starbucks. They're all the same."

"They're not all the same. In Seattle the green logo girl has tits and nipples showing."

"Really? What do you care about tits and nipples?"

"Many queers like tits and nipples, and women are more likely to show them to us than to you. It's another perk of our superior lifestyle."

"I've seen bulletin boards in a coffee shop. Recently. When I was walking around between two victims' apartments."

"Get help."

"How hard can it be to find a non-Starbucks coffee shop with a bulletin board?"

"Let's go."

They jumped in a cab and headed over to the non-Starbucks the Little Fool remembered. They had to drive around in a circle for a few blocks to find it. The Little Fool couldn't remember exactly where it was. The sign over the door said, "Dave's," but the cardboard sign in the window said "Any Place But Starbucks" and that's what everyone called it. The Little Fool was in a trance. He could smell the killer. The Little Fool had him. Right in the entranceway were two huge bulletin boards. It was all punk bands, spiritual massages, bass players and roommates wanted (who *wants* any of those things?). The Little Fool was reading it like the Torah; he started at the upper right and moved across. He had his finger touching every word; he didn't want to miss one thing on the board. His heart was racing. His certainty that he'd find what he wanted had no relation to how likely it was that he'd find what he was looking for. The Little Fool had become a full nut, and nuts are always sure of everything. Nuts go with feelings. "It's all clear to me now" is one of the sure signs of being a nut (cutting your own hair is the other). I saw the light. No more in darkness.

But he had a chance on this one. Tommy couldn't stand looking at the Little Fool. It was like watching someone waiting for his HIV test results. The Little Fool was flop-sweating and reading every word aloud. At first it was a mumble: "Wanted bass player for heavy metal/rap working band. All originals. Do not need original material from bass player. Must have own equipment. Call after two A.M."

Tommy was fidgeting. He walked to the counter to get them some hot chocolate. He was at the counter and the Little Fool was getting louder and louder. People pretending to think about chess moves were now distracted by the Little Fool's coffeehouse bulletin board insanity. He was now editorializing. "Another fucking bullshit massage. New-age fucking shit. Jive. Is there release during this massage? Is she going to jerk me off? That might be worth her fucking fifty dollars an hour. That would direct my energy into her face. Makes a great gift. I got your great gift hanging. I'm looking for a fucking roommate who smokes and hates animals—anything on the board for me? Where's the fucking Dean Martin tribute band that's looking for a Kenny Lane impersonator who can't play the fucking piano? That's what I need."

At a flea market in Stormville, New York, a friend of ours, a magician who was working on a new act, talked to a booth owner/operator about his animal trap collection. This friend was considering an act called "King of Animal Traps." The old trapper told a story about seeing a bear with his foot crushed in a bear trap. The trapper said the bear was standing up and screaming. "What do you mean, 'screaming'?" our friend asked. "He was standing up on his back legs and . . ." and then the flea market guy did an impersonation of the bear in agony. We never heard the trapper do it; we heard our friend do it, and I assume he was holding back. And we know the trapper was holding back from what the bear did. It was an impersonation that made us laugh and made the Little Fool's blood stop and pound in his ears. There's a level of true emotion where there is no difference between a bear and a human. It's the moment in the "Pinky the Cat" video you see on the Web where the animal ranger wearing the Smokey the Bear hat has a "very loving, male cat" crawl up the ranger's leg, dig its panicked, feline claws into the ranger's leg, and bite the friendly man's right testicle. The portly ranger throws his head back and just screams. It's not a scream of attack. It's not a scream of fear. It's not a scream of anger. It's a scream of pain. A bear-in-a-trap scream. A pure scream. In a few moments, Tommy would hear the Little Fool yell with excitement, and attack, and revenge, and heroics, but right now, as Tommy is holding two hot chocolates, one with non-fat milk and whipped cream, it's just that amazing sound. The Little Fool was standing by the bulletin board. In his hand he clutched a flier with tiny writing that he had ripped off the wall. Every one of his muscles was tense. His head was all the way back. His mouth was wide open. His eyes were full of tears. The Little Fool was screaming. Wherever the bear and the ranger were, they both could hear him. The people in the apartments upstairs could hear him. It was an animal scream. If the perp was within ten blocks, he would have heard that scream and just tipped his king over. The game was over. The scream wouldn't stop. The Little Fool no longer needed to breathe in. He needed to yell. Way. Down. In. Side.

The Little Fool was now reading aloud in a scream: " 'The Proust Questionnaire. How would you answer? Let's get together and talk about it. Literature and philosophy can get you out of your funk. If you need advice, get it from the greatest minds ever. What are your answers to these questions? Not everyone is thinking only about the latest hip hop song!' "

The volume dropped a little, but the Little Fool was still reading aloud. Everyone in the shop was listening.

One. What is your present state of mind?

Two. What is your greatest fear?

Three. What is your idea of perfect happiness?

Four. Which historical figure do you most identify with?

Five. What is the trait you most deplore in others?

Six. What is the trait you most deplore in yourself?

Seven. What is your greatest extravagance?

Eight. What is your favorite journey?

Nine. On what occasions do you lie?

Ten. Where would you like to live?

Eleven. Which historical figure do you most despise?

Twelve. Which living person do you most despise?

Thirteen. Which words or phrases do you most overuse?

Fourteen. What or who is the greatest love of your life?

Fifteen. What is your greatest regret?

Sixteen. When and where were you happiest?

Seventeen. If you could change one thing about your family, what would it be?

Eighteen. If you could change one thing about yourself, what would it be?

Nineteen. What do you most value in your friends?

Twenty. What is your principal defect?

Twenty-one. What to your mind would be the greatest of misfortunes?

Twenty-two. What would you like to be?

Twenty-three. What natural gift would you like most to possess?

Twenty-four. To what faults do you feel most indulgent?

Twenty-five. What do you consider the most overrated virtue?

Twenty-six. In what country would you like to live?

Twenty-seven. What do you consider your greatest achievement?

Twenty-eight. What do you regard as the lowest depths of misery?

Twenty-nine. What is your most treasured possession?

Thirty. What is your most marked characteristic?

Thirty-one. What is the quality you most like in a man?

Thirty-two. What is the quality you most like in a woman?

Thirty-three. Who is your favorite hero of fiction?

Thirty-four. Who are your heroes in real life?

Thirty-five. How would you like to die?

Thirty-six. If you were to die and come back as a person or thing, who or what do you suspect it would be?

Thirty-seven. If you could choose what to come back as, what would it be?

Thirty-eight. What is your favorite color, flower, bird, and occupation?

Thirty-nine. Who are your favorite writers, composers, painters, and poets?

Forty. What is your motto?

The Little Fool was hoarse. The non-Starbucks was silent except for The Little Fool's reading. He was spitting out every number. He paused for a moment and then went back: " 'Thirty-five. How would you like to die? Thirty-five. How would you like to die? Thirty-five. How would you like to die?' " He threw his head back in the bear trap position and yelled, "Well, asshole, tell me! How would *you* like to die?"

Tommy put down the hot chocolates, dug into his tight hip-huggers and pulled out a twenty-dollar bill. He started laughing the-atrically and ran across the non-Starbucks to the Little Fool. Tommy stuck the double sawbuck into the Little Fool's face as the Little Fool continued to scream, "I want the answer to question thirty-five! Maybe I can help you!"

Tommy jumped up to the Little Fool's face with the twenty and yelled right back at him, "Okay, brother, you win! Here's the twenty. I didn't think you'd have the balls to do it, but you read the whole board aloud at the top of your lungs. Here's the twenty. You are amazing. You're a nut. You'll do anything. You kill me, man, I love you." Tommy stuffed the twenty into the Little Fool's shirt pocket and threw his arms around the Little Fool in the most manly, sports-bar hug our Tommy could manage. He stuck his mouth in the Little Fool's ear and spoke like the parent Tommy would never want to be: "Listen, baby. Listen to me. You can't make a scene. You're close to catching the motherfucker. Don't blow it. Don't be crazy. You do *not* want these people talking about whatever you found on the board. Don't scare the asshole away." Tommy was just barely getting through. The Little Fool could almost hear him. Tommy continued, "Trust me, baby, trust me. I love you, please trust me. You don't have to understand—just do what I say. Right now. Laugh and high-five me like a jock. Please, baby, please. You have to. For Nell. Laugh. You were kidding. High-five me."

Tommy managed to stop the mental-ill momentum. The Little Fool was able to see himself for just a moment. He had no idea what he was doing, but he felt love through the craziness. The love quieted him. His mind slowly processed the command. He laughed. It was an okay laugh. It wasn't crazy. It was forced and goofy, so it passed for jock-like. He did a real old white guy's high-five with Tommy. Tommy took it from there. "You won fair and square."

Tommy took the sweaty, crumpled flier out of the Little Fool's hand, put the flier back on the bulletin board, and spoke softly: "Pull it together, baby. If you want to catch this motherfucker, you have to think and you have to let me help. Remember, I'm your Watson-whatever. We're going to walk over to the counter and enjoy our hot chocolate. I want you to smile and be a little embarrassed, but still proud. You got that, crime-fighter?"

They walked over to the counter and picked up the hot chocolate. The goatee was very impressed. "Hey, the beverages are on me. That was great, man. I dug it. Was that just a gag, or have you done acting before? Man, you seemed really into it. You're great. Did you happen to notice any new bands needing a bass player on that board?"

The Little Fool and Tommy sat down at a chessboard table and started sipping their hot chocolates. The Little Fool spoke quietly: "That's the motherfucker. That's him. That's the whole thing. It's Proust, for christ's sake. It's like self-help garbage, but it also looks like an opportunity to meet some people and talk about important questions. There's no phone number, there's no address. There's nothing. There's that little box there where you put the question-naire after you fill it out."

"Then what happens? I don't get it."

"You put a contact number or email address on the flier. The freak reads the questionnaires and if he thinks it's time for you to die, he gets in touch with you, meets you, and kills you."

"Is it a club?"

"No. The people never meet each other. If they'd met each other, the cops would have figured that. The victims just think about their questionnaires, fill them out, drop them in the box, and then meet him for coffee or something. He goes from there to killing them."

"Are you sure? How do you know?"

"I'm lost. I'm empty. I'm worried. I have no family left. I see that questionnaire and I really want to think about it and fill it out and talk to someone else who feels that way. And that's just what I'm going to do. I'm going to fill out a questionnaire."

"It's time for your Hitchcock question: Why don't they go to the police?"

"We might go to the police. We might do that. I might still be sane enough to do that. But I think we need to find out a little more, first. We need to talk to someone here and see who puts those up. But we can't do that now. We've made too much of a scene."

"We?"

"Yeah. If we ask now, it'll look fishy. We'll have to ask tomorrow who puts those fliers up. We'll find this guy."

They sat sipping hot chocolate. The place had calmed down. Fame is fleeting and no one even remembered the nutty performance art bit. They were just drinking their sophisticated beverages and sketching in their expensive notebooks.

Tommy was worried. "How are you doing, baby?"

"I'm feeling lonely and confused. I think I'm going to grab one of them there Proust fliers and fill it out."

CHAPTER THIRTY-SEVEN

Bait

1. *What is your present state of mind?*

2. *What is your greatest fear?*

3. *What is your idea of perfect happiness?*

4. *Which historical figure do you most identify with?*

5. *What is the trait you most deplore in others?*

6. *What is the trait you most deplore in yourself?*

7. *What is your greatest extravagance?*

8. *What is your favorite journey?*

9. *On what occasions do you lie?*

10. *Where would you like to live?*

11. *Which historical figure do you most despise?*

12. *Which living person do you most despise?*

13. *Which words or phrases do you most overuse?*

14. *What or who is the greatest love of your life?*

15. *What is your greatest regret?*

16. *When and where were you happiest?*

17. *If you could change one thing about your family, what would it be?*

18. *If you could change one thing about yourself, what would it be?*

19. *What do you most value in your friends?*

20. *What is your principal defect?*

21. *What to your mind would be the greatest of misfortunes?*

22. *What would you like to be?*

23. *What natural gift would you like most to possess?*

24. *To what faults do you feel most indulgent?*

25. *What do you consider the most overrated virtue?*

26. *In what country would you like to live?*

27. *What do you consider your greatest achievement?*

28. *What do you regard as the lowest depths of misery?*

29. *What is your most treasured possession?*

30. *What is your most marked characteristic?*

31. *What is the quality you most like in a man?*

32. *What is the quality you most like in a woman?*

33. *Who is your favorite hero of fiction?*

34. *Who are your heroes in real life?*

35. *How would you like to die?*

Slowly and in a lot of PAIN to prove I WON'T cry out to GOD!

36. *If you were to die and come back as a person or thing, who or what do you suspect it would be?*

37. *If you could choose what to come back as, what would it be?*

38. *What is your favorite color, flower, bird, and occupation?*

39. *Who are your favorite writers, composers, painters, and poets?*

40. *What is your motto?*

At the bottom he wrote a brand-new, temporary email address.

CHAPTER THIRTY-EIGHT

Another Basket for Some Eggs

They filled out another Proust questionnaire, filling out every blank and putting another temporary email address at the bottom. This questionnaire was in Tommy's writing. It was perfect. He'd practiced every answer in one of his notebooks before he wrote on the xeroxed sheet.

"Are you trying to impress a murderer?" the Little Fool sneered.

"Well, we don't know what sets him off. If he kills people for bad penmanship, we have that covered. Maybe he kills people who give a damn about the way they present themselves to the world. We need both kinds of bait. I'm the queerbait, but that hasn't been said about me since high school."

They filled this one out pretty straight, if any form that contains references to Bette Midler and James Dean can be considered straight. Tommy insisted on writing down *Ben-Hur*. That wasn't particularly gay, but it was very Tommy. The Little Fool and Tommy figured they had to seem Atheist and sad, and they were Atheist and sad, so they pretty much just filled it out. No big surprises. The serious bait was really just two questions.

1. *What is your present state of mind?* Lonely

35. *How would you like to die?* Soon.

Tommy folded this questionnaire very neatly and put it in a nice, pink envelope. "Should I put on a drop or two of Old Spice? I do that for shits and giggles on all my sweet letters. The Old Spice makes me think of the big, sexy, seafaring Dad I never had."

"I don't think our bait needs cologne."

"You catch more flies with honey than with vinegar."

"With Old Spice, you just catch crabs."

Tommy said he'd run out and drop the sparse, psycho questionnaire at Any Place But Starbucks. They were going to drop the neat one off a day later so as not to look fishy, and so Tommy would have plenty of time to sneak on the aftershave.

Tommy took a cab over to the bulletin board while the Little Fool did a search of Renée's emails. He'd read all of them, but that was before he knew what he was looking for. He mostly just got sexually excited; he didn't retain many nonsexual images from her notes. He searched for "Proust." Nothing. He searched for "questionaire." Nothing. He tried "historical figure." Nothing. He pulled out the extra questionnaire he'd copped to see what else he could search for. He was pulling out key phrases and getting ready for another search when he looked at the top of the page again. "Stupid, motherfucking programmers. Why don't they build spellcheckers into the 'find' programs?"

He then searched Renée's emails for "questionnaire." Speaking of spelling, how about B-I-N-G-O? There was an email to one of the guys she'd had a lot of cybersex with.

. . . So, I found this Prouste [sic] *Questionnaire at the Starbucks* [sic]. *It's not self-help bullshit; it's literature or something. It's all these heavy questions. Good ones to think about. Filling it out made me think a lot about myself and what's important. I guess there's some sort of group of people who get together and talk about this. I'm so fucking sick of talking about nothing but Howard Stern at work; I need to talk about anything else. I just want more. I need to be a little heavier. I like thinking about this shit. I really do. I filled it all out and I think I'm going to drop it back off. I filled it out pretty honestly. I put one joke in:*

26. In what country would you like to live? France

27. What do you consider your greatest achievement? French.

I was kidding about France, it's a sucky place, but I sure like to suck cock. You don't think anyone would think from that that I mean I speak French, do you? Or that I like France? Dude, that would be awful. BTW, shouldn't I be sucking your cock right now?

    Well, you're not here, so I guess I'll just watch a Seinfeld *rerun, it's a funny [sic] one tonight.*

That email had been sent just a little over a week before she'd been fished out of the drink. I guess this was the time that sane people would have turned the message over to the police. But what would the police do? He'd been through Renée's emails a million times. He'd dug around in her trash. Even with this information, he couldn't get a thing. Not even a reference to a webpage. He checked her address book. Nothing unusual. The perp must have used a temporary address that Renée had deleted. The Little Fool had no phone number, no email address, no snail-mail address. He had nothing. The Little Fool wasn't sure of much in life right now, but he was sure that whoever the perpetrator was, he believed one of the women he'd murdered spoke French. Oh lord, please don't let me be misunderstood.

CHAPTER THIRTY-NINE

Crime-Fighters in the Big Situation Comedy

Tommy later reported to us what had gone on during his part of the adventure.

Tommy didn't want anyone at Any Place But Starbucks to see him put the paper in the box. For all Tommy knew, the killer was right there sipping a latte. Tommy didn't have the Renée information the Little Fool had, but Tommy was still pretty sure he was about to open communication with the killer. There were people sitting and talking at the tables, and no line at the counter, so the employees were watching everything out of boredom. Tommy didn't want anyone to see him drop the folded questionnaire into the little cardboard box. He glanced at the bulletin board. Yup, the ad and the box were still there. He was afraid that, after the Little Fool's giant performance art piece, the killer would get spooked and take down the display. It might have been better for the plot if he had. Is this too direct a line to the climax? If you take one of those fiction-writing courses at a community college, don't they teach you that the hero has to have one more surprise obstacle before getting to the McGuffin? There's that big, Hollywood, weekend-seminar guy who teaches that *Terminator* is the perfect script, and doesn't the hero have an extra problem or two before the ending?

This story doesn't really have a McGuffin. There isn't a secret formula, or a computer chip, or a piece of microfilm hidden in a diamond by a beautiful blonde, all of which everyone wants. There's nothing that anyone wants in this story. There are just a lot of dead people. And who wants dead people? What were Tommy and the Little Fool trying to accomplish? They were trying to find a killer. And what were the Little Fool and Tommy going to do with him when they found him? What are you hoping for? Do you want them to do the right thing and bring him to justice to get that "fair trial that the victims never got," or do you want him to be killed with the Little Fool as judge, jury, and juggler? Which cliché do you want? I don't want to give too much away, but Nell is still going to be dead at the end of our story. We're not going to bring her back to life. It's bad enough we have a typing sock monkey. None of the dead people the Little Fool loves are going to come back. In all the excitement, punk, I kind of lost track myself.

Tommy was part of a team of real crime-fighters, and the rest of the world was in a situation comedy. Howard Stern isn't a show. It's not like Jean Shepherd telling stories on the radio in the middle of the night. Howard Stern is like a really smart and funny co-worker who knows everything, sitting around the water cooler, chatting. *Seinfeld* isn't a comedy where the characters learn something and move on. It's not a play or a movie. The characters are going to come back the next week pretty much the same as they ended this week. It's modular. The characters are likeable: You like to have them in your home (or, in Howard's case, in your car or workplace). But their ersatz friendship comes with a price. It seemed to Tommy as he sat in Any Place But Starbucks and waited for a break to make his move, that Shakespeare's mirror was working backwards. People were acting more like TV. Lucy, you gotta lotta 'splainin' to do!

Cartoons don't make people more violent. Cartoons just make little boys make slightly different noises and use different names when the little boys play. Fantasy sex and fantasy violence do no damage at all. Morality is very strong. It's built into our genetics and it's taught by parents and peers. We have lots of good reasons to treat people well, and those reasons aren't going to be taken away by a stupid movie or TV show (or even a great movie or TV show). TV shows can't make you kill. Radio can't make you hurt

other people. Rap music can't make you a gangster. If we're talking about what kind of music is going through the heads of most
killers, it's Sinatra. Sinatra is real violent music. How many hit men
were whistling "Fly Me to the Moon" while they whacked (in
both senses)? But that isn't Sinatra's fault. When the spokesheads
for "Industry" talk about being responsible, they're just self-
aggrandizing. Hollywood believes Hollywood helped the religious
people kill on 9-11. Hollywood believes they gave people cancer
because the characters smoked in *Basic Instinct*. That's just not true.
I'm a cop-killer. Fuck police brutality.

Nope, you can't change the big stuff, but you can change the little
stuff. And that's where the sadness is. Our lives are little stuff. We
don't care about kids using slang. That's just fun. What's really both-
ersome is people talking to people they love as though they were in
a situation comedy. Morality doesn't stop you from doing that. It
comes in under the radar. These jokes that aren't jokes and don't
mean anything, but have the gloss of wit. There was a woman sitting
with her young child at the coffee place. The boy had a container of
apple juice in front of him, but he was much more interested in the
toy he'd just gotten. She was talking loudly enough for Tommy to
hear, so he could know how clever she was. "Have you heard 'Patience is a virtue'?" she said to the child, who'd of course never
heard that, but she was unwinding her joke for the rest of the world.
"Have you heard, 'All good things come to those who wait'?" He
hadn't, but the set-up was done. "Have you heard, 'If you open that
before you get home, Mommy is going to throw it away'?" This was
a chance for a mother to talk to her child, but instead she was doing
bad situation-comedy schtickala. No, TV didn't cause the Twin
Towers to fall. That was religion. TV didn't cause cops to be killed.
That was the drug war. But TV did cause a Mom to talk to her kids
as if she were a Harvard graduate comedy writer writing for an ex-
model in a way that would justify the live audience laugh track and
not anger the network. That moment was gone forever. All Tommy
found out about the Mother and the son was that she watched situation comedies. Bury the rag deep in your face.

Tommy heard all this as he sat sipping, waiting to fight crime. Finally he had his break. There were customers, and no one was watching the board. He walked over casually. He was pushing the nonchalant thing. He might as well have been singing Curly Howard's "la da dee, la da da" to himself. Tommy went to stick the questionnaire in the box, but he saw one already in the box. He pulled out the folded questionnaire and stuck it in his pocket. He took the one the Little Fool had filled out and put it in the box. Tommy looked around. No one had noticed. He walked out the door. I'm begging you to beg me.

The Little Fool would have taken the questionnaire and ripped it up without reading it, but Tommy did unto others. He opened the questionnaire. He read it as he walked down the street. He spoke quietly to himself. "Hey, look! *Ben-Hur!* We got another chariot fan!"

CHAPTER FORTY

Übermensch

The Little Fool and I had to piece together what happened with Tommy. He was gone a lot longer than he should have been. How long could it take to drop off a questionnaire? It seemed he must have wandered around a bit on his way back. When the Little Fool re-read Renée's old email and became certain that Tommy was off to make contact with the real killer, the Little Fool and I got really worried. We got really nuts. The Little Fool was getting antsy waiting, so he went out for a walk. Just after the Little Fool left, Tommy walked in. You say, "Good-bye," and I say, "Hello."

Tommy came in with his story all prepared. He knew just what he was going to say when he got home. He'd spent the last block of his walk rehearsing. He wanted his story to be perfect. He wanted the Little Fool to see him as the perfect crime-fighter. When he realized the Little Fool was gone, with no note, Tommy's mood changed dramatically. He was a different person when he was alone. That's true for everyone, but more so for Tommy. It's the thing about being too comfortable with yourself. He played it big in life. He had lived as a woman for years. When you're man enough to hide your genitals, you're man enough to not have to hide anything at all. But when Tommy was alone, it was different. There's a different kind of alone when you're planning on seeing someone and you have a story to tell and no one is there. That's when you're really alone. What do you do when your love is away.

Planned alone is different. Maybe you're going to read, maybe you're going to watch TV. Maybe you just want to shut your eyes, take a bath, doze off. That's the kind of alone that you plan when you know you're going to be alone. And sometimes someone calls during alone time and they see a gentler, more pensive side of you. Alone time is a good time to fall in love. When you've settled in for the night. When there's no booty call. When maybe you feel just the first scratching of a sore throat. When you brew up a big pot of tea and get a big bubble bath going and plan on reading some poetry in the tub. Real poetry, like haiku or something. Basho, not some Jewel crap that you read for a goof, but something that's a little over your head. And you have the phone by the bathtub, mostly because if you start to drown and have to call 911, you want it ready. The phone is there just as a bubble bath lifeguard. Well, if that phone rings at about 11:00 P.M., and it's someone you met recently and thought, maybe, about dating, and all of a sudden he's in your head, talking through your phone. . . . You're naked and you're alone and that voice comes over the phone and you start talking. . . . Well, it's an easy way to fall in love. You have nothing in your head that you're planning to say. You have no stories ready. You don't have an agenda. And that person on the line will sense your mood and he'll feel safe. Finally someone is listening to him. And he might tell a story about his nutty old Aunt Millie. And you might listen to the story. And you might get a little glimpse into another human heart. And when you get that glimpse, when you listen without thinking about what you're going to say next, that person on the phone can own you. And when you listen to someone, you automatically own him or her. I can't tell you, but I know it's mine.

That's how fortune-tellers work. You want to know the secrets of the spiritualists that Houdini fought? It's very simple; you don't need to know anything sneaky. All the "I see a kind woman whose name begins with a J" doesn't mean anything. All psychics really do is listen. They listen and they watch. They are the only people who are engaging other humans just to get information and not give it. If you're a skeptic, you'll watch the tape of the "reading" and say, "See, see, it's such bullshit, that phony piece of shit is just saying the same stuff back to that poor bastard." But that's the whole point. When a loved one dies, there are all sorts of people who are willing to talk. The clergy will tell you that that's the way of the world and the loved one is in a better place. Your friends will say that you have to take care of yourself. They'll tell you life goes on. But a psychic will listen. She'll look into your face and into your eyes and she'll listen to every sobbing word. And she'll tell you back what you said. And that's a revelation. A real revelation has to be something you already know, something you just said. Next time you're on an airplane or a train or bus, or even in a park where you happen to be sitting next to a stranger, decide that you're going to find out all you can about that person. Don't think anything about yourself. Don't think about how you're going to present yourself, or what you want out of that person. Don't think about affirming yourself. Don't think about your favorite stories, or what's been bugging you lately. Don't think about you. Think about that stranger. Before you talk, check him out. How much does he make a year? Is he married? What does he do for a living? What CDs does he own? There are hints all over. And start a conversation. Let him steer. Bend over and let him drive. Hang on his every word. Simply restate to him whatever he says and watch the eyes for any positive or negative. Watch the eyes flash and then dull, and adjust it as you speak it back. Learn as much as you can. Guess what? You're psychic! And your sucker will fall in love with you. You can sell him anything. He'll lick you. You'll own him. Knowledge is power. Knowledge about another person is love. If we want to put every charlatan out of business, all we have to do is listen to each other. All the victims are paying with money, memories, and dignity just to get someone to listen. Busted Madame Marie for telling fortunes better than they do.

Tommy was in the inverse position. He was the fraction to the integer. He was 1 over lonely. He had come home expecting to be with the Little Fool, and instead he was alone. He had a story all planned. He hadn't planned a bubble bath or a lay down; he had planned to talk, and think, and be with the Little Fool. Tommy was excited, scared, and jacked up. He needed to talk to someone. He didn't have a monkey, so he spoke to himself. And when Tommy talked to himself, he was a very different guy. When Tommy was in the world, the world was butch, and Tommy was the touch of nelly to round the edges. That was his role. A little nancy to the world of football and Iraq. But when he was alone, he didn't have to balance, he didn't have to scoot up on his teeter-totter seat to balance the big macho dick on the other end. Macho had jumped off and left him bouncing on his ass. Now he could sit where he wanted. When Tommy talked to himself, he wasn't silly. He didn't mince. He didn't play it big. When Tommy talked to himself, he wasn't Tommy. There's a place you can get where your name is nonsense. When you're in that place, you can say your name over and over and it means nothing. Above and beyond. Tommy. Tommy. Tommy.

Tommy was no longer Tommy. He was someone who was a little butch and a little fag like everyone. He was a little bit me and a little bit you. He was all of us. Not having the Little Fool when Tommy needed him had jacked him into someone else. The retard buddhists try for this. They think it's becoming one with the universe. What they're really doing is sitting on their asses when there's work to be done. If you really want nirvana, just seize the mood when it's given. The timing was right—Tommy was knocked out of himself. No more good-natured, joking-around Tommy. I'm gonna wash that man right out of my hair.

Many nights right before Tommy went to sleep he would lie on his back and for the first time of the day he would feel his muscles holding his face as Tommy. He would be aware of what his face was doing. He would feel the half-smile; he would feel himself holding in his cheeks. He would feel the slight wrinkle on his nose. And in one moment, he'd let it all go. One big release and Tommy would be gone, like mucus with a deep sneeze on a sunny day. Let all the tension go out of his face. And when he did that, when he relaxed, he would feel Tommy fly off into the room and through the ceiling, gone and nearly forgotten. He would feel the mask go away. We all have a face that we hide away forever.

And as he lay there in the dark, he would imagine his face as a blank. As blank as a fourteen-year-old model in a makeup chair in Paris, still on heroin from the night before and far away from Mom and Dad and all those small-town people who didn't get it. Pretty vacant. Vay cunt. And blank is one with the universe. For a moment, he would think about willing Tommy back into his face. Could he do it? Could he remember the half-smile? Could he remember how he held his eyebrows and his cheeks? No. His face was now blank forever. He was now everyone. Any attempt to pull Tommy back into this pure shell was a washed-up impressionist on the Vegas Strip, holding a cigar in his hand, licking his lips, saying "Gracie" and pretending he in some way had a hold on George Burns's soul. Tommy was gone, and the one-world, one-life, puppet body that now lay in Tommy's place couldn't fake it ever again. He couldn't remember how to be Tommy. And this being, this pure life-force without barriers, without a name, would slowly drift off to sleep and would dream, not for Tommy, but for all of us. A candy-colored clown.

The übermensch that most of the time allowed his body to be used by Tommy walked around the apartment. This was one of those times that wasn't for sleep. It was time for action. He had a job to do. He moved around the apartment. He didn't go up on his toes when he walked. He simply moved. He didn't play with his hair. He didn't pick up any of the Little Fool's dirty clothes and put them where they belonged. Tommy didn't make tea. He didn't wash dishes. He didn't turn on the local '80s station to dance like Cyndi Lauper. He just moved across the room, directly over to the computer. He typed his password into the screen saver. "#1cocksucker" meant nothing. It was just touch-typing, the mnemonic device had gone away, it was just QWERTY to him now, a dance his fingers did by rote. He didn't see Tommy's cute Barbie and Ken desktop; he went right to work. He opened the Little Fool's special remailer account. From here Tommy could send a message that could never be traced. He reached into his pocket and pulled out the questionnaire he had copped from the box at Any Place But Starbucks. The questionnaire was wrinkled from ass sweat. Übermensch didn't even think about it. He was robot Arnold Schwarzenegger landing naked in the garbage of the past. Tommy was no longer fastidious. He looked over the questionnaire. He invaded privacy. He read every answer slowly and carefully. He mouthed the words. He tried to become the person who had filled out the questionnaire. He could role-play a football star or a homophobic pipe-smoking '50s guy from a driver's-ed film, but becoming someone a bit like Tommy was harder. He couldn't let Tommy back in. Not yet. He wanted to be this other man. He had to take on this personality; the sad, desperate personality that had filled out a questionnaire and dropped it in a box on a coffee shop bulletin board. He had to compose this email very carefully. Tommy, can you hear me? Tommy? Tommy?

CHAPTER FORTY-ONE

I Love Lucy and Tommy

It wasn't going to take Columbo and Perry Mason together to analyze the scene the Little Fool walked into. There was the man we know as Tommy passed out in the computer chair. The Little Fool ran over to the slumped figure. The Little Fool remembered all his cop first-aid training. He would have called 911 and then started CPR, but the Tommy-figure was breathing. He was sleeping. He was sleeping very soundly, but it was just sleep. The Little Fool went from the dead panic run to the nursery sneak. It was time to take care of his friend who had fallen dead asleep, probably from the pure exhaustion of fear. Let him sleep. The Little Fool would never look at anyone else's computer screen. Never. He would never read a note not meant for him, never. That's why he had Tommy. Tommy was the nosy one. But there was a note in front of the computer, and the Little Fool suspected it might be for him. Tommy might have left a note before blasting off in the computer chair for the land of nod. Rocket number nine take off for the planet. For the planet.

The Little Fool picked up the crumpled, ass-sweated, piece of paper and looked at it. A murderous questionnaire. It wasn't Tommy's writing. These weren't Tommy's answers. There were things on this questionnaire that we knew Tommy didn't know. Tommy had collected a stranger's questionnaire. During CPR classes in cop school, they taught the Little Fool that a heart attack was "no time for modesty." It was a time to throw politeness to the wind, rip the

189

victim's shirt off, and give him a lip-lock. No time for modesty. The Little Fool had to look at the computer screen. This was an emergency. He carefully reached around the head in front of the keyboard and wiggled the mouse. He typed "#1cocksucker" when prompted, and a half-finished email popped up. It was the Little Fool's account. It was the remailer account. It was the secret account. The "to" address matched the address on the bottom of the strange questionnaire. The "re" said, "Proust," and the message started, "I can tell you're going through a tough time. Maybe I can help. I read the questionnaire that you dropped off at Any Place But Starbucks and found it very upsetting. I'm hoping I can help—" Then the typing stopped. The author had fallen asleep or passed out. The Little Fool did what any well-trained ex-policeman would have done. He felt all the blood drain from his head. He felt the room grow cold. He felt like he needed to sit down. He felt he should sit down. He should find a place to lie down. He had to sit down. He really needed to lie down. Can't wait. The Little Fool fainted. There were two unconscious bodies around the computer and a helpless monkey across town. When the truth is found to be lies.

We're in the middle of the "Lucy Problem." There is a big misunderstanding between Lucy and Ricky Ricardo. He's just planning a surprise party. He isn't seeing another woman. That sexy woman really is just the new Cuban vocalist. But the husband and wife never talk. And a half-hour situation comedy goes by. A half-hour for people who are desperate for nostalgia, for people who think a woman other than Phyllis Diller is funny, a half hour they spend sitting and laughing with the track. But the situation is just stupid. Just talk to each other. Forget the surprise party, just forget all your plans, and talk to each other as human beings. Don't string us along. We're not stupid. We know how we'd solve this. Why can't Lucy figure it out? That's not funny. That's just stupid. Tell me, momma, what is it?

The Little Fool came to with Tommy cradling his head. Tommy wasn't afraid; he knew there was stress around. He was no longer übermensch; he was now Nurse Tommy. He had a cool washcloth and a glass of water. "What's wrong, baby? Are you okay? What can I get you?" The Little Fool had passed out next to a killer and come to in the arms of his dearest friend. Split personality is a plot device that can be used once, and Hitchcock beat us to it. Tommy wasn't Norman Bates and the Little Fool wasn't Lucy. The Little Fool and Tommy talked. "What the fuck were you doing with that fucking questionnaire?" the Little Fool asked. "What the fuck. What the fucking fuck, you fuck? What?" he elaborated. "Fuck, jesus, fuck. What the fuck are you doing?" he further inquired. "Fuck!" he exclaimed. You may be a lover, but you ain't no dancer.

Tommy felt he had to stop the killer from killing anymore. He had the questionnaire in his hand, but he was afraid. He was so scared the man whose questionnaire was covered with Tommy's ass sweat would get in touch with the killer another way. Tommy didn't want anyone else to die. Not this guy. Not the *Ben-Hur* guy. "I've kinda got a crush on this guy, C.B. I like his answers. I feel close to him. Look, his favorite journey is hitchhiking anywhere on an autumn day. How adorable is that? I was afraid, C.B. I was scared. This is the first one that I felt like I knew *before* he died. This is a life we can save. I want to warn him. I love him so much. His life is so precious. Please don't stop me from warning him just so we can catch the guy in a trap. This guy isn't bait. This is a human being. He's got cute writing."

"You've taken the questionnaire out of the box. The killer can't find him. You've saved his life, Tommy. You saved his life. You've done it. You saved a person's life. You don't have to write to him. You have the questionnaire. Tommy, you saved him. He's okay. Jesus, Miss Drama, cool it."

"Why did you faint, you pussy?"

"I thought you were the killer. I thought you were the killer. It seemed so perfect, that the killer would be right next to me. It seemed like perfect horror."

"Are these the eyes of a killer?" Tommy was back in control of his face. He didn't have to think about how to hold his face. He didn't have to remember how to smile. He helped the Little Fool into the chair. Tommy went to make a pot of tea. He picked up the Little Fool's socks and dropped them off in the laundry closet. Home where my love lies waiting.

"Now, if I tell him I saved his life, doesn't he owe me a blowjob?"

CHAPTER FORTY-TWO

A Bite!

From: Proust030305@HotMail.com
Date: Tue, 05 Mar 2003 14:55:01 EST
Subject: Questionnaire
To: Proust182@Yahoo.com
X-Mailer: AOL 5.2 for Mac-Post-GM sub 147

Proust182,

You are in a lot of pain. The answer, as you know, isn't self-help. It doesn't work on anyone and you're smart enough to know that. For a clear-thinking Atheist like yourself, the answer can only be found in literature, art, and friendship. That's what our little Proust group offers. It's a chance to get together and discuss the things that really matter. This is perhaps the only group that doesn't talk about 12-Step Programs, our lack of privacy from the government, or what's on TV. We don't talk about movies. We don't talk about fashion. It's not a good place to meet potential dating partners. It's a good place to talk about things that matter. It's a good place to rise above the mundane details that eat our life alive.

Our little circle is a chance to talk about the only things that make life worthwhile: art and humanity. I see myself as benevolent, but I am certainly the despot of this organization. I like to meet each member alone a few times before he or she goes to group so I can make a reasonable guess as to how well he or she will fit in. If we're not right for you, we won't help you, and you sure won't help us.

I trust you understand.

How important is this to you? That's one of the things I need to find out. You sent your mail from a temporary email address. That's wise. We all get enough mail about sexy underage lesbians who'll make our penises longer (I'm sure even women get those messages). You're very protective of your privacy and your time and I respect that. I'm sure you respect that quality in others. My email address is temporary as well. I opened the account just to send this mail. I will not receive mail at this address. You cannot write back to me until we meet and you're part of the group. At that point you'll only be allowed to use your real name and address and you'll get a password. It will then be time for trust.

Obviously, I don't meet with everyone who drops off a questionnaire. There has to be a connection. That little questionnaire tells a lot about a person. I am capricious. I "go with my gut." I'm looking for someone who knows literature, who knows real art, and who is at a crossroads in his or her life. I'm looking for real seekers without god.

You don't fit the pattern of anyone I've found acceptable. But I found your ignoring of all but the one question very arty. Intense. Stark. A bit dada, maybe. It gave me a chill and made me laugh. Maybe we can all enrich each other. You seem like a good bet to me.

The others might not approve, but it is not a democracy. I'm Caligula, and I think you're going to fit in perfectly. Let's meet and begin our search of lost time.

10:17 P.M. Thursday the 7th—meet me at the New York City trapeze school in Hudson River Park. I like to go and watch the business people pretend to conquer their mislabeled minor fears. They're just starting up for the year. The classes finish at 10:00, and the 17 minutes will give me time to collect my thoughts in preparation for our meeting.

Why 17 minutes? Seventeen is the first number that feels random. 1,2,3,4,5 are obviously special. Add in 6,7,8, and 9 (for a total of 45) because there's just something interesting about every single-digit number. They live on our hands. Some of us can visualize most of them. Ten is our decimal; much too obvious. Eleven is too close to ten, the first number with matching individual digits. Twelve is the quaint dozen. Thirteen is the number of bad luck for the traditionally superstitious. Fourteen is two sevens. Fifteen—three fives. Sixteen is a nice square and a standard increment of an inch. But 17—there's nothing special about 17. What are you going to say, it's one of the two two-digit numbers whose digits add up to the lowest cube? I don't think so. Seventeen is a random number. So, at 10:17 I will be waiting to see how interested you are in the bigger issues of life.

Does that whole 10:17 thing seem too crazy? Fine. Go watch a rerun of *MASH*. I don't care.

I am well aware that you owe me nothing. You are in no way obligated to show up. Please forgive the deep presumption of stating that you don't owe me anything. That is obvious, and stating the obvious always runs the danger of underlining the point enough to call it into question. You do not owe me anything, and if you don't show up I'll enjoy a little night air alone and my email will never again darken your inbox.

If you feel like joining me for a get-acquainted chat, pick up a nice, sophisticated, hot beverage from Anyplace But Starbucks on your way downtown, and nurse it. You can sip it slowly in the cab or on the subway. Try to make it last until our meeting. I'll know you by the cup. Carry it with you to fight the early spring chill. Make it an "Xtra Large" (so much better than Venti) and hold it in your right hand. We'll introduce ourselves, and we'll be off.

If you have something more important to do at that time, do it, and thank you for your indulgence and your time.

CHAPTER FORTY-THREE

Hit Me!

"Don't pout. We put yours in the box a day later. We might get an email to your fake address, too. We'll keep checking it."

"He's a snob. I should have just written '*Ben-Hur*' or 'the *Ben-Hur* film' and not 'that *Ben-Hur* movie.'"

"It's no insult not to be chosen. He's deciding who to kill, remember. Maybe Old Spice takes the fight out of him. Or maybe he's enough of a psychopath to like Old Spice. Maybe that manly scent saved your cute little ass."

Why don't they call the police? Just call the police. You have enough information. You've solved the crime; you know where the bad guy is going to be. Yeah, your old police department still thinks you need to get psychological help, but they'll listen. You have all the information. You can prove it. Maybe not in a court of law, but you can prove it enough to get a few of your old buddies from the force to go in there with an Xtra Large cup of Any Place But Starbucks coffee, a wire, and lots of backup over behind a tree. Please please please. You're not playing with kids. This is no place for the Little Fool Crime-Fighter Players. I could scream until my gray spackled face with the big red grin turned blue. Little Fool, you're probably bigger than the bad guy. You're undoubtedly stronger than him, but you're not a killer and he is. Experience counts for a lot. No matter what cops you send in, they won't have the experience of this guy. This evil, sick, lost creep knows what it feels like to kill. And he likes it now. The first kill has to be the hardest. He must be getting better at it. Try to remember the first time you put the regulator in your mouth and cautiously walked into the pool. No matter how badly you wanted to be a scuba diver, no matter how much you had read, you needed a few dives to feel it. So few people actually kill another human being. So few. So few really have that experience. The first cut is the deepest.

David Packer is an actor in Los Angeles. He was over at Dominique Dunne's house the night her boyfriend murdered her. Packer was over there to work on a scene for a TV show he and Dominique were doing together. They were going to act together. He ended up hearing the fight she had with her boyfriend in the other room that moved out into the yard where the boyfriend killed her. David Packer called the police. Some macho actor types, self-appointed posthumous friends of Dominique, have this semi-public fantasy that if they themselves had heard the yelling, they would have walked out and saved her. Let's forget for a second that a couple of showbiz lovers screaming at each other doesn't mean one of them is going to kill the other. That's a nutty conclusion to jump to, even when it's true. Let's assume you know something really bad is happening and you walk out there to help. Who are you? You're Ron Goldman, that's who you are. No one is a match for a killer. Never. His adrenaline has a head start on yours. Tangle with a killer and you're going to die. That's what killers do: They make people dead. But somehow I got stuck between a rock and a hard place.

Ever try to kill an animal? I don't mean popping a squirrel with a .22 when you're a kid, and I don't mean hitting an armadillo with your SUV. I mean really killing an animal, mano a paw. The Little Fool had a pet rabbit when the Little Fool was a teenager. The rabbit got sick—cancer or something. The rabbit was really suffering. Anyone could see the rabbit was suffering. The Little Fool got all philosophical—he could pay the twenty bucks to have the bunny "put to sleep," but he wasn't going to do that. He had cared for the rabbit in life; he would care for him in death. He would usher him to death's door and carry his bunny love across the big threshold. That was kind of the idea. It was very heavy. The Little

Fool had given it a lot of thought. It's hard for me to remember exactly what phase the Little Fool was in at the time, but the last goodbye to the rabbit had been very serious. He was going to commune with the rabbit one last time and then he would drown the sick, dying, suffering old rabbit in the bathtub. He didn't tell our Mom and Dad his plans. He waited until our parents were out. The rabbit's name was Ralph. He'd been the Little Fool's pet for a while. The Little Fool didn't talk to Ralph from his heart like he talked to me, but they were close. The Little Fool took Ralph into the bathroom and closed the door. The rabbit was shaking. He was suffering. But the Little Fool held him and felt his still soft fur. The Little Fool's touch brought Ralph some comfort. Ralph sensed nothing amiss. The Little Fool filled up the tub with warm water. The Little Fool said, "Goodbye, Ralph" and with tears in his eyes lowered Ralph with great ceremony into the tub. The plan was to hold Ralph under until he was dead. Death of a loved dumb animal with dignity. Seasons don't fear.

There was never a moment of dignity. It was awful. Did you know that rabbits can scream? You don't ever want to hear a silent creature scream. Ralph fought for his life. Ralph fought to breathe. He was no longer weak, old, and suffering. Prey becomes very predator-like when trying to keep its head above water. The Little Fool was bleeding from Ralph's flailing claws. The Little Fool's arms got sore from fighting with a sick old bunny. It didn't take long for the Little Fool to realize that this death-with-dignity home-version idea was very bad. But in that little bit of time, having someone else do the job was no longer an option. Ralph was really suffering now. Oh, it had been cruel. Of all the dead bodies the Little Fool has washed out of the drink, of all the horrible images he's seen in his life, it's this one that stays with him. He had decided to kill Ralph, but the Little Fool hadn't decided fast enough. It's a horrible image. Do you see what I'm saying? The Little Fool couldn't kill a cancer-riddled old bunny rabbit without out a great deal of trouble and angst. Would killing a human be easier? Is there any chance the killer would fight less than a sick rabbit? You've heard about the Boston Strangler. I ain't one of those kinds.

Here's another piece of information you need to have. I was holding this back. I didn't want the Little Fool to look like Alan Alda. I didn't want you to dismiss the Little Fool as someone who takes the soft-rock records of the '70s too seriously. I tried to paint the Little Fool as tough. And he is tough. He can handle dead bodies. He was able, after a while, to kill his own pet rabbit. He can live with parasites in his gut. He can take a lot of pain. But the Little Fool has never hit anyone. Never. We have to define "hit." There have been pats on the backs and punches in the arm. He hit a male teacher's hand that the Little Fool felt was on his shoulder in an inappropriate way. When the Little Fool was filling out his personal scorecard and wanted to get it just right, he would say he'd never "hit a person in anger." It sounded as if he was talking about roughhousing with the boys, but he was really talking about sex-play with the girls. It got tricky. There were a couple of girlfriends who liked to be slapped. I'm not talking about a loud little spank on a tight little ass; I'm talking about a nasty, hard slap across a begging, slut face. A really hard slap, as if maybe she could possibly get a little bit of a black eye; maybe a little. Actually, as we come to the end of our story, let's let it all hang out. She wanted to be hit, in the face, hard, right when she had an orgasm. She'd been on top of him, she asked, and he listened. She screamed, "Hit me!" and he did. Afterward, in their little post-sex discussion, she complimented him on "not being a pussy." She was *very* happy with his brutality. He did it all for her. At least the first time. He wanted to be a good lover, and, whatever she wanted, he tried to give her. He wasn't selfish; he wasn't vanilla. If she liked it, he'd do it. And, hey, guess what? He liked it. He really liked it. They had sex for a few months, and she liked it harder and harder. The Little Fool's passions rose to the occasion. Fire away.

But he drew a line. He drew the line before "hit me" was followed by "with your car." Once, she'd really wanted to have sex when they were angry at each other. They were in the middle of a

big argument, and she wanted to have sex right then. The Little
Fool performed fine in the genital area, but he couldn't hit her.
He couldn't hit in anger. She thought the hate would give her more
love, but the Little Fool couldn't work himself that way. He could
enjoy the hitting only if he could convince the zookeeper in his
mind that he wasn't really hurting anyone in any real sense. When
his powerful moral sense that held the chains of the beast inside him
knew it was in control, then he could beat her senseless, but only
then, when love and trust would take the safety off. How was that
self-training going to pay off with a real killer who wanted him
dead? We hope he would go into the meeting with his superego
safety clicked off. But would the killer be able to convince the Little Fool in a very short period of time that the killer really, really
needed to die? Hit me slowly. Hit me quick.

He knows being hit in the face can be sexy from the other side,
too. The Little Fool hasn't been hit much. He doesn't do any contact
sports. He's big enough and loud enough and aggressive enough to
bluff his way out of most fights. But not all. In high school he'd
been walking with a girlfriend to Friendly's ice cream shop. They'd
spent a lot of time talking, but they really hadn't gotten around to
any sex. The Little Fool was dressed out of fashion. It doesn't matter what he was wearing or how his hair had been cut; all that matters is that it was different than what was accepted by these
particular fellow students at this particular time. There were no
adults around when four boys approached the Little Fool and his
date. The boys taunted him. They questioned his sexuality. They
didn't care that he was the one with the girl. It hadn't bothered the
Little Fool at all, and that bothered the four boys. Finally, one kid
pulled himself out of the quartet and stepped in the Little Fool's
path. It's hard to imagine that the way this kid looked could ever
be in style, but the boys had believed they were closer to fashion
than the Little Fool was, and the dress code had to be enforced.
The self-appointed cop-kid was a lot smaller than the Little Fool.
There seemed to be no way the kid could lose a fight with our
hero. The kid was going up against the biggest guy in the school.

Win or lose, the kid would look cool. He taunted some more and the Little Fool asked him politely, with only a little bit of sarcasm, to get out of the way. The Little Fool wouldn't bite. The Little Fool watched the smaller but angrier boy pull his fist back. The Little Fool hadn't put his arm around the girl yet. He hadn't been that close to having sex with her. Both of his hands were in his pockets. The Little Fool watched the wind up for the hit in slow-motion, and didn't prepare himself in any way. It was sexy. The Little Fool kept his eyes locked with the eyes of the boy who was about to hit him. All through the swing they tracked each other. The Little Fool's hands didn't even tense up in his pocket. The Little Fool didn't turn his head. The last twelve inches that the fist traveled to the Little Fool's mouth, the replay would show that the would-be little bully knew he had lost the fight, and lost badly. But there was no way to stop his hand. He might have been able to do it physically, but there was no way socially. He knew he'd lost before contact. Only as the Little Fool's head snapped from the blow did he break eye contact. The Little Fool had him. It must have hurt the Little Fool a lot. His mouth filled up with blood and his nose started pumping snot down the back of his throat. It probably hurt the bully's hand just as much or more. The Little Fool's teeth all stayed in; they hadn't given a millimeter to the boy's unprotected hand. The hand would be bleeding.

The Little Fool knew the fight was over. He whipped his head back to regain eye contact with the boy. He sucked the postnasal drip flowing into his mouth, to join the blood pouring into his mouth from his cheek. He coughed a little, opened his mouth, and spit out a mouthful of blood and snot on the sidewalk. For the first time, he removed one hand from his pocket and brought it up to his mouth. He hadn't felt the pain. He didn't comfort the area. He didn't rub it. He simply used his bare finger to clean some blood off his lip, brought the finger down, and wiped it on his shirtfront. He went back to the same, exact eye contact. The boy's face was full of terror. His cheering section was silent. The Little Fool said, "So, are you done, asshole?" His hand went directly from wiping the blood on his shirt, back up and around the girl, who now as a woman would give herself in every way to the Little Fool. His mouth again filled with the blood of the alpha male. The tiny would-be bully got out of the way. His friends said nothing, and the Little Fool began walking in the same direction, but the destination had changed. The Little Fool and the teenaged woman were no longer two teenaged friends heading to the ice cream shop. They were now the big strong silverback and his mate, going over the hill for the mount. It would be the best sex of their lives. She'd fully lubricated in her jeans before the spit-blood had whacked on the sidewalk. He'd been fully ready for sex before his hand slid around her back and rested on her breast. As their pace picked up to get to the backseat of her car for the best time of their past or future lives, the Little Fool said, "I hate violent assholes." She stopped, went up on her toes to reach his face, and very gently licked some of the blood from his lip. They continued their walk even faster. Nothing would be negotiated. There would be no hesitation or even an awkward moment. Nothing would be said until she pulled her Mom's car up to the front of the Little Fool's house and said, "You might want to put some ice on that," and the Little Fool thought, years later, that he should have asked, "Put ice on which?" I've seen the toughest souls around.

So, the Little Fool knew it was sexy to hit and be hit. Sexy. Call the police. Oh, if only calling the police were sexy. Not even 911. Just call one of your friends. Please. The Little Fool did have a gun. He had to have one as a police officer. The department wanted him to carry it all the time, but he couldn't remember ever carrying it. He was a diver, and guns don't work underwater. He didn't even keep the gun handy by the bed. He hadn't fired it since cop school. He didn't even know for sure where the gun was. One-eight-seven on a motherfucking cop.

Tommy knew nothing about guns. The Little Fool found his gun, loaded it, and told Tommy he just had to point and pull the trigger. Tommy would take the gun and follow. That was their entire plan.

Together they weren't even worth one man with a plan. Panama. Tommy would be packing on the streets of NYC, and the Little Fool would meet a killer. Unarmed. Thinking hitting was sexy. Quack, quack. Sitting ducks. Death march. The beginning of the end. And you, you will be my queen. We can be heroes just for one day.

CHAPTER FORTY-FOUR

Stupid Stupid Stupid Stupid Stupid

He must have been sitting at Any Place But Starbucks even before 9 P.M. He probably wasn't nervous at all. He must have looked like nothing. He was watching people. He wasn't watching the hip-huggers and bouncing breasts on the young girls. He wasn't smiling to himself at the boys trying to look cool. He wasn't writing descriptions in his head of the people that walked by. He wasn't gathering a funny story or two for a friend he would meet later. And he sure wasn't downtown watching the trapeze school practice. He was just watching customers and patiently waiting. He was sipping his decaf 6-shot Americano and watching. You can't go to jail for what you're thinkin'. Just standing on the corner, watching all the girls go by.

Getting dressed was always an event for Tommy, and this time he had a gun to hide. He wouldn't use a holster. He got in his head that nothing is sexier than a gun just stuck loose into the back of a pair of jeans. But they had to be the right jeans, and that took more than a few tries. He'd have to wear a baggy shirt to cover the gun, and he'd worked hard on his abs and arms, so he didn't like to cover up too much. He chose a tight, ribbed, dirty green tank top that he believed made him look like Bruce Willis in *Die Hard*. Tommy put a billowy, white shirt on over that, and that covered the gun in the back. If Tommy had ever seen a cheesy magician in a billowy, white shirt, Tommy would have had to change again. But chance was kind. To everyone he meets, he stays a stranger.

Tommy's and the Little Fool's lives would have been very different if Tommy hadn't been smart enough to want practice following the Little Fool. If they had walked in together, talking about the meeting, the bad guy would have been gone forever. He never would have showed at the meeting. The Little Fool and Tommy would have been saved. The bad guy was in the business of killing the lonely. It hadn't crossed the Little Fool's and Tommy's stupid minds—their stupid, stupid minds—that telling the victim where to buy his coffee made it easy to keep an eye on the victim before he knew he was being watched. But Tommy wanted to practice. He wanted to follow the Little Fool from the apartment to the coffee place, and then all the way downtown to see which distance felt right for not being noticed. They were barely smart enough to realize that the killer would move the Little Fool after they met, and Tommy wanted to be ready to follow.

So, the Little Fool walked in to get coffee alone. Tommy wasn't close enough yet to see him make his purchase and feel the weight of the cup in his hand. He now had his ID badge that the killer would recognize. But the killer already had him made. Tommy was a ways behind. They had no communication between them. The Little Fool kept fingering the knife he'd put in his pocket. It was a gravity knife. It provided no comfort. He didn't know how to use it. He wasn't ready to use it. It just pumped up the fear. He could open it fast and the blade would lock. None of the victims had been shot. He wasn't bringing a knife to a gunfight. Tommy was following, bringing a gun to the knife fight. Tommy was the Little Fool's advantage. Tommy was the Little Fool's only hope. Tommy, the only joy in the Little Fool's life, was going to be the only thing that would keep him alive. That's all they had. Not a brain between them. That's why I'm leaving it up to you.

A neon sign over the Little Fool's head with an arrow flashing "victim" wouldn't have made him more obvious to the man who was waiting. The killer sat at his table with his decaf and watched the Little Fool. The killer studied the Little Fool. We don't know what the killer thought about the Little Fool. He probably felt nothing.

He didn't kill for pleasure. There was no pleasure. It was his calling.

The Little Fool checked his watch every forty-five seconds. He sat down and he got right up again. He walked around the shop. If he had looked around the shop, he would have seen the obvious neon sign that said "Killer!" with the arrow blinking and pointing to the man alone at the table. But the Little Fool didn't look around. It wasn't time yet. The show hadn't started and he wasn't on yet. He was still preparing. He was psyching himself up. He checked his watch again. He felt the knife in his pocket. He thought about Nell. He thought about Ralph the rabbit. Years ago, on a light news day, there was a fluff piece the Little Fool remembered. It was a piece on "Clown College" in FLA. Victor Gaona was teaching clowns acrobatics. In his Mexican accent, he had said, "You change-a your mind, you break-a your neck." (Is that Mexican? It sounds Italian.) Anyway, his warning is about commitment in the air. The Little Fool was about to attempt a quadruple somersault without ever having tried a single, double, or triple before. He couldn't change his mind in mid-spin. He had to commit. This couldn't be a Jack Black half-assed-with-a-wink performance—this had to be Andy Kaufman. The Little Fool had to be all the way. Make it real, or else forget about it.

The three of them headed downtown to the park, the Little Fool in the lead with Tommy and the killer following the Little Fool close behind. We're dealing with a full cast of stupid people here. It never crossed the Little Fool's mind that the killer might follow him. How could the killer know that the Little Fool might bring someone else? Tommy wasn't looking for anyone else sneaking around. Everyone knew something the others didn't know, and no one knew enough. The Three Stooges heading for a very messy denouement. "Are you sure you three guys know what you're doing?" The Little Fool was scared. The killer was committed to his mission. Tommy was looking good in his billowy, white shirt. The Little Fool had told Tommy not to monkey with the gun; just leave it. The barrel was almost in the crack of his ass. The gun was loaded. Tommy kept the Little Fool in sight and never saw the creep walking beside Tommy. Larry is heading downtown, Moe following him with a plan, and Curly has a gun. I love him. And where he goes, I'll follow. I'll follow. I'll follow.

CHAPTER FORTY-FIVE

I Kinda Like This Guy

The Little Fool looked around the trapeze area. New York City trying to have sawdust. Real acrobats don't practice near a modern skyline with a river flowing by. Real flyers don't make mid-six-figures. Real acrobats don't train anyone they're not fucking or related to. This was just a classy NYC park with rich people circus-slumming on a perfect urban night. The Little Fool clutched his cup of coffee and waited for his first glimpse of the murderer. The killer watched him, and Tommy watched him. The Little Fool knew that the next person he was going to speak to was a murderer. The killer didn't know that the Little Fool knew that. The Little Fool didn't know he'd been followed. The Little Fool didn't know what was going to happen, but he knew it was pretty likely that the next person who spoke to him would try to kill him. Tommy was about to watch someone try to kill his friend. Tommy had a gun in his pants. His job was to save his friend. Rocket in my pocket and the fuse is lit.

The killer walked up from the other side of the park. As the Little Fool watched the killer walk up, the Little Fool knew that Lee Harvey Oswald had single-handedly shot John F. Kennedy. That mystery was solved in that instant. As this man—this man who had done so much evil and hurt so many people—walked up with a smile, the Little Fool knew that huge events could have insignificant causes. Little tiny flaps of hateful butterfly wings causing hurricanes of pain to rage through lives. You didn't need a conspiracy of the

CIA, the FBI, the Mob, and the Cubans to plan it all out. You didn't need people to hide umbrellas and whack anyone who saw anything. You didn't need the existence of a personal satan or a nebulous evil. You just needed one fucking nut. Just one fucking nut. One fucking nut. There is no evil in the world; there's just a single guy walking toward the Little Fool. Who needs an abstract evil when you have one fucking nut? I am the god of hellfire.

Tommy kept the gun in his pants and watched from a safe distance. He believed it was important to be able to describe the killer. Tommy wanted to get that clear in his head. He stared and squinted and one word kept going through his mind. The word was "happy." The killer was a happy guy. He was confident. As little like a movie bad guy as you can imagine. Just an okay guy. The killer wasn't tall or short; he wasn't fat or athletic. He was about forty. He was dressed— Who could tell how he was dressed? He was confident and strong. He walked over to the Little Fool. Tommy couldn't quite hear the killer. Tommy got a word here and there. It was a strong, confident voice, but the killer was just a little too far away. Tommy could hear that the killer sounded happy. Like you were walking onto a yacht.

I can see by your coffee that you are a cowboy. Hi. Everyone calls me "Smitty," but my surname isn't Smith. When I was a kid, I wanted to be special. My name was Robert Jones. A fairly unspecial name. I didn't like "Robert." I wouldn't allow "Bobby." I wanted "Rob," but "Jonesy" was starting to catch on with my friends. I thought those around me to be so unimaginative that I made one last plea for a name that was in some way special. They said, "Jonesy." I suggested "Smitty" just to be perverse. It takes constant vigilance, but I've made it stick. Call me Smitty.

Smitty stuck out his hand. The Little Fool shook it and gave his own name. No interesting story; just his name. He put his well-shaken hand back into his pocket and felt the gravity knife. Smitty turned to indicate the trapeze, and the Little Fool ran his eyes all over Smitty's body. Where was the weapon? Oh, the shark bites with his teeth, dear.

That's the trapeze school up there. You been watching the businessmen conquering their fears with a safety harness and a net?

Smitty probably had a scalpel in his pocket. Or a knife. Or a blunt object. Or all of the above. What a nice voice. The Little Fool's attention went right up to the trapeze before he was finished casing Smitty.

Listen, your Proust was not an invitation to small talk and witty banter. "Slowly and in a lot of pain to prove I won't cry out to God" would be written by someone heavy. Are you heavy . . . ?

He used the Little Fool's first name with the familiarity of an uncle. It fit so well in Smitty's smiling mouth. The Little Fool tried to remember the question he'd hardly heard. He liked the sound of his name in Smitty's soothing voice.

What are you pondering, my newest friend? That reminds me. I was speaking at a seminar in Ohio. I said, "Why is it that people in Ohio don't understand the concept of a rhetorical question," and three people raised their hands while blurting out, "Oh, oh, I know! I know!"

I comment on the conspicuous absence of an invitation to small talk, and then I tell a silly, apocryphal anecdote. The truth is you make me a little nervous. That was a very intense questionnaire you turned in. Let's see if you're going to fit well in my little club. There's a bench right over here. Walk with me, will you?

As Smitty gestured, the Little Fool sneaked another peek. It was kind of a baggy suit jacket. Smitty could have some surgical equipment in there. Could he have some blunt objects in there? His clothes were very well tailored, except for his jacket sleeves. They were a little long. Did he literally have something up his sleeve? He was planning to kill. What equipment did he have? The Little Fool fingered his knife. Tommy felt back for the gun under his shirt. Smitty was perfectly comfortable. He didn't fidget, he didn't sway, he didn't shift back and forth on his feet in that dance that cops and circus elephants are so fond of; that irritating dance of someone who knows he's going to be standing for a while. Smitty was comfortable. Smitty would be comfortable barefoot on broken glass listening to a scientologist Amway salesman pitching a time-share. The Little

Fool felt his own hand relax on the knife. He and Smitty were walking side by side toward the bench. Not too many yards away, a figure in a white shirt shifted. The Little Fool saw Tommy plainly. He was wearing a billowy, white shirt. It was a white shirt. A white, billowy shirt. It was like being secretly followed by the Sloop John B. My grandfather and me.

Pascal's Wager. Let's talk about it. "Slowly and in a lot of pain to prove I won't cry out to God." Usually I need to have a conversation to know if a person is right for the group, but you were very efficient weren't you? Very efficient. What could you possibly add to that answer? I know you. So, this can be a monologue. We don't need to talk. I need to talk to you. This isn't going to take more than one meeting. I know all I need to know. Get ready to go to . . . school.

Okay, so school and hell were the same thing. The Little Fool agreed with that. He had no doubt this was the killer, but what was his move? It couldn't hurt to listen. What? Of course it could hurt to listen. Run. Get the police! What more do you need? Why are you listening to this guy? Run!

The Little Fool didn't listen to me. He listened to Smitty. He wanted to listen to someone and he chose a strange man over his monkey. Smitty would talk forever and the big fucking fool would listen forever. I'm an idiot for you.

I want you to know that my group is heavy enough for you, so let's start there. Pascal didn't go far enough. The most important question is, "Is there a God?" There are people who claim to never think about that question. People on both sides of the debate who claim never to think of that question. People who think it's too confusing, and there are too many haircare products to buy to worry about that hard question. Some of these people live as theists, and some live as Atheists. You are an Atheist and you lead with that. It's all that matters on a questionnaire you send to a stranger. So, you are an Atheist who cares. The not-caring Atheists are very smug with this POV. They are the non-combative Atheists. They are the Atheists that all the religious want Atheists to be. Hedonists. Party boys and girls. They might be fun to have sex with. They're great to have as a boss—but don't talk to them. They wallow in life's lack of meaning. They've made peace with emptiness, and that's a peace that will leave you forever falling down a well. The wonderful, strong feeling of weightlessness with no pay-off. They dismiss the whole question, and you and I will dismiss them. Playing an eye for an eye with the already blind.

How about agnostics? It's a dodge term created by Darwin's pit bull, Huxley, as a different "A" word. It seems smarter and less dogmatic. It means "I don't know." The problem is it never answers the theological question, only the epistemological. Someone asks the question, "Do you believe in God?" and you answer, "It can't be known." But the question isn't "Can it be known?" It's "What do you believe?" "Do you like country western music?" "There isn't a radio playing right now." Everyone is agnostic. "Agnostic" is for people so solipsistic they believe theology is the place to wear their false humility on their sleeves. All the world religions can join together with the Atheists and dismiss the agnostics. We ask them what they think on the most important question of life, and they answer that it can't be known for sure. They have no default setting.

So, we care desperately, and we're not wimps. What's our next move? Do we believe that our belief should be the belief of our parents? Is theology based on geography? Thank the Christian God I'm a country boy and thank Allah I'm a Bedouin? Or are Allah and Yahweh the same? Are there many paths to truth? Can x and not-x both be true? Is it just our little minds that make that seem impossible? Were the pious men flying into the World Trade Center serving every idea of God that has ever been? It's nonsense, of course. But that's where the Atheists fall apart. It's supposed to be non-sense. All the religious writings celebrate nonsense. A little learning is a dangerous thing. So, Darwin has a cute theory as to how we got here, and it makes sense. We can prove it. And Screaming Steve Hawking, the cripple who we can look at in comfort because he's not retarded like the rest of them, he'll probably prove the Big Bang or something else that makes sense. He'll do that. But what started the Big Bang? Who will answer that? We worship the God of the margins. The God that answers all the questions that science and sense haven't gotten to . . . yet. But surely they will get there. They have to. While the religious will continue to dodge and weave. They'll have God guiding evolution. They'll have God starting the Big Bang. They'll have God guiding the hand of Huxley as he writes the word "Agnostic." God is the Jell-O of our brains, and there's always room for Jell-O. Just nod. Are you with me?

Here was something the Little Fool never expected. The killer was right about everything. He nodded. He really nodded. He nodded like a suck-up student in the front row of a class he had to pass. He was on board for the duration.

So, we get the drift, and we're Atheists. We see the direction. We see the people who have died for these ideas; we read about Copernicus and Newton and the church beating them up. We see the statistics. We don't really think Bill Gates believes in God, do we? Nah. And see that African-American sitting in the shotgun shack in Mississippi who can't spell "Mississippi" without the little singsong in his head? See him? We know he believes in God, don't we? So, I'll line up a bunch of people and you pick out the Atheists for me. They're the smartest. They're the best dressed. They're the richest. They all have nice watches, don't they?

Let's imagine that David Letterman says, "Jesus Christ," in disgust on his late-night laughfest on CBS. He takes the Lord's name in vain, which, of course, is the only way to take it. He says those syllables that mean nothing. He says, "Jesus Christ." Well, you know he's going to get letters. And you know there's a letter-writing network, and CBS knows how many letters they're going to get. CBS can tell you how many letters they'll get before he even says it. And they'll tell Dave how many letters he's going to get, and that'll stop him from saying it. But you know what they won't tell you? Do you know? They won't tell you what those letters are. A number of them—I don't know that number, but a number. A real number. An integer. A positive number—a number of those letters will be written in crayon. Yup, crayon. And most of them will have misspellings. Yeah, some will be emails, but there will also be a lot of lined paper. A lot of handwriting. So, David doesn't say, "Jesus Christ." Is it because of money? No—people who write in crayon don't buy Lexus cars. They don't buy the shit he's selling. He's not advertising beef jerky and fucking pork rinds. He's not advertising vests for middle-aged fat women to wear over a turtleneck when they want to look "nice." They have no financial impact on him at all. Hey, Dave, say, "Jesus Christ." Do "The Top Ten Ways to Keep the Virgin Mary's Hymen Intact," and have number one be "Fuck the Mother of God in the asshole until she bleeds." It won't cost you a penny! Not a fucking red cent. And all the executives know that. They know that pissing off PETA will cost them coin, but the Christians have no real power of the purse. So, fuck them, and fuck their crucified God.

But David won't do that. And the reason he won't do that is Pascal's real wager. Yeah, there might be a God, and there might not be a God. If you bet there's a God and there isn't, so what? So, maybe you wasted a couple hours every week in prayer and you don't get to say, "Ohmygod," all the time like a teenager. But, if you bet there's no God, and there's a God—well, maybe you'll go to hell. But, nevermind hell, that's not the worst part. Maybe you've pissed away a chance at eternal life. But that's not the worst part. The worst part is that in that instant that you die you realize that you've missed the meaning of life. And that's a gamble that's hard to take. It's a big gamble. It's what makes people say, "Agnostic," and stops David Letterman from making fun of Jesus. Letterman doesn't believe in God, but he won't make fun of it. Even the comics that got busted for blasphemy won't go all the way. Not all the way. Bill Hicks talked of a higher power. Sam Kinison was a fucking preacher and Lenny Bruce was a Jew. They wouldn't go all the way.

Are we alone now? Look around. There's that homosexual man over there behind the tree. In the white, billowy shirt. Don't look, but he's over there and he keeps reaching back to feel his ass. He's watching both of us, but I bet it's you he's checking out. Maybe he's a size queen. How tall are you? Six foot six? So, other than that size queen, do you see anyone else within earshot? That's not a bad use of language: "to see anyone within earshot." Do you see anyone who might be able to hear us? Are we alone? I think we are. We are alone with a stranger, being watched by a billowy shirt. And we're talking about God.

God is, by all reports, infinite. And our thinking is finite. So, there you go. We are told over and over again that we can't possibly understand. We can't understand. We cannot understand. All of the religions have that in common. They say we can't understand. That's why science and religion don't need to fight: because science is about what we can understand, and if we understand everything we needed to know last week, we can imagine something we can't understand now, and that's where God lives. God lives in our reach exceeding our grasp. Who started the Big Bang? Who made it so life could evolve? Oh, you know the answer, and it's not a who, it's a what. Now what caused the what and who caused that what? Am I talking too much? It's not a conversation is it. That's okay. This is all the easy stuff. You already said so much more with one simple answer.

The Little Fool smiled and waved him on. Now I was on board. We were both insane. We wanted to hear more.

There is nothing more full of hate than tolerance. Nothing. "I don't mind Christians as long as they're not trying to convert me." That's the conventional wisdom. "As long as they don't preach, they're okay." "As long as they respect my right to my own opinion . . ." But I contend that all tolerance is hate and condescension. What idea is more lacking in human respect than "Go ahead, believe that nonsense if it makes you feel better"? And what about the tolerant Christian? Imagine that as we sit here there's a truck coming at me. And you see the truck. And you hear the truck. And you smell the truck. And you taste the smoke of the truck. And you feel the truck rumble the ground under your feet. And you know the truck is real. And it's coming right at us. And you move out of the way, and you're okay. And I look at you and say, "I don't see the truck." Do you say, "Well, you're entitled to your opinion?" Remember you can feel the fucking truck. Do you smile and nod? No. You mention the truck again. You say, "Get out of the way." You preach the gospel of getting out of the way of the truck. And if I still don't listen, and if you love me like you should love all men, do you shrug and say, "Well, it takes all kinds"? At some point, if you're a good person, you grab me and knock me out of the way of the truck. You hit me and you drag me and if you have a baseball bat you use it and you get me out of the way of that truck.

But that's just to save my life from a truck. Life doesn't matter. But the religious, those who know there's a God, those who can see God, and smell God, and taste God, and hear God and feel God, know that it's not just the loss of life they have to stop; it's the loss of eternal life. If you would pull someone you didn't really know out of the way of the truck, how could you not pull a person out of the way of the Atheism that would snuff out eternal life?

I talk to God. I talk to Jesus. I talk to Yahweh. I talk to Jehovah. I talk to Allah. *Atheists use the argument that everyone is Atheistic to all the Gods but one, but that's not true. I believe in Zeus. I talk to Zeus. I believe in Buddha. I believe in nirvana. I believe in the God that stops David Letterman from going all the way against God. You, you are an Atheist. You know there's no God. But there are times. I know there are times. There are times. Do you have kids? You don't. I can see it in your eyes. You don't have true love. And sometimes you wake up in the morning and you're still a little tired. You haven't gotten the rest you really need. You'll never get that rest. Your weariness is not physical, is it? You know that life is wasted, and you feel empty. And all the "life is all we got so let's make what we can of it" just doesn't fucking work. And friendship and humanity, and all the humanism and art and* Moby-Dick, *and Miles Davis playing "Sketches of Spain," and Van Gogh's "Starry Night," and the Monkees' "Last Train to Clarksville," and* Citizen Kane, *just aren't enough. And shooting your cum into the mouth of a really sexy twenty-year-old, and a banana split and riding fast on a motorcycle and The New Rhythm and Blues Quartet playing live and loud just aren't enough. And when you feel empty. When that's not enough, then you're missing God.*

And I'm too smart for the Bible. I know that's all bullshit. And I'm too smart to believe that saying, "Fuck Jesus hard and cream on his crown of thorns," would send me to some fiery hell. And I know that the end times aren't predicted in Revelation, *and I know that those guys flying the World Trade Center planes aren't going to get virgins or even a box of raisins in the afterlife. I know that angels aren't among us and I know that no one is watching over me. I know all of that. And I was able to be a good, full, no-fucking-around Atheist, except for the problem of faith. Because all the religions say that thinking won't do it. You have to have* faith.

Have you ever been in a business meeting when you're really tired? An important meeting? And you start to doze off, and there are images in your head. And you fight those images. And that night when you want to go to sleep, you try to welcome those images so they can take you to dreamland. And you know there are voices in your head that say you can talk to your dead Grandmother, or at our age, maybe your dead Mother, and she's still with you. And you can talk to your dead friends. And you know that you should go on hoping and wishing, and then your little, tiny mind that's just

*a little bit bigger than the others around you says, "That's all fantasy.
That's make-believe. Those voices in my head— Those ideas are just voices
in my head." You've done that; you've fought them. But, over thousands of
years, before the first written word, in a time of religions and stories that are
no longer remembered, the very wise men let themselves go. And God talked
to them. And God told them what to do. To be an Atheist, you have to work
all the time. To believe, to live forever, to do what everyone from the pope
and Bin Laden to David Letterman know know know deep inside when
they're alone— That's what to believe. Don't believe in Jesus Christ. Don't
believe in Allah. Don't believe in the tooth fairy or Santa Claus. Don't believe in UFOs and your toaster talking to you at night. Just believe in God.
Don't you want to believe in God?*

*We're practically alone. Don't tell me you're a Christian, don't tell me
you're a Jew or a Muslim, don't tell me you're a Scientologist. Just tell me
that you have heard a voice—any voice—inside your head. Look me in the
eyes and tell me that. You're not so fucking smart that you know everything.
Isn't there a nagging voice in your head telling you that you don't know
everything? Don't you worry that you could be wrong? Don't you? Well, just
for a moment, here alone, just tell me that you've heard that voice, and look
me in the eye!*

*You don't know everything. You can't know everything. Listen to the voice
inside your head. I see the truck. The truck is coming at you. I smell the
truck. I feel the truck. You need everlasting life. I know God, and He wants
to save you. YOU NEED TO KNOW GOD! TELL ME ONCE
AND IT'LL BE TRUE FOREVER. TELL ME THAT YOU AC-
KNOWLEDGE SOMETHING THAT COULD POSSIBLY BE
CALLED GOD AND ALL YOUR WORRIES WILL BE OVER!*

The Little Fool looked in Smitty's eyes and nodded slightly. The
Little Fool was so lonely. He was so empty. He was so lost. "It's a
great life if you don't weaken," Mom had always said, and the Little Fool had weakened. And it all happened so fast. Right as he
made eye contact, he felt a second of cold on his neck. Smitty had
cut him. Smitty cut into his neck. The Little Fool grabbed the
gravity knife in his pocket and tried to pull the knife out. Smitty
was already taking the scalpel to the Little Fool's gut. The Little

Fool had the belt buckle that his Dad had given him, but it always stuck into the Little Fool's potbelly, so he wore it over to the side. Smitty went to stab him in the side and hit the top of the buckle. At that exact instant there was a gunshot. Tommy shot hot lead down the crack of his ass. The bullet flew right along his ass crack and missed all the ass meat. The bullet came out the bottom of his pants like an x-rated cartoon fart. Tommy was crouching, and the bullet went right into his heel. There was a yell as Tommy fell. Smitty heard the gunshot and the scream and knew that Tommy could be trouble. The Little Fool was gargling blood, so Smitty prioritized. He ran over to Tommy. And I put my arms around you and I tumble to the ground.

Tommy was shot in the heel and it hurt. He felt the bone shatter. He threw down the gun. Tommy yelled at himself, "You stupid, fucking faggot."

Scream out to God! Scream out to God! Offer your pain to God!

Tommy needed to find the gun. He had to grab the gun. This perfect salesman was coming at him with a blade covered in Tommy's friend's blood. "Stupid cocksucker. Stupid faggot. Queer. Loser. Find the fucking gun!" Tommy was screaming at himself. And he picked up the gun. He closed his eyes and shot the gun at the evil. The pain was shooting through his foot. The bang banged in his head. The bang was so fucking loud. It hurt so much. He was screaming and firing. His eyes were closed. Smitty was very cool, but he had no move on this chaotic chessboard. Tommy wasn't firing as fast as he could. Well, he was firing as fast as he could, but he wasn't firing as fast as anyone else could. He was firing really slowly. The shots were much too far apart. It was as though he had to figure out how to use the gun every time he pulled the trigger. The pain was blinding *and* his eyes were shut. He was shooting like a girl and he hated himself for it. "You stupid faggot, fire the gun." And all the hatred from all the jocks over all the years was firing out the end of the gun. The first bullet had hit his own heel. The second went high into the air and would come down on the roof of a condo building in New Jersey. The third bullet hit a nearby tree. The Little Fool held the wound in his neck. He had to stop the bleeding. He had to get air in and, more important, he had to help Tommy. The Little Fool stood up and tried to run with one hand on his neck toward Smitty. Smitty was all over the place, watching Tommy's random gun, and trying, coolly, to second-guess every bullet. Smitty was bobbing and weaving. There was no way to predict anything coming from Tommy. There were gunshots and deep, homophobic screaming every few seconds. The Little Fool, with one hand doing direct press on his neck, used his other hand to grab Smitty from behind. Smitty's scalpel went up to stab the Little Fool's hand. The fourth bullet shot the Little Fool in the left forearm. The bullet went through the forearm and into Smitty's collarbone. He dropped the scalpel. The fifth bullet went into the ground. There were several more in the clip, but Tommy threw the gun like a villainous girl throwing her gun at Superman. Smitty's collarbone shattered. Smitty's cool evaporated. The Little Fool was holding his neck together with one hand, and his forearm was shooting blood into Smitty's face. The Little Fool was kicking and kneeing and biting and spitting. The Three Stooges had all pissed and shit their pants. Pieces of the shattered collarbone finally took Smitty into unconsciousness. The Little Fool kept kicking. Smitty stopped moving. The Little Fool crawled. He crawled and he found Tommy. Through the blood, he saw Tommy's heel torn to pieces. Tommy was crying and shaking. The Little Fool wasn't human. His pain was amazing. He was fighting just to stay alive. But he couldn't think of anything except Tommy's suffering. The Little Fool crawled to Tommy's heel and placed his mouth against the bloody, torn shoe. He had one thought in his mind: "Kiss it and make it better." Lullaby and good night.

CHAPTER FORTY-SIX

Yeah, the Monkey Did It

Don't you know, little fool, you never can win. Use your mentality. Wake up to reality.

Yeah, the monkey did it. It was Dickie all along, but not the way you might have thought. It wasn't a stuffed, grinning sock toy coming to life like some *Night Gallery* doll and biting with art-directed, blood-painted teeth. It wasn't the Little Fool dressing up like Dickie the Sock Monkey and normanbatesing innocent people in the big NYC shower. But all these people had been killed by the sick, pleasing idea of an imaginary friend: the pure evil, anti-science, anti-human idea that the truth inside you is more important than the truth outside you. It's a pernicious, personal evil. Don't ever deny your feelings. Feel love and hate and everything in between, and crawl all over the sides of those feelings, but don't feel things you should think. Don't ever try to feel the truth. Don't let things in your head tell you what to do.

My name is Clayton Fraser Benz. No one has ever called me "The Little Fool." That's a name I used to use when I was talking to Dickie, my imaginary friend. It was a name to remind me of my childhood. To remind me of a time when I wasn't good at anything. I'm big enough to love being called "Little" and, well, only a fool talks to a sock monkey. I am not Dickie. There is no Dickie. I'm Clayton. Some people call me "C.B.", some people call me "Cotton Balls," or "Mister Balls," but most people call me "Clayton." I'm a grown-up. My Mom and Dad are dead. That's just true. I can remember them, but they'll never talk to me again. They won't watch over me. There are parts of them in my genes, my habits, and my memories, but there's no soul or spirit. My parents are part of me in ways that are much more real than any spirit or soul. Nell is dead. I can still love her and remember her, but she can never love me back again. My childhood is over. I can remember it, and learn from it, and cry about it, but it's over. I'm not a Little Fool, I'm a big man. Dickie is a toy, a sock monkey that sits on my bed. I can use Dickie to remind me of memories. I can hug and hold that sock full of pantyhose. It's okay for me to look at Dickie, think about my Mom and Dad, and cry my eyes out. That's life. That's real, that's now. It's even okay for me to talk out loud to Dickie. But it's not okay for him to talk back. That's just not okay.

It doesn't matter which imaginary friends talk to you when you close your eyes. It doesn't matter if it's allah telling you to fly someone's plane into the World Trade Center, or it's jesus telling you to offer your suffering up to god. It doesn't matter if it's some monkey that's a combination of your Mom, your Dad, your old friends, your sex partners, and all the pop music you've pumped into your head. We're not alive for long, and we have to learn as much as we can about the world outside of us. There's such a short time to really love real people that we can't afford to waste time inside ourselves. We don't live long enough to live inside ourselves. There isn't a lot of spare time to talk to a sock monkey. Listen up, I have the right to preach—god stabbed me in the neck.

Faith is the enemy. Faith and hope say it'll be okay. There is emptiness and hopelessness and pain and suffering, and faith can mask the pain, but faith can't really take it away. It's an anesthetic, not a cure. It won't really be okay. We're all going to suffer and die. It's going to get worse. But it's also a great ride. Fight the faith. When you want something to be true so badly that you can feel it, that's the time to question. Oh, faith feels good, the heroin of the born-again. The E of the higher power. The dope of a sock monkey.

Dickie didn't get into me too deep. He wasn't in as deep as Smitty's god. But Dickie had a start. And the faith felt good. Faith always feels good. It probably feels better than heroin, and that's why faith has done so much more damage. If I'd spent a little more time with Nell and a little less time with Dickie, I might have a few more precious memories of her. And if I spent a little less time with my memories, I might have a little more future joy. I'm sure going to look for it. I'm looking for things that are real, things that are outside of my mind. Dickie was a gateway drug to the heroin of god, and I kicked the reefer before I was in the gutter blowing dogs for wine change.

What's the difference between god and a sock monkey?

There is a sock monkey.

CHAPTER FORTY-SEVEN

Leaving Only Me to Tell the Tale

Well, I lived. I have a really sexy scar on my neck. With a couple of bolts glued on, I could look way Frankenstein's monster, but I choose to see the scar as sexy. Chicks seem to dig it. What more do they want? I got it fighting a serial killer. The scar is white, smooth, and raised across my throat. Maybe I should get the scar tattooed to look like a snake wrapped around my neck and biting its tail like my Grammy's old mink stole.

Tommy limps. Man, does Tommy limp. He blew off his whole heel, the whole back of his foot. Tommy walks like a pirate. He's able to tell the story in a way that, if I'm not there to heckle, does not make it clear that his wound was self-inflicted. But when I'm there, I point out that the bad guy never laid a glove on him. He just shot himself in the foot and then he shot me. He can make it sound better than that if I'm not there to help. He's got that spin down and now he's trying to find a way to make his limp look sexy. He's breaking new ground. Captain Hook and Ratso Rizzo aren't useful role models.

You fire a gun five times in a NYC park and cops will eventually show up. They got there barely fast enough to save our lives. We were all unconscious in a big, bleeding heap. I had my mouth over Tommy's trashed heel, and our blood was all flowing together all over my mouth and face. We are three-quart blood brothers. But then again, our love for each other is that much deeper than any two-drop Boy Scouts with a penknife. We needed three quarts to hold our friendship. We mixed a lot of bodily fluids that night on the ground, so I guess I've slept with everyone that Tommy's slept with over the past fifteen years. I'm pretty fucking proud of that. I'm very proud of that.

The tabloids played up the angle of the insane, incompetent gay crime-fighters. We went on a couple of TV shows to talk about our adventure. Tommy loved being on TV. He loved the makeup and picking out his wardrobe, and I—I loved it all just as much as he did. They played us up as a gay couple and I was really afraid that if we tried to clarify we would make it look like that was something to be ashamed of. So, we kinda shut up. It didn't get in the way of us getting laid. No one in Boy's Town worries about me when he picks up Tommy, and I've met a lot of women who want to spend a few nights trying to turn me straight. Yeah, I'm dating again. I'm dating a lot. Hey Nell isn't the only . . . dead body fished out of the sea? No, that's not right. What I mean is, there are other wonderful women in the world, and I'm paying attention now. I'm going to find her.

Tommy and I have grown apart the way really close friends grow apart. He'll always be my closest friend, but we don't need to see each other or talk that much. Every time we get a chance to hang, it's wonderful, but we often have other things going on. We used to call each other every day. Now, it's a lot of email.

Smitty shared our fifteen minutes of fame. I guess he was kind of "Son of Sam," and Tommy and I were like that guy who caught Son of Sam, see? The guy who caught Son of Sam was a little less famous than Sam. I don't remember the captor's name. That's okay. My name doesn't matter. "Those two crazy gay guys" is fine with me. Smitty lived. He got a lot of my blood and little parts of my arm blown into his shoulder. He has pieces of his collarbone all over his chest. It was a long trial, but the jury was out for about two hours. It was an easy call. Tommy and I spoke against the death penalty for him, but New York isn't a big snuff state anyway, so we probably weren't needed. Smitty will be in jail forever, and that's right and good.

SOCK

I tried to use my fleeting fame to point out that it was Smitty's faith in religion that made him do it. I tried to say that adults shouldn't have imaginary friends, but that just convinced everyone that I was a crazy gay guy. I guess I'm not good at bringing my message to the people.

I kinda, sorta have my old job back. I can't really dive with the bad arm and neck, but I work. I do paperwork and I fill tanks and stuff. Cops can retire young, which means I'm not that far from retirement age anyway, so I'm not sure I'll ever get back into the filthy NYC water I love, and the water is pretty clean now anyway. Maybe I'll retire to Bonaire and take rich tourists diving in warm, clean water. I'm thinking those resort dive guys—even the crazy gay ones—must get a lot of pussy. I still haven't entered the gene pool, but I still love fooling my body into thinking I'm entering the gene pool. I'd like a wife and kids, but I don't want to settle down. But I'm available.

I go to the prison almost every week to visit Smitty. We've become friends, I guess. I liked him from the moment we first met. We play chess by mail and we chat. We also talk. And we argue a lot. He's still trying to convert me, and his intellectual challenges help keep me honest. I'd like to get him to give up his imaginary friends, but the prison system encourages the very beliefs that made him kill. It makes my job harder. If I do ever win him over, he'll have to face some serious issues. He works hard to believe that the people he killed are in heaven. He tries to believe that what he did was very wrong, but even so his victims are in a better place. It's so much easier to believe that he's going to hell than that he sent so many people to nowhere. He'd like to believe that even if his suffering will be forever, his crime stopped when their hearts stopped. I believe that at some level he knows there's no better place, but faith, as always, makes him feel better. That heroin soothes his nonexistent soul. We killed that one woman together, and she didn't even hear Smitty's speech. She wasn't lonely and sensitive. She had kids, goddamn it. I stole the note, and that made him kill. I have no way around that. She's dead. She's missed. Her loved

225

ones still suffer for the mistake Smitty and I made together. I feel worse than Smitty does.

You could ask what harm there is in his believing his victims are in the afterlife. He's never going to get out of prison. He's never going to kill again. He won't even try it in prison. He wouldn't even try it if he were out of prison. He's harmless. Let him have his peace. But I won't do that. He killed the woman I love, and he tried to kill a man I love, and Smitty tried to kill me, but I still don't hate him enough to condescend to him. He deserves what he never gave his victims. He deserves the truth. I have no right to decide what's best for him. I just have to try to tell the truth as I see it. And that's what I'm doing. But we don't always argue. It's not all heavy. Sometimes we tell funny stories from the past and he tells me jokes he hears from the guards. Sometimes Smitty and I just talk about music. We both love Dylan and Sinatra. Smitty is teaching me about Coltrane, and I'm turning him on to Half Japanese. Smitty is my friend. It's just a friendship. I think it'll continue. I always know where to find him.

And Dickie? He's moved from my bedroom to my office. He sits on top of my computer monitor, and I look at him often. And when I look at him I remember my youth and all the people I've loved and what they mean to me. And I remember that all Dickie is is me. That's all I really have. And I love that tough, motherfucking little monkey.

Thanks

The dead woman in the book is named Nell because my dear friend Nell Scovell made me write the damn book. I have no idea why, she's just a friend, but she wanted it written. She pushed me hard and I sent her every chapter as I wrote it. I thank her, but you can't blame her.

My sister, Valda Stowe, was the first one to ever say I could be a writer. She's supported me from the day I was born and she's still there for me.

There were others that joined the cheering section and mean the world to me: Kelli Kirkle, Jonesy (Mike Jones), Dino Cameron, Mickey Lynn, Farley Ziegler, Anne Buchanan, Shari Getz, Sandra Cox, Aye Jaye, Colin Summers, Spicoli (Pete Golden), and as always, EZ, Krashner, Glenn, Blaire, Teller, and the Jungle. Gary Stockdale is doing the music.

Thanks to T. Gene Hatcher for taking the first pass at fixing the grammar. Thanks to Renée French for her impassioned handwriting. And to Kim Scheinberg for understanding the book and editing it so that you might have a chance of understanding it, too. She got all but two of the pop references that set the tone for each paragraph without even looking them up.

Thanks to Elizabeth Beier and the people at St. Martin's who decided to publish a novel by a Vegas comedy magician. They seem to like it. They were the first ones to read it that never met me. Thanks to Dan Strone for selling the damn thing.

It's all fiction. No one in the book is real. I'm tall but I'm not a fucking police diver. Some people's lives inspired me a lot. John Norton taught me the Ding Dong life, which turned out to be all life. David Packer let me use his real name and his story. I didn't use Lynda Youngs's name, but she's there. I have to thank Matt Tafoya for a lot of beautiful conversation that popped up in the book, and Doc Swann for a period of his life that I'm afraid I just ripped off.

The character of Nell is every woman I've ever loved and hoped for. Maybe I'll really get it together with her before she's killed by a psycho.